THE CURSED PRINCE

AYA LING

INTRODUCTION

Can a disabled mage save a prince from a terrible fate?

When she was fourteen, Gabi promised she'd do anything to protect Prince Alrik of Arksar. Including falling in love with him, in case true love's kiss is needed to break the curse. But six years later, Alrik hasn't expressed interest in any woman. He is content to flirt, but never showed a strong attachment for anyone. And now the witch who cursed him has returned after years in exile...

Time is also running out in Savony, where trolls have broken out from underground, terrorizing the castle. More help is needed to defeat the trolls, but with half the mages tasked to protect Alrik, how will Alix, Sybil, and the princes band together and save their kingdom from an unprecedented crisis?

This is the third and final installment in the Reversed Retelling trilogy. It is highly recommended that Book 1, *Till Midnight*, and Book 2, *The Beast and the Beauty*, are read prior to starting on this book.

CHAPTER 1

She was beautiful, with olive skin and black hair and sparkling eyes, with only one thing that marred her beauty: her right foot was crushed, mangled, so that with the misshapen lump at its end, her leg no longer resembled a normal human limb.

A middle-aged woman with graying hair crouched in front of her and took a long, hard look at the girl's foot.

"It's beyond what magic can fix." She shook her head, tears in her eyes. "I'm sorry, child."

Gabi didn't reply. Painkilling spells kept her from fainting away, but her heart and mind were numb at the moment. In a distance, next to the smoking remains of poplars and feather grass, lay her parents, both of them dead. They had an unexpected battle with a power-hungry mage, and the epic clash had ended in tragedy. It took the lives of her parents and the evil mage. It took her foot—the mage targeted her to make her parents surrender and her mother died saving her life, though an errant bolt of magic bounced off and struck Gabi's foot.

She winced when she remembered what happened earlier.

Her mother's shriek echoed still, her body falling lifeless to the ground, burned and bruised from the impact of magic. Her father lying close by, his face bearing so many wounds that it was barely recognizable.

"I'm sorry I wasn't in time to save them," the woman said. "We weren't close, but I knew them because they were the few other mages in existence. My name is Freja." She lightly touched Gabi's shoulder. "I live in Arksar. If I hadn't heard that a certain witch was lurking in Masaro, I wouldn't have come."

Arksar was thousands of miles away, separated by an ocean. Gabi was in luck that Freja happened to be here, or she mightn't be alive.

But she was too devastated to speak. A lone tear trickled down her cheek and landed on her collarbone. She didn't notice, didn't bother to wipe it away.

"Come with me, child." Freja waved her hands. A cart rolled over the ground, stopping in front of them. Another wave, and Gabi was levitated into the air, landing gently in the cart. "In the future, your home will be with me."

* * *

MANY DAYS PASSED before they reached Arksar. They could've gone faster, but Gabi's foot kept them from traveling at a normal pace. During the journey, Gabi behaved like an automaton. The bone-deep grief from losing her parents had seeped into her soul, leaving her hollow, with no desire to want or hate. At night she woke up frequently, sweat running down her forehead and neck, with the remnants of a nightmare surrounding her like a ghost. In her fourteen years of existence, she had never been without her parents. She had never imagined what life could be without them. And now they were gone —forever.

2

Freja was sympathetic. She cared for Gabi's foot with well-constructed spells, saw that Gabi ate enough to stay healthy, but she lacked the loving care of a mother. Not that it would make any difference. They were strangers still, and while Gabi was grateful to the older mage for saving her life, her bereavement prevented her from any emotional reaction.

One day they arrived in the bustling sea port. Freja engaged a small carriage and helped Gabi climb in.

"Need any more painkilling spells?"

Gabi shook her head. There was a dull throb in her right foot that wasn't unbearable. Besides, the painkilling magic sometimes came with side effects—she'd feel dizzy or drowsy.

"There is something of utmost importance I must tell you before we arrive in Brek, the village where I live," Freja said, folding her arms together. "It is not only important; it must be kept secret. I will have to bind you to a silencing charm."

Gabi raised her head. However devastated she was, she couldn't ignore Freja's words.

"Yes, a silencing charm. If you speak anything related to the secret, your voice will die away," Freja continued. "Even if I have your word and you vow not to speak of the secret, I cannot risk a slip of tongue. Will you agree? It won't be long—only for about seven years. But if you are unwilling, I shall seek an ordinary family and let them adopt you."

As a mage, even a young one whose magic wasn't fully developed, Gabi knew of the difficulties and risk that posed when living among ordinary folk. Long ago her parents instilled in her that the "non-magic" looked upon mages as a be-all-and-end-all solution to their countless problems.

"If they know we can perform magic at will, rather than concocting spells with ingredients, people will come begging for us to do everything for them," her father had said. "A house infested with rats and mice, a missing horse, even an itch on the back. They'd become little better than an infant. We cannot help them with everything."

Gabi took a deep breath. "I agree to the binding."

Freja looked pleased. "I thought a mage would." She held up her hands. Green-and-gold sparks gleamed from her fingers. "Are you ready, child?"

"I am."

"Open your mouth."

The sparks flew into her mouth. A peculiar taste, sweet and bitter like a special brand of Masaro chocolate, spread from her tongue to her throat.

"Repeat after me: I, Gabriella Donato, daughter of Valentina and Pasquale, solemnly promise that the following details will not be repeated or conveyed through any method, such as oral, writings, or gestures. Any attempt to do so will result in obstruction. My voice will fade away, my quill run out of ink, my hands go numb and unable to move. Release from the promise will be granted in seven years."

Gabi repeated it word for word. Freja looked at her, eyebrows raised.

"Every word is spoken verbatim, and I have spoken only once. Have your parents taught you the silencing charm?"

"Never." The bittersweet taste faded as the spell took effect. "I was born with an exceptionally good memory."

"So if I were to give you a thousand-word essay, you'll be able to memorize it after reading it once?"

She could, in fact, memorize a book, but Gabi didn't bother to reveal that. Freja would find out anyway. "Yes."

"Hmm. This could be useful. But for now—" Freja's gaze swept over her face "—it is something else I have in mind. Do you know anything about the king of Arksar?"

"Not much." Gabi's parents had kept her well-sheltered in a remote town in Masaro. She didn't even know much about their own monarch, much less the Arksan king.

"Everyone knows he has a daughter, Iliana, who is around ten years old. Everyone also knows he had a son, who was cursed by a witch and died when he was a month old. But what everyone doesn't know is that the prince is alive."

Gabi's attention was fully arrested. "There's a prince of Arksar?"

"He was born with the name Alrik, but for caution's sake, I call him Eric. It is a common name in Arksar. Walk down the streets of Linberg or Trond, shout the name Eric, and at least one man will turn around."

"So he doesn't know he's the prince?"

"I'd not leak the truth before he is twenty-one. I have told him that his parents died in a fire, and that I was a neighbor who happened to be there on time. You see, the original curse stated that Alrik would prick his finger and die on his twenty-first birthday. When I arrived, it was too late to remove the curse. But I modified it and made it less threatening. If he happened to injure himself, he'd fall into a deep, permanent sleep instead."

It didn't sound much better to Gabi.

Freja drew her brows together. "I lied to him—I told him that he had hemophilia. That if he were to injure himself, his wounds would not easily heal, and a deep injury could make him bleed to death. I had fooled him a few times with magic, making blood run from a minor wound, so he'd believe that he was afflicted."

Gabi nodded.

"To keep him alive, I'd do anything. Anything, including less ethical methods. Lying to him about his body condition is one thing. But there is another, in which I hope that you—" the mage's gaze was piercing "—may prove to be useful."

"How?"

"When I told you that I modified the curse, there is one way to wake him from permanent slumber."

A line flashed through Gabi's mind. She had read about the curse many years ago.

"True love's kiss," she said.

"Yes. I had to hide him in Brek, a small village on the eastern border of Arksar, surrounded by a thick forest, so he wouldn't attract attention. But on the other hand, there are no girls close to his age in the village. There's a town called Kardi a half day's drive away, but there's work to be done on the farm and we don't visit Kardi often. If you're living with him, chances are likely that he will fall in love with you."

Shock filled her mind. She was fourteen—she had never even thought about anything like romance, much less making a prince fall in love with her.

Freja continued, as if she were making innocuous remarks about the weather.

"You're pretty enough, and even though that foot is debilitating, I doubt it will make you unattractive in his eyes. I have raised him since he was a baby, and the lad has a good heart."

"I...I don't think..."

"Please. I know it's asking a lot of you, child, but we need extra precaution. It's possible that he won't ever prick himself, but if there's the chance he does, you will be able to wake him from permanent slumber. Do not worry—you're not playing with his feelings. You're saving his life—increasing his chances of survival."

"Suppose..." Gabi started. While it seemed impossible to her to make a prince fall in love with her, she knew she was pretty. And Alrik—Eric—didn't know he was a prince. "Suppose he does fall in love with me. Then what happens after he returns to the palace?"

Freja shrugged. "That is a problem we'll worry about later. The most important thing is to keep him alive."

"What shall I do, then?"

"Be kind to him, but don't throw yourself at him. I daresay

that he will be attracted to you soon enough." Freja held out her hand. "Will you help me, Gabi?"

Gabi paused. Part of her was intrigued, part of her felt it was unwise. But she was young and impressionable, and while she disliked the idea, she owed Freja her life.

She grasped Freja's hand. "I will."

CHAPTER 2

Six and a half years later...

"Where's Alrik?"

Gabi emerged from the kitchen, her apron splattered with grease and crumbs. She stood on the landing, where a flight of rickety stairs led to the basement.

"He said he's going to Matthias's house," Freja said from the foot of the stairs. Her graying hair looked frazzled, and there were patches of dark purple under her eyes. Despite being a powerful mage, she was not invincible. Considering what she had to do—weave a countercurse that could control more than two hundred vicious trolls—no wonder Freja was looking exhausted recently. "He prefers their cooking."

"Again?"

There was compassion in Freja's eyes as she came upstairs, but all she said was, "If he wants to gorge himself on Matthias's cooking and come home with a stomach ache, it's his choice. Is lunch ready?"

"Yes." Gabi snapped her fingers and her apron became sparkling clean—something she wouldn't have dared to try if Alrik was around. She took off her apron and limped to the kitchen. The sting of Alrik's refusal to stay at the cottage bothered her, but she pushed it to the back of her mind. She excelled at many skills, thanks to her remarkable memory, but somehow the art of cuisine eluded her. It was surprising that she couldn't cook well, since she had come from Masaro, which was famous for its desserts. Gabi couldn't bake a cake without filling the kitchen with smoke. But then, she was first and foremost a mage, and for her, magic mattered more than anything else. "It's on the table, Auntie."

She sank onto the wooden chair, glad to rest for a while. Freja had fashioned an artificial foot for her, but she disliked the *clunk, clunk* of her wooden foot hitting the floor, so she only used it when going to town. Looking around the kitchen, where three stools were set around the table, she was reminded that Alrik was spending less and less time at home. He went off to other villagers' houses whenever possible.

Alrik. She had failed to make Alrik fall in love with her. She had tried, but she wasn't a natural flirt, and when living with him for nearly seven years, it was hard not to reveal her true nature. She quarreled with him, nagged him for slacking off in farm work and household chores, and he in turn complained she was difficult to live with and frequently criticized her cooking.

Sometimes it made her confidence ebb. She wasn't a dazzling beauty that appeared only once in a generation, but still a lovely girl by any standards: eyes and hair the color of rich dark chocolate, flawless olive skin, and a sweetness in her features that remained even when she was in a temper.

Yet Alrik treated her more like a bossy sibling. There were a few times when she thought he cared for her. Once, when her wooden foot was caught in a rabbit trap, he had crouched beside her and insisted on carrying her home. There was a rare tenderness in his gaze. But when they arrived home, he shut himself in his tiny, one-room cabin near the farm, and when he emerged for dinner, it seemed nothing had changed. He was indifferent when she tried to engage his attention, and after the meal, he went straight back to hauling firewood.

It hurt. Not just because she had failed Freja, not just because Alrik might fall into permanent slumber, but because she had fallen in love with him. She loved his lighthearted, easygoing grin, loved his carefree laugh, loved his ability to see humor in bad situations. Sometimes, her disability and the stress of worrying for Alrik's life drove her to bouts of moodiness and despair, but when he appeared in the doorway with a glow in his eyes and a curve in his lips, it felt as if he brought sunshine that chased the rain clouds away.

And yet—there was a relief in her failure. If Alrik loved her and wished to marry her, he'd meet numerous obstacles. What would the people say to a queen who had to limp everywhere, clinging to her husband's arm?

"You all right, child?" Freja said. She entered the kitchen and poured two cups of warm milk. "You look like you didn't sleep much last night. Go and take a nap before Alrik returns."

"I'm fine." Gabi rubbed her temples. "Just a little hungry after getting up early this morning. And speaking of weariness, you don't look too well, Auntie. How is the countercurse coming along?"

Freja grimaced. "About a hundred more to go."

A few months ago, the princes of Savony had contacted Freja. Underneath the Savon castle were more than two hundred trolls, who had lived there since the founder of Savony, the great King Antoine, had made an agreement with the trolls. Unbeknownst to the public, Antoine and his descendants were cursed to fight the trolls every fortnight. Recently the princes broke the curse; they were no longer forced to fight the trolls, but on the other hand, the trolls were alive and well, remaining a formidable threat.

Just a few days ago, Freja received news that two trolls had broken out from their underground lair. They killed one and injured another before they were discovered and demolished.

"That's less than half the amount needed," Gabi said. "Let me help you, Auntie. I can make a perfectly decent collar now."

"Not at the moment," Freja said. "If Alrik sees you frequently going down to the basement, he'll get suspicious and follow you. Until he turns twenty-one, I'd rather that he remain ignorant of the dangers out there."

Gabi's hand closed tightly on the fork. Alrik's birthday was next month.

"Any news about the witches?"

"So far, none." Freja waved her hand—the loaf of bread on the counter came floating to the table. "After they battled Lorenza and Julong in Finsoor, I expected that they'd lie low for a while. They might be hiding in a distant region in Masaro and aren't anywhere near Arksar."

Gabi desperately hoped so. Freja had enough on her plate weaving the countercurse. They had hoped Moira and Sorcha had disappeared forever, ever since an epic battle twenty years ago, but they had re-appeared. Great timing.

"What worries me is that they have the Peerless Knife." Freja dipped a piece of bread in the stew. "If they harvest the energy in the knife, we won't stand a chance against them."

The Peerless Knife. It was said to be able to cut through any material, including diamonds—the toughest substance known to humans. It was also infinitely magical, which was why the Savon princes were able to break their curse. They used the Peerless Knife to cut down an ancient tree, where the magic of the curse originated. But when Moira captured Prince Gerald, she gained possession of the knife. Which meant she had an almost endless reservoir of magic.

"But enough about the witches." Freja set down her spoon. "I invited Clara to come stay with us. She should be arriving today or tomorrow."

"Clara? Isn't she the sister of that girl Ronnie is engaged to?"

"That's the one. I made a trip to Kardi to see her before I came back from Linberg. She's just as pretty as Marianne."

Gabi chewed on her slice of bread. A sour feeling rose in her chest.

"It will only be for a month," Freja said. "Perhaps love at first sight will happen this time."

"But isn't Clara too young for Alrik?"

"She turned sixteen last month. I overheard her mentioning to Marianne that she found Alrik handsome, so she'll make an effort to attract him. Of course, it's only for the curse. Even if Alrik falls in love, she can't become queen."

Just like Gabi. Anger reared in her mind—anger at herself, at Alrik, and at Freja. She was angry that she fell in love with Alrik. She was angry at Freja for making her "seduce" Alrik for the sake of saving his life. And now, Freja was targeting another innocent girl. If Clara fell in love with Alrik and vice versa, she would be compensated handsomely, then dismissed. A pawn for "the greater good."

"I'll do the dishes," Freja said. "I need to clear my mind after weaving the collars. You take a good rest, child. Don't you need to tutor Alrik this afternoon?"

Her anger abated. Freja's plan, however heartless, was formed with good intentions. Better a heartbreak than a life taken. As much as she resented Freja's idea of "seducing" Alrik, she owed Freja her life. And were someone to ask her if she regretted coming to Arksar and living with Alrik, she couldn't say yes. Whatever frustration he caused her, she'd rather endure it than never meeting him.

* * *

ALRIK RETURNED about two hours later, looking fairly satisfied. Matthias and his wife had no children and treated him like a son. Every time Alrik went there, he was urged to eat as much as he liked. Famine was rare in Arksar, and while none of them in Brek were rich, the villagers never had to worry about starving.

His cheery whistle came first, then he entered through the back door. A tall, strapping lad of twenty, soon to be twenty-one, he was growing more and more like King Tyrell. With ash-blond hair and twinkling blue eyes, a strong jaw, and a well-built body from farming and training, he turned heads whenever he visited Kardi, or the ancient oak, a trading point where caravans from Lulan passed on their way to Arksar or Savony.

But much to Freja's disappointment and Gabi's secret relief, he was charming to all girls but never grew attached to any. It seemed that Alrik's motto for life was to enjoy himself while he was young. Marriage? That could wait until he was thirty. As long as he kept his good looks, he'd have no problem attracting women.

Gabi was annoyed as she looked at the clock. Alrik's good mood only made her more cranky.

"You're late," she said, not bothering to keep the irritation from her tone. A man who couldn't be punctual and who criticized her cooking didn't deserve to be treated nicely. "Have you forgotten how much work we have to do today?"

He yawned. "Aw, Gabi, it doesn't hurt to relax for a bit. Did you get out from the wrong side of the bed today?"

"My bed is right next to the wall," she snarled. "In the main room, now. You've got a load to catch up today and if you delay my schedule again I'll…"

"Feed me with stew?" He pulled a face. "Now that is a dire threat." And he made for the main room in a few quick strides, while she limped after him, repressing the urge to trip him up with a well-placed spell.

The main room of the cottage served as living room, sitting room, and parlor. A quarter of the room was used for storage.

Freja could've easily bought a larger house, but the last thing she wanted was to attract attention in this tiny village. Even in Brek, Freja made sure that they lived at a twenty-minute walk from the nearest house. No villager should know she and Gabi were mages, much less Alrik the prince who lived.

In the corner of the main room was a desk and chair, and a clay tablet with chalk. Alrik draped himself in the chair, placing his elbows behind his head, with the languid ease of a cat. Gabi silently positioned herself at a reasonable distance from him. Even her remarkable memory failed her occasionally when she met his intense blue gaze.

When both Alrik and she were fifteen, Freja suggested that they both learn Arksan history and geography.

"The boy needs to be equipped with knowledge to rule," she told Gabi, while Alrik was away at Matthias's house. "We'll tell him that I have an old friend working as a bookkeeper's assistant at the palace, who plans to retire in a few years. I'll tell Alrik that if he studies hard, he can take the job when he reaches twenty-one."

In the beginning, Freja had taught them both. Gabi, being from Masaro, knew little about Arksan history. But her superior memory allowed her to remember details quickly and correctly. She only had to flip through one book, read carefully, and then she could recite its entire contents word for word.

Within months, Gabi was able to master all the books Freja taught—indeed, she was able to remember details that her "aunt" didn't. So Freja suggested that Gabi take the role of instructor instead. For several times a week, Gabi was to tutor Alrik. Besides preparing Alrik for his future role, Freja had hoped that Gabi's tutoring would draw the two of them closer.

Now, as she took her place behind the table, she felt a pang. Was she not pretty enough? No, there wasn't even a woman close to Alrik's age in Brek. Was it her intelligence? But Alrik rarely seemed intimidated that she could recite facts and details right off her head. Indeed, often he'd sit back with a look of admiration. Was it her foot? But he was always ready to lend her a helping hand, even carrying her across mud when spring showers were plentiful, but he never followed up with a desire more than friendship. Only chivalry. Maybe it was her personality. He was a man, after all, and most men would not pick an intelligent, outspoken woman for a wife.

"Are we going to start or not?" Alrik drummed his fingers on the table. "If you don't feeling like teaching, I wouldn't mind skipping it altogether. I need a nap."

"No chance." Gabi placed a hand on her hip and glared. "I am not letting you out of this room until you can recite today's lesson by heart."

A flicker of emotion passed through his face—what was he thinking? Did he think she was flirting with him?

"Can't bear to part with my company?" he said, smirking. "Surely it isn't that you underestimate my intelligence, Gabi. If I were to put in the effort, we'd be done in an hour."

Heat flooded her cheeks. "I...I'm just saying, Aunt Freja wanted..."

"Oh yes, I know what you mean." His voice dropped cold. "It's necessary that I gain knowledge to be prepared for that government job."

"Don't you want to have a different life rather than staying in this tiny place?"

He shrugged. "I don't mind re-locating to the city. But how about you? Will you move to Linberg as well?"

She couldn't give a definite answer. Since she had failed to make Alrik love her, Freja suggested that she meet another mage: a young man called Morkel, who lived with his sister in the south of Savony. Freja had known their parents.

"Pure mages are dying out," Freja had said. "When a mage marries a non-magical person, their children's magic will be diluted. So think about it—you and Morkel can get to know each other. I'm not going to ask you to marry him, but you can do worse. And he understands what it's like to be a mage and having humans depend everything on us."

Gabi thought about a small pile of letters tucked in a drawer in her bedroom. A year ago, she and Morkel started corresponding. He seemed nice, but one couldn't switch affections like trading goods.

Just at this moment, a brisk knock sounded from the front door.

"I'll get it." Alrik sprang up and was at the door in a second. Was he eager to get away from the lesson, or was it simply chivalry on his part? It was the latter, Gabi decided, unwilling to think the worst of him. Alrik might banter and tease her, but he was always a model knight when it came to her foot.

He swung the door open.

Outside stood a young man who was a few years older than Alrik. He had a plain, sun-baked face, though his muscular arms and trim waist indicated an impressive physique. Next to him was a young woman of remarkable beauty. Her hair was braided, crisscrossed on top of her head, and there was a tiny heart-shaped birthmark on the left side of her throat.

Like most Arksan women, she had blond hair and blue eyes, yet her features were so exquisite that one might wonder what she was doing in Brek. She ought to be dressed in silk and velvet, sweeping majestically in the palace. The homespun gown and kerchief around her head seemed an insult to her beauty.

Ronnie and Marianne. Ronnie had grown up in Brek, but a few years ago he moved to Kardi to serve as a bricklayer's apprentice. Marianne was a shopkeeper's daughter. Gabi had met her only once, when she visited Kardi to buy some magical ingredients for Freja, but she recognized Marianne instantly. Few people could forget a face like Marianne's.

"Eric!" Ronnie clapped Alrik on the back, then frowned.

"What're you looking so surprised for? Didn't you get my letter?"

Alrik looked toward Gabi. She realized that neither she nor Freja had told him about Ronnie's letter, which contained a message about Clara. They had received it while Alrik was taking the cows to the pasture.

"We couldn't let Clara travel on her own, so Rianne and I borrowed her father's wagon. I guess we're a day early, but you should've known we were coming."

"Clara?" Alrik said, still looking bemused.

A young girl stepped out from behind Marianne. Although she was several years younger than Marianne, it was clear that the two shared a resemblance. Alrik's eyes widened.

Clara, the girl Freja invited in hopes of making Alrik discover true love, had arrived. And she was already gazing at Alrik with adoring eyes.

CHAPTER 3

S he wasn't jealous.

She was NOT going to be jealous.

But to be candid, Clara was stunning. She reminded Gabi of a water lily—tall, pale, and fair. Her sweet, doll-like features would make her an ideal model for a glass figurine, the kind traded and sold among caravans. The girl wasn't flawless—she hadn't lost her baby fat, but one could imagine what a beauty Clara would grow into when she was older. As she limped slowly toward the girl, Gabi suddenly felt small and insignificant, not to mention awkward. Dressed in a bright pink gown, her silky blond hair braided in pink ribbons, Clara seemed to bring spring into the house.

To make things worse, Alrik was openly staring with his mouth half-wide. Gabi considered prodding his back, but Ronnie got there first and slapped his arm.

"Quit staring, you oaf," Ronnie said, wagging his finger. "Am I invisible, or are you hit by lightning?"

"I'm blinded with the abundance of beauty."

Ronnie rolled his eyes. "Have you met Clara?"

"Perhaps once or twice, when she was a child, but she looks much different now." Alrik grinned and held out his hand. "Pleased to meet you, Clara. And this is Gabi. Don't be afraid— she reserves her bossing around for poor me."

"I do not boss around," Gabi said with a glare. "And if I do, it's because you did something that deserved criticism. Ask Auntie."

Clara laid a cream-white hand in Alrik's and smiled at him. One thing was for certain: she wasn't shy, like Marianne was. Gabi remembered how awkward she was when she met Alrik at fourteen, with Freja's request ringing in her head, telling her to make Alrik fall in love. "I'm glad to be here."

"We're glad too." Gabi held out her hand, telling herself there was no room for petty jealousies. Alrik's life was their priority. If Clara truly made Alrik experience the deep, everlasting power of love, she would only be grateful. "Welcome to our humble dwellings."

Clara stepped into the main room, her limpid eyes taking in the table piled with books, clay tablet, and ink bottle. She picked up a book and wrinkled her nose. *Trade and Commerce in Arksan History*? Is this what you read during your spare time, Eric?"

"Clara," Marianne said, her voice gentle but firm. She laid a hand on her sister's elbow. "You are a guest."

Clara shrugged and put the book down. Although she resembled her elder sister, their characters seemed worlds apart. Marianne was always introverted and shy—when she worked at the shop, she preferred to stay in the back room doing paperwork, rather than handling the purchases at the counter. She was self-conscious of her looks, preferring to cloak herself in gowns of dark colors. Clara, however, appeared the opposite.

"Is Freja in?" Ronnie asked. "Should let her know that I've brought Clara, safe and sound. My, you should've seen the men who stared when I hitched the cart and drove her all the way from Kardi. You'd think they never saw a girl."

"Freja's taking a nap," Gabi said, knowing that the older woman didn't want to be disturbed while working on the collars. "But she asked me to give you this."

She handed Ronnie a small jar filled with purple ointment. "This is a cleaning spell Auntie developed, as a thank-you for bringing Clara. It'll remove the dust on the floor in no time. Just rub the ointment on your broom and it'll pick up every speckle of dust, even larger pieces of trash."

Knowing it was impossible to keep Alrik ignorant of her ability to cast magic, Freja had long ago claimed that she was a decent magic user. To explain her occasional trips to Linberg and other places, Freja said she was hawking her newest spells, though she stressed that she worked on mundane magic, such as beauty spells that made pimples disappear for a while, or heating charms that kept one's hands warm in Arksar's freezing winter. She warned Alrik that the basement was her bastion, and unless in the case of an injury involving blood or the house catching fire, he should never darken the doorway.

Ronnie's ruddy cheeks glowed. "Gee, thanks. I'm sure Mari-anne'll find it useful after we're married."

"You found a house already?" Alrik asked.

"I'm a bricklayer. We'll build our own house. Can't start on it right now—I've still got a few months of my apprenticeship. But we'll get married once I finish."

"Congratulations," Gabi said. "Would you like to stay for dinner?"

"Sorry, got to get back before it's dark," Ronnie said with a grin. "But I wouldn't say no to a bit of grub on the road."

Gabi limped to the cupboard and pulled out a loaf of bread and cheese. While she bundled the food in a large kerchief, Alrik filled up the water flask.

"Gee, thanks." Ronnie grabbed his cap and jammed it on his head. "Marianne and I are discussing when to have the wedding, but it oughtn't be later than a month. I'll let you know when we set the date. You all must come to Kardi for the ceremony, and Eric, you must be my best man."

"Of course," Alrik said.

Gabi was unsure if it was a good idea. What if he were to cut himself by accident, especially when the drinking and merry-making started? Moira cursed Alrik to prick his finger and die on his twenty-first birthday, but neither Freja nor Gabi wanted to take any chances. He could still fall into permanent sleep when the date was so near.

But seeing Ronnie's happiness, she was reluctant to step in and tell him that Alrik shouldn't go. She decided to leave the matter to Freja. Alrik, for all his don't-care attitude and occasionally rebellious nature, rarely dared to defy Freja.

Ronnie packed the food and water in a burlap sack and headed to the door, Marianne following him. She had barely spoken while in the house. "Well, I'll see you soon, mate. And you, Gabi." He waved at Clara. "Don' worry, lil' sister. We'll tell your parents the first thing we get back to Kardi, so they'll know you've arrived safely."

"Thanks for bringing me." Clara's voice was clear and sweet, like a nightingale's. Gabi had no doubt that when Clara came of age, her father would receive just as many, if not more, requests to court his daughter as Marianne had.

When Ronnie and Marianne disappeared down the grass-strewn path, Alrik looked toward Gabi with a question in his eyes.

"Auntie has been feeling weary recently," she quickly explained. "I can't do all the work with this leg, and you have lessons to prepare and the farm to take care of, so she invited Clara to stay with us until you depart for Linberg."

There was a slight frown on his face, but he nodded. "Whatever Auntie says."

He didn't appear to be as delighted as she had imagined. What was wrong with him? Clara was the prettiest girl she had seen. Not that she had seen many, but no one could object to the girl's fresh, natural beauty.

On the other hand, Clara was stealing looks at Alrik. At least the girl found Alrik attractive.

Still, Gabi hoped that the girl wouldn't fall too hard. As a shopkeeper's daughter, Clara had even less chance than Gabi of becoming queen. According to Freja, Moira cursed Alrik because she detested the ancient royal custom of Arksar.

"The king of Arksar is always supposed to marry a woman of noble birth and distinguished standing; it is considered that commoners will 'taint' the blood of the offspring. But I think this is merely an excuse that Tyrell used to reject Moira. Look at his grandfather. He didn't bother with this custom when he met Helene, who wasn't anything but the daughter of an Arksan bookkeeper and a Savon seamstress. The combination of Arksan and Savon features made her so beautiful that he vowed to make her queen, custom or no custom."

"Carry her bags to my room," Gabi said, gesturing at Alrik in the bossy manner he often complained about. Since he didn't care for her in a romantic way, she had no qualms bossing him around. "And we'll give her a tour of the house."

The tour of the farm and cottage shouldn't have taken long, but for a town-raised girl like Clara, everything seemed novel and wondrous. She kept up a steady stream of questions, mostly directed at Gabi, but it was Alrik her gaze rested on most often.

"The hens won't peck at your heels as long as you stand straight and let them know who's master," Gabi said, when they came to the chicken coop. Clara wrinkled her nose and shifted a bit closer to Alrik, who was looking as bored as he did in his lessons. "Since I can't run, I've learned to stay put and glare."

Clara giggled. "I don't think I can do that. That brown one over there seems real protective of her eggs."

The Kardi girl seemed less ruffled when they entered the cow's stall, where the inhabitant was peacefully drinking water and swishing its tail, but she did look hesitant when Gabi suggested that she learn how to milk the cow.

"Eric will teach you," Gabi said firmly. "Knowing him, he'll be eager to dump his duties on others."

Alrik, however, merely raised an eyebrow. How he managed to raise one eyebrow without moving the other was a skill no one knew how to do, not even mages. "I thought she was here to relieve Freja of her work."

Oops. She couldn't tell him the real objective of inviting Clara.

Gabi put her hands on her hips and glared. "Actually, what Auntie meant was that Clara could help wherever it was needed. And since your lessons are more important than running the farm, she wants you to concentrate on getting knowledge in that bloated head of yours."

"He's taking lessons?" Clara said, tilting her head. "Is that why he has those books in the main room?"

"Auntie wants him to take an assistant clerk's position in Linberg," Gabi said. "She has an old friend who's going to retire soon. But just because Auntie knows someone doesn't mean that Eric can slack off. People in the capital don't want an ignorant worker. He could still lose the job if he doesn't work hard."

"I don't see the point of learning so much," Alrik said, with an insolent shrug of his broad shoulders, "since you can do it for me."

"I'm not always going to be around to save your skin," she said bitingly. "I suppose it's time we head indoors. Freja ought to be up from her nap by now."

Freja was yawning—she must've been working hard on the collars, but she welcomed Clara with a heartfelt smile.

"Child, how glad I am that you've come to stay with us," she said, giving Clara a pat on the shoulder. "It's been a bit lonesome down here, and I'm longing for more company than these two. Their squabbling brings me headaches."

"We don't squabble," Alrik interjected with an injured, indignant look. "We merely choose to have intelligent discussions that happen to start with disagreement."

Gabi rolled her eyes. "Five minutes in your company would drive anyone to start an intelligent discussion."

"Only you. I get along perfectly well with Ronnie. And Ulfred. And Rolf."

"Rolf is nine years old. You'd have to have the mentality of a nine-year-old if you quarrel with him."

"That's enough," Freja said, looking like an exasperated parent. "Gabi, it's high time that you start dinner. Clara, you're too thin—you need more flesh on those skinny arms."

Clara flushed, though she didn't seem offended. "I'll help Gabi with the cooking; I'm not that tired."

"Please do," Alrik said. "The only food Gabi can make is stew, stew, and stew."

Clara giggled. "I can cook something different," she offered. "Marianne and Mother used to teach me plenty of recipes. Some are from Savony."

"Savon cuisine!" Alrik looked as if Clara was his savior. "You should have come to us earlier, Clara. We need someone like you."

Clara flushed and looked pleased. She had the kind of skin that reminded Gabi of roses and cream. Gabi didn't have a mirror, but she knew too well of her own olive complexion, which was smooth and blemish-free; but for the typical Arksan standard of beauty, a pink-and-white complexion was more enticing. Gabi knew she was pretty, but next to this young girl like early spring, all fresh and vibrant, she felt ordinary.

As it turned out, Clara was an excellent cook. Using the

vegetables in the storage shed, she whipped up a golden-brown casserole that had Alrik going for third and fourth helpings, until Gabi snapped at him and reminded him there were three other mouths at the table.

Freja did not say much; she looked thoughtful as she ate and watched the interaction between Alrik and Clara. When dinner was over, she asked Gabi to come down to the basement.

"I need to unearth extra blankets for Clara," she said. "There's going to be a chill tomorrow, and the temperature will drop."

Once in the basement, Gabi closed the door, set a locking charm and muffling charm that made it impossible for anyone to overhear, even if their ears were pressed on the key hole, and turned to Freja.

"Well?" Freja said. "What do you think about Clara? Does it seem likely that she'll fall in love with Alrik?"

Just like Freja. As one of the more powerful mages in the kingdoms, Freja was more attuned to magic and spell-making than to human emotions. She didn't even notice that Gabi was in love with Alrik, though Gabi thought she did well to conceal her feelings.

Three years ago, Alrik had told Freja that he could never see Gabi as more than a sister. When Freja relayed what he said, Gabi had shown disappointment, but she was careful not to reveal how much pain she actually felt from the rejection. Since then, Freja had tried to find another candidate who could perform true love's kiss in case there was need for it.

"I think it looks promising," she said reluctantly. It pained her a little to see Alrik and Clara together, and also pity for Clara's doomed feelings, but it was necessary to prepare for Alrik's survival. "Clara seems to like Alrik already. Did you see how she blushed during dinner?"

Freja frowned. "Not particularly. The collars have been keeping me distracted."

"But the bigger issue is that Alrik needs to reciprocate. When you modified the curse, it said that the kiss must come from someone he loves. It can't be only from a person who loves him." If it worked that way, Gabi's love for him was enough. In fact, she wished that he weren't a prince. If only he were an ordinary peasant Eric, they wouldn't have any obstacles. But on the other hand, if he were an ordinary peasant, Freja wouldn't have taken him under her wing.

Fate was cruel and twisted.

"There's another thing I'm concerned for," Gabi said. "When Ronnie brought Clara here, he mentioned he's getting married to Marianne soon. Do you think we should let him go to the wedding?"

Freja paused. "Did Ronnie ask him to be best man?"

"Yes."

"Hmm. If Ronnie already asked Alrik to be best man, and Alrik said yes, I can't see how we could prevent him from going. They grew up together."

"But Auntie, if it's a risk on Alrik's life..."

"It's a wedding. Not a battlefield. Alrik can take care of himself; we've warned him of his hemophilia."

Gabi nodded, though she still felt a bit uneasy. Whatever might go wrong, might. Could it be coincidence that Moira had made a re-appearance just a month before Alrik turned twenty-one?

"I'll make him a pair of gloves and put an impenetrable spell on them. As long as he doesn't take the gloves off, nothing will pierce his skin."

"Unless it's from Moira. A magic-infused blade can still harm him, irregardless of the gloves. And how about his face? We can't cover his face."

Freja shook her head. "Don't worry too much, dearie. You'll be there at the wedding and keep an eye on him. Now, we'd better get Clara's bedding, or they'll be wondering why we're taking so long."

Clara probably wouldn't mind that they didn't return to the first floor for some time. As Freja carried the blankets upstairs and Gabi followed her, clinging to the railing for support, she prayed that Freja's optimism was justified.

CHAPTER 4

Everything appeared to be going to plan. For the next few days Clara stamped her presence in the farm, latching herself to Alrik and occasionally to Gabi. The cow kicked over the milk pail and she had no idea how to calm it down. The hen refused to let her reach the eggs. The woods looked dark and deep—she needed someone to accompany her. Alrik responded to her distressed requests with amiable assent, coming to her aid with a cheerful disposition.

Once, when she limped to the stalls to call them for dinner, Gabi saw Alrik patiently explaining the habits of the cow to Clara, while she gazed up at him adoringly. The scene stirred a bitter resentment in her heart, and she had to take a deep breath to compose herself before opening her mouth.

This was why she failed. This was what worked with men— she had to act vulnerable, helpless, in order to make Alrik feel like she couldn't do without him. She had ample opportunity with her leg. But such was her nature; she disliked having to rely on others for things she could do herself.

As if to console her feelings, there came a knock on the door. Freja had gone to the trading point for magical ingredients;

Alrik and Gabi were gathering berries and nuts in the woods. Gabi limped to the door and paused for a second. She summoned her innate magic and sensed that the person outside was ordinary, non-magic folk. With less than a month to Alrik's birthday, she had to exert extra caution.

Opening the door, she found a man with a grizzly red beard. He looked terrifying when he didn't smile, but when he did, it was an infectious smile that made even children smile back.

"'Lo, Gabi," Ulfred said. He was a retired palace guard and lived with his young grandson, Rolf. Ulfred also knew that Alrik was the prince; sometimes he kept an eye on Alrik whenever Gabi or Freja were busy. "Just you in the house?"

Gabi told him where the others had gone. Ulfred frowned. "They oughtn't have left you alone. It's far out here, but you'd never know when a tramp shows up, and you can't run due to that leg of yours."

"You forget I'm a mage," Gabi said, smiling. She had enough magic to overpower a dozen tramps. "Did you come to see Alrik? You can wait in the main room; he should be back before long."

A few years ago, Freja had asked Ulfred to give Alrik lessons in strengthening and self-defense. Alrik needed to grow stronger, she said, due to his hemophilia. Her real reason was to make Alrik capable of fighting. A future king couldn't be a weakling. Arksan kings were known to be warriors rather than scholars.

"Naw, I just came to deliver this." He tossed an envelope, smudged and worn, into Gabi's hands. A quick glance at the handwriting told her it was from Morkel. "Got an admirer?"

"Oh no, it's just a friend," Gabi said, trying to look nonchalant, but Ulfred hadn't spent forty years in the palace for nothing.

"Maybe 'just friends' now, but it could be more in the future, eh?" He grinned. "Thought you and Alrik would make a match of it one day. Pity it's not to be."

"He doesn't see me more than a bossy sister," she said. The rejection from Alrik still burned in her mind.

"He used to be real fond of you."

"If he did, he grew out of it."

Once Ulfred disappeared down the path, Gabi shut the door and limped to the rocking chair. She liked to sit there and relax when she didn't have chores to do or lessons to plan. Drawing the letter from her apron pocket, she tore the flap open and started to read.

"Dear Gabriella," Morkel wrote. "How does it fare in the great Arksan forest? We have arrived in Reine, a small town about a day's journey from the Savon castle. Traveling non-stop is exhausting, though I doubt we'd have much time to relax when we arrive. You must have heard from your aunt that two trolls have broken out from underground and killed a servant girl, and seriously injured a few others. It happened that the servant girl's family lives in the very same town, and they have been in a state of shock and mourning. The mother is confined to bed, so great is her grief. I wish I could employ magic to numb their minds and make them forget the pain, but I know it is unwise to tamper with emotions."

Gabi shut her eyes for a second. She knew what it was like to lose a loved one.

"What are you reading?"

A familiar voice drawled. Like a child caught stealing candy, Gabi quickly stuffed the letter into her pocket and glared at him. Alrik had just come in the main room, carrying a basket. Clara followed close behind. She was so engrossed in reading the letter that she hadn't heard them enter.

"Is that another letter from your admirer?"

"He's not an admirer," she said sharply. "He's a friend."

Alrik smirked, but there was no mirth in his eyes. "A friend who you've been corresponding with for nearly a year? Where is he from?"

"I..." she began, then stopped. She didn't owe him an explanation. She had every right to correspond with Morkel. "Since when are you so interested in my affairs, Master Eric? Who I write to is my business."

Alrik looked like he wanted to deliver a heated retort, but shut his mouth tightly. He set the basket of nuts and berries on the table and vanished. Clara, glancing at his retreating back, looked at Gabi.

"Is he all right?"

"Don't mind him," Gabi said, not bothering to repress her irritation. She got up, limped to her bedroom, and shut the door. Really, Alrik could be so annoying. Now who was being the bossy one?

* * *

Alrik was all smiles at lunch. Clara had made roast beef, fried potatoes, and sugar-glazed carrots that had Gabi scraping her plate.

"Aren't you a culinary goddess," he drawled, ladling a third helping of the beef. "I wouldn't mind having this every day."

Clara flushed and giggled. "It isn't anything special. At home, Mother and Marianne could get up a feast. You should come some day, Eric. They'll be glad to have you."

"I can't wait," he said, with another grin that made Clara blush.

It seemed that Alrik was pacified, and he no longer was bothered about Gabi's letter. But once it was time for their lesson, his cloudy mood returned. He lounged on his seat with eyes half-closed, his fingers playing idly with the quill, and looking like he wanted nothing but to be done in ten minutes.

Gabi silently took her place on the other side of the table.

"Turn to page forty-two."

He didn't move.

"Eric."

With a sigh, he opened the book. Gabi went through the lesson, her picture-perfect memory enabling her to recite facts without much effort, though inside her emotions were twisted with anxiety and curiosity. Was he even listening?

"And so, after the great King Bjorn conquered Trond, he united all regions that we call the kingdom of Arksar today." Gabi closed the book with a snap. "Any questions?"

Alrik, who had his elbows crossed over the back of his head while she gave him the history lecture, loosened his posture and placed his elbows on the table. His gaze, intense and piercing, rested on her face. Messy sun-gold hair framed a handsome, chiseled face that strongly resembled the current king, Tyrell. As she saw Alrik grow more and more like his father every day, Gabi prayed that no one in their tiny village, Brek, would discover the connection.

"I do have a question."

She crossed her arms and waited.

"Who is the man you're corresponding with?"

"This has nothing to do with our lesson."

"Then let's make it relevant," he said, leaning forward. His sky-blue eyes were like a lake, peaceful yet deep. She averted her eyes, ignoring the heat that was crawling up her face. Peasant or prince, he had a magnetic presence that no one could ignore. "Give me a test. If I get all answers right, will you answer me that question?"

She drew in a breath. "You're not a child, Eric. I am not using that outdated method of dangling carrots in front of you to make you behave."

"Who cares about the method if it works?" he said, doing a greatly exaggerated gesture of yawning. "The facts are dry and mundane, and the way you teach is boring. How am I to have the incentive to learn unless there's some fun involved?"

Gabi hesitated. From how he barely seemed to be listening while she imparted the lesson, she doubted how much he absorbed.

"Fine. If that'll make the facts lodge in your brain." She closed the book with a huff. "Tomorrow afternoon, I'll set you a test with twenty questions."

"I have to go to Ulfred's tomorrow," he reminded her.

"Very well then, the day after tomorrow."

Gabi limped back to her room. She shoved *A Brief History of Arksar* into the shelf above her bed and collapsed on the sheets. Why was Alrik suddenly showing interest in her letters? He couldn't be jealous. He probably was only irritated that she was keeping a secret from him. And if this would make him study harder...all the better.

A while later, when she found Clara boiling water in the kitchen, Gabi leaned against the wall and coughed to get the girl's attention.

"Clara, I need you to bake enough bread and scones to fill a basket, and I need you to take it to Ulfred's house tomorrow with Eric."

CHAPTER 5

Alrik was irritated. Not that he exhibited it—he was known to be charming, and charming he must remain on the outside, though inside he was seized with the urge to shake Gabi's shoulders. As he headed to Ulfred's house, Clara hanging at his side, his mind drifted continuously toward Gabi. This morning she had sent him off to Ulfred's with a smile and a wink at Clara, saying, "Have fun, you two."

Was she deliberately trying to make Clara and him a pair? He didn't understand. It wasn't as if he were a catch. As an ordinary farmer—well, a well-educated farmer but not rich by any means—Clara could have better prospects.

The idea irked him to no end—for he had harbored a secret, burning affection for Gabi that had taken root since he first laid eyes on her.

He had been working in the garden, pulling up weeds with Ulfred, when Freja returned from a long trip. She occasionally took trips to Linberg, visiting a friend who worked at the palace.

There, sitting in the well-worn wagon, was a girl around his age. She didn't look much like the villagers—it was the first time he had encountered anyone with dark hair and olive skin —but it didn't matter. She was as lovely as a summer dream, and would've been even lovelier, if not for the desolation in her eyes.

"Both her parents died, and her leg was injured badly in an accident," Freja whispered to him, while Ulfred came forward to lift Gabi off the wagon. "She has no family now, so I decided to adopt her. Be kind, Eric."

He was not a saint by nature, but at that moment he was filled with sympathy as well as intrigue for this new addition to the household. Alrik wanted nothing else but to make her smile.

It took almost two months. Matthias gave him a fat puppy with mild brown eyes and a cute yipping that endeared it to everyone. When he carried the puppy indoors and set it on the ground, Gabi was sitting in the rocking chair, placidly knitting as if she were seventy instead of fourteen. The puppy scampered across the floor with muddy paws, stopped in front of the girl, and wagged its fluffy tail with a few barks, as if expecting her to produce a meaty bone.

A smile blossomed from the corners of her lips, bringing a sweetness to her features and a glow in her eyes.

He had never seen anything so beautiful.

Alrik decided then and there that he wanted to see her smile again. Again and again. He tried everything he could, from bringing her flowers to learning useless but flashy card tricks. It worked sometimes, and he was rewarded with the prettiest smile that ought to be painted, framed, and hung upon the wall (in reality, her smiles were kept treasured in his dreams). Other times she retreated into her moodiness. But as Gabi gradually learned to live with the anguish of losing her parents, she resembled less of a drab, gray winter evening, and came to reveal more of her true character—a vibrant, clever young woman who might be a tad bossy at times, but nevertheless set up permanent residence in his heart.

Someone tapped him on the arm, jolting him out of the wandering direction of his memory.

"Eric?" Clara pouted. "Are you walking with your brain shut off? I've been trying to talk to you and you barely respond."

"Sorry, sweetheart," he automatically responded, with an obligatory smile that charmed almost every maiden he met. "It must've been something that Gabi put into breakfast this morning. My stomach isn't receptive to the food she makes sometimes."

"Then let me cook tomorrow. I can cook much better than she."

"Trust me, sweetheart, I'd love nothing less, but then she'll have to do your job, and she'll have far more trouble skimming milk and driving the cows to pasture with that leg of hers. Anyway, what were you talking about? Compliments of my manly strength and looks, I bet."

She pinched his arm and giggled. "You are such a hopeless flirt, Eric."

He grinned, but in his mind he wished that it was Gabi walking (or to be more specific, limping) at his side. But then, Gabi wouldn't flirt with him. She had stopped showing him anything but platonic friendship since he made it clear she was only like a sister to him.

"Gabi said that you take boxing lessons," Clara commented, gazing at his broad shoulders with shining eyes. "That is *so* manly."

Alrik gave a hardly perceptible nod. Several years ago Freja claimed that he was too skinny for his age and needed more flesh on his body if he were to work on the farm. And so she made an arrangement with Ulfred, a retired palace guard. She'd pay him to teach Alrik how to fight and Ulfred would earn some money to raise his grandson.

Thanks to Ulfred's training, Alrik grew from a scrawny teen to a man with an impressive body that any maiden would appreciate. Gabi would blush scarlet whenever he returned to the cottage with his shirt off, after a particularly rigorous bout of training. She'd throw a shirt at him and tell him to stop strutting around half-naked.

The memory made him smile. Every time he left Brek, whether to visit Ronnie in Kardi, or to trade with Lulan merchants at the ancient oak tree, he thought about Gabi. They had lived together for nearly seven years. For some people, they might have grown to be like brother and sister, but for him, he knew that it wasn't brotherly affection.

She was smart, incredibly so with her razor sharp memory, and despite the numerous times she scolded and chastised him, he sensed she cared and wanted the best for him. Some men might regard her crippled leg an inconvenience, but Alrik barely found it a flaw. He loved her and wanted to spend the rest of his life with her.

But he was hesitant to take the next step. His blood problem was a hereditary disease, and he didn't want to risk the chance that it'd pass down to his children. And so, while he was madly in love with Gabi, he held back. If only he were fully hale and healthy, he'd have courted her.

Alrik let out a sigh as they approached Ulfred's house. Perhaps it was just as well that Freja wanted him to take up a job in Linberg. It was torture being around Gabi all day, yet unable to express his true feelings.

"Eric!" They hadn't even reached Ulfred's doorstep, when the door flung open and Rolf greeted him with eager eyes. The boy must have seen him from the dormer window. "I've been waiting for you!" His eyes widened at the sight of Clara, who looked fresh and pretty in a flower print dress, her golden hair in two braids.

"Hello," she said in a cheery voice and dipped her hand into the basket. She handed him a cinnamon-and-apple bun, still warm from the oven. "You must be Rolf. I'm Clara, and I made this especially for you."

Rolf accepted the bun and sniffed it with appreciation. Alrik gave him a nudge, indicating that he should say thank you. "Are you visiting, Clara? Or are you staying?"

"Freja hired me to help in the house and on the farm. I don't know how long I'll be here, but she has promised me at least a month's wages."

Rolf brightened. The child was won over by a mere cinnamon bun.

"Where's Ulfred?" Alrik said.

Rolf pointed to the back of the house. "He's waiting for you."

In the yard, Ulfred was waiting for him impatiently. Despite his age (near sixty), he was as lean and powerful as any thirty-year-old. Ten years ago he retired from his post as the head of palace guards—rather early when he still maintained excellent strength and health. When Alrik asked why he chose to retire in a quiet village like Brek, Ulfred merely shrugged and said he was tired of city life.

"Eric!" Ulfred said, clapping him on the back. "Heard from Freja that you're planning to go to Linberg soon?"

Alrik nodded. "Freja said I should go after my twenty-first birthday."

"You'll like it, I'm sure. Need to see more of the world instead of being cooped up in a tiny place like this. Now, show me what you learned last time."

Alrik demonstrated a flurry of punches and kicks.

"Not bad," Ulfred said. "You need a bit more speed—have you been running every morning? That's an area you've got to improve on. Your strength is decent, and if someone were to fight you, he'd go down pretty quick. Except in the case when someone's wielding a weapon. Even I wouldn't dare to fight bare-handed when someone is armed."

Freja had made it clear that while she wanted Alrik to gain strength, the training was NOT to draw blood.

"Anyway, I'm going to the woods now. Got to hunt some game for dinner. When I come back, we'll have a proper duel."

"Sure thing. By the way, I've brought a girl. She's playing with Rolf at the moment."

"Ah, so she's finally arrived." Ulfred nodded. "Marianne's younger sister, isn't it?"

"How did you know?"

"Freja mentioned it a while back." Ulfred grinned and nudged his arm. "What do you think about the girl, eh? As pretty as Marianne?"

Alrik raised an eyebrow. "She's only been here for a day and you're already plotting like a matchmaker?"

"What else is there to do?" Ulfred's tone was light, but there was an earnestness in his gaze that made Alrik a tad confused. Why was Ulfred so concerned about Clara? "So are you interested in her?"

Alrik shrugged. "Like I said, she's only been here for a day. Time will tell." He wasn't even twenty-one, and here Ulfred was acting as though if he didn't take an interest in Clara, he was going to remain a bachelor for the rest of his life, a thought that was frustrating and depressing. With his blood condition, the bachelor prospect was very likely.

"Well, don't dally too long," Ulfred said. "Girls don't like it when you behave wishy-washy around them."

From his experience, girls were more likely to be irritated if he tried to make a move too fast, except for a few who were clearly into him. But Alrik didn't bother to explain.

Ulfred vanished. Alrik stood looking after him for a while. Ulfred knew about his condition; surely he would know that Alrik would not—could not—be interested in girls.

But it wouldn't hurt to flirt. Life would be dull indeed

without pretty girls. Might as well make the most of the chance while he was young and good-looking.

Alrik started warming up. He kicked, he punched, he did sit-ups, he did push-ups, and he rolled across the ground, as agile as a deer. He wondered what it was like to work in the palace. What about Gabi? Would she end up with the mysterious man who was corresponding with her?

Jealousy stung through his mind. Alrik jumped and kicked at a tree so hard that he heard the bark splinter.

Two hours later, sweat soaked through his collar and tunic. Alrik grabbed a towel and wiped his neck and forehead, breathing heavily.

Footsteps echoed behind him, and a hand was on his arm, followed by a frantic whisper.

"Eric, you've got to come now." Clara's fingers dug into his sleeve. Her voice trembled a little. "There's a man here—he says he's Rolf's father, and he won't leave until Rolf goes with him. D'you know him?"

Alrik had never seen Rolf's father, but he had heard unsavory tales about the man. The boy's mother died of typhoid fever, and the father abandoned him due to heavy drinking and gambling. The last time Rolf saw of his father was in prison; his father had beaten up a gambling partner in a drunken rage.

In the living room, a middle-aged man with unkempt hair and a thick beard was pounding on the table with a fist, while Rolf cowered behind a chair in the corner.

"You come home with me this instant," the man growled. Another punch, and the table shook. Alrik was surprised; he'd expect Ulfred would have a sturdier table. "Get out of that corner now and stop shaking. You're too soft; a good whipping will toughen you up."

"Shut up," Alrik said loudly. He stepped in front of Rolf, shielding the boy. "If that's how you used to treat your son, no wonder Ulfred had to get him away."

The man whirled around. His eyes were bloodshot, his skin sallow, and he reeked of sweat, manure, and alcohol.

"I don't want to go with him," Rolf said in a low voice. "Every time he came back he wanted money. When Mama refused, he hit her."

"He won't hit you." Alrik rolled up his sleeves and faced the man. "Get out of here while you can."

"Don' yer tell me what to do with my son, you pup!" the man yelled, his face purple with rage. "If he knows what's good fer him, he'd be comin' home with me this instant. The law's on my side; he can't stay here."

"The law makes an exception for scum like you," Alrik corrected him. At that instant, he was grateful that Freja insisted that he study the laws of Arksar. "You've been in jail, and you haven't mended your ways. Do you think in court the judge will allow your son to be brought up by a criminal?"

The man swelled up like a bullfrog. "You dare lecture me? You weren't even born when I was beating up thieves and robbers in the streets."

"True, which means that at least twenty years your junior, I wouldn't have trouble beating you up."

With a snarl, the man reached into his pocket and flashed a curved blade at them. A dagger, rather peculiar in shape, but the gleaming blade signified danger nevertheless. Clara gasped and moved closer to Alrik.

"I'll cut this pup up and take yer away before that nosy grandfather of yours returns!" he yelled, waving the dagger in the air.

Alrik pushed Rolf as far away from him as he could—toward the wall, shouting, "Clara, take him and run to the kitchen. Lock the door. I'll take care of this drunk."

The man leaped at him, swinging the dagger. He wasn't a trained fighter, but the dagger gave him an advantage. As Ulfred had warned, a man with a weapon was more dangerous even if he wasn't skilled or strong.

By instinct, Alrik grabbed the table and used it as a shield. The dagger hit the wood with a crunch—the man pulled out the blade and howled.

"I'm taking my boy, and you ain' standing in my way!"

The man kicked at Alrik, who dodged. He was about to use the table again, when the man rolled on the floor and slashed at him. Alrik backed away, but not before the gleaming blade cut through his trousers, drawing blood.

Clara screamed. For a moment, Alrik felt as if a heavy shadow passed before him. He barely felt pain—it was too brief—but as he felt blood start flowing from the wound, alarm crept up in his mind, blotting out all senses. He was going to bleed to death, he was going to die at twenty, and he'd never live to see Gabi arrayed in a wedding gown, smiling at him...

The door opened. Ulfred came in, his face as black as thunder. The former palace guard grabbed a chair and threw it at Rolf's father, who tried to duck, but it was too late. The leg of the chair clipped him on the head and he let out a grunt of pain. Ulfred followed up with a swift punch on his stomach and wrenched the weapon out of his grasp. The dagger dropped to the ground with a clatter.

"What—are—you—doing—with my grandson!" Ulfred punctuated each word with a blow.

"Grandpapa, wait!" Rolf shouted. "It's Papa—stop beating him, you'll kill him..."

Ulfred stopped, as if he had hit him over the head. "Oh." He blinked. "Sorry—haven't seen him for ages—my memory's not as good as it should be. But what's he doing, waving a weapon in my household? And Eric! You're bleeding!"

Clara rushed for a bandage and brandy. Rolf's father, bruised and bleeding, crumpled to the ground.

Alrik pressed a cloth to his wound, his fingers trembling. To his surprise, after a while the bleeding stopped.

"Is this normal?" he asked Ulfred, who was muttering to his son-in-law that he was a disgrace and he should never come to Brek again, or he'd find himself behind bars again.

"What?"

"The bleeding stopped." Alrik looked at his wound. It wasn't deep, but the dagger had drawn a long and jagged wound across his leg. Tiny droplets of blood dribbled, but it wasn't the same as what he remembered in his childhood. "When I cut myself with the butter knife, back when I was about nine or ten, the blood wouldn't stop. Aunt Freja brought handkerchiefs, and the blood soaked through all of them. This wound is even worse, so..." He shook his head, puzzlement clouding his mind. Did he remember incorrectly? But although the memory was from ten years ago, it stood out vividly in his mind. He had thought he was going to bleed to death, and Freja had given him an hour-long lecture and sent him to bed without supper.

Ulfred opened the door. Warning the man never to come to Brek again, he shut the door with a bang.

"How did that scumbag hurt you?"

"Rolf was teaching me how to spin a top," Clara said, starting to clean Alrik's wound with a bottle of brandy. Alrik gripped the arms of his chair and resisted the urge to make any sound. If it were only Gabi and him, he wouldn't have trouble letting loose a grunt of pain, but in front of Clara and Ulfred, he needed to keep a tough exterior. "Then that awful man came knocking on the door. I didn't want to let him in, but when he saw Rolf he just forced the door open and strode into the room. I knew I couldn't stop him, so I ran out to get Eric. The man tried to take Rolf, but Eric wouldn't let him, so he attacked with a knife."

Ulfred let out a string of curses that shouldn't be said in front of Clara, much less his grandson. He apologized, though Clara merely giggled and Rolf looked oblivious.

"Everything all right?" he said, leaning over and staring at Alrik's wound.

"I think so." Alrik frowned. "Maybe this means I'm cured?"

"If Freja said you had a problem, don't assume you're off the hook. Always be safe than sorry, lad."

"What problem?" Clara asked.

Alrik explained.

"But you healed," Clara said, pointing at the wound. She had put the bandage over the wound with a deftness that he appreciated. She was, after all, a shopkeeper's daughter, not a noblewoman who hardly did a day's work. There was a red stain, but no more blood trickled down his leg.

"True." He scratched his head. "But back when I was a child, I was bleeding seriously."

Clara stood up. "I know a doctor in Kardi. When we go for Marianne's wedding next week, I can bring you to that doctor."

Alrik nodded. Hope—bright and beautiful like the midday sun—filled his mind. Was it possible that his bleeding problem had faded away with time?

If he no longer had the disease, then he probably wouldn't worry about his children in the future. He'd have no qualms courting Gabi. He'd be able to stop fighting his attraction to her, and simply go ahead and confess his feelings.

But it had better be soon. That letter correspondent seemed to be a young man that Freja approved. He had to act fast and claim Gabi before she was promised to another.

CHAPTER 6

*A*lix emerged from healer's ward and headed to North Tower. A breeze sent new leaves fluttering to the ground, and the faint scent from the garden drew butterflies and bees circling over the crocuses and primroses. Normally, a day like this would be pleasant, but a tension hung in the air like a fog. Few servants were in the garden, and the ones who passed through walked quickly, their heads bowed and voices urgent and anxious.

"Did you see those green-skinned monsters yesterday?"

"My heart was beating like mad. I thought I was going to keel over and die!"

"So that's what the princes have been dealing with—the poor things."

"I don't think I can stay here any longer. The pay is good but I ain' risking my life staying here."

"When they said there were trolls underground I didn't believe it, but when those two monsters came out I..." A maid let out a sob. "I'm quitting today; I ain' gonna hang around and get gobbled up."

Alix watched as the maid wiped her tears and stalked away.

Her heart felt heavy as iron. She couldn't blame the maids for being scared—anyone would be.

She quickened her pace, not wanting to relive what happened the night before, but the horror was so vivid, so terrible, that it crept up like a phantom, messing with her mind, despite her determination to banish it from her memory.

She could still hear the screams that ripped through the air, filled with terror. She was staying in a private chamber in Central Tower with a window facing north, and when the screams woke her, she dragged herself out of bed and peered outside.

Selma stumbled out of the tower, blood pouring down her face like a red river, staining her front. Seconds later, an eight-foot troll burst out, a human leg dangling from its jaws. It lumbered toward her, red eyes wild, as if it had been starved for days.

A wordless cry emitted from Alix's throat, her body frozen in shock. The troll lunged forward and made a grab, its long green fingers missing Selma by an inch. An arrow embedded in his arm, the feathers quivering.

Theo stood in front of the tower, bow and arrow in hand. He released a second arrow, which flashed through the air in a silver blur and lodged in the troll's thick neck. It howled, and the sound was worse than ten hellhounds braying.

By that time, dozens of servants had gathered outside, their expressions filled with shock, horror, and disbelief. Alix knew there was skepticism when the queen announced the trolls' existence. Now, no one would dare question whether the queen was deluded.

The rest of the princes appeared, and while their expressions also spoke of fear and shock, they had sufficient experience dealing with trolls. Enzo and Ethan charged forward, one armed with a shield, the others swinging two broad swords. The troll roared and attempted to impede them with a powerful blow, but it suddenly froze. A few seconds later it crashed to the ground, an enormous spear sticking out of its back. Julian, his dark hair covering half of his face, slowly lowered his arm. Theo approached his younger brother and clapped his back.

A shaft of bright sunlight shone in her eyes when the shadows of the building ended. Alix blinked; the present came into focus.

Sounds of men shouting reached her ears. On the other side of North Tower, Theo was directing soldiers. Large slabs of stone were being hauled from the mountain behind the castle, forming a wall around the tower.

Theo saw her. His eyes were bloodshot, indicating he barely slept last night, and there was stubble on his chin. Her heart went out to him—he had suffered this pressure for years. Breaking the curse gave him joy and respite, but it was only temporary.

His jaw relaxed a little—no matter how exhausted or angry or frustrated he was, whenever he saw her, his mood would lift, even if just a little. Knowing that she had a positive influence on his character was gratifying.

She slipped her hand into his and gave an encouraging squeeze. "Did you have any breakfast?"

"One bowl of oatmeal."

Alix tilted her head, giving him a quizzical stare.

"I swear I did. Ask the twins."

"I meant that you need to eat more." Alix jabbed his chest. "You probably ate only because the twins threatened to force-feed you in the dining hall."

Something like a smile ghosted his lips. "You know me well." He tucked a lock of her nut-brown hair behind her ear—a rare gesture of tenderness for him. He gazed at her, a soft light in his dark eyes. "My turn to interrogate you. Did you sleep at all last night?"

"I wanted to, but I couldn't," she confessed. "We knew the trolls were coming, but it's so...soon."

"If only Mother had predicted the trolls would break out last night. We would have been better prepared for the attack."

Strangely, since her last prediction, Queen Marguerite returned to her old self, making ridiculous predictions about the weather or even what gown Alix would wear. But then, according to Duchess Claudia, true seers only were able to make genuine predictions several times in their lifetime. Perhaps Marguerite had used up her quota.

"How's Selma?"

For him, Selma was not just a servant. She was a mother to him and his brothers, looking out for them when the queen was unable to do it. She shielded them from the prying eyes of other servants, only wanting to see them safe.

"Odeon said that while her injury is deep, it isn't life-threatening. Beatrice will tend to her and make sure that she recovers in time."

Relief spread on his face. "Thank the magi that we arrived and killed those trolls."

"Beatrice is also trying to analyze the trolls' corpses. Ferdy brought them to her this morning, and she said she'll try to discover if there's anything about the composition of the trolls that could help us, any weakness that could give us an advantage."

Theo looked doubtful, but he nodded. "Wasn't Beatrice scared when she saw the trolls?"

"I think Ferdy was more squeamish when Beatrice was examining the corpses."

They shared an understanding smile. Ferdinand was much taller and stronger than Beatrice, but if asked to bet who was mentally stronger, Alix would place her money on the latter.

"I need to send a message to Freja." Theo rubbed a hand over his forehead. "That wall won't be able to hold off the trolls for long. We need the power of a mage." He regarded her with a thoughtful look. "You're dressed for going out."

"Fabio wrote me yesterday."

Theo frowned. "Everything all right with him?"

"I hope so." Last time she saw him, he seemed happy. He had saved a good deal from working as the queen's favorite tailor. He even talked about buying a house. "I need to see Auntie anyway, and she doesn't live far from his house."

A soldier approached them with a question about building the wall. Theo turned, but not before giving her a swift kiss on the cheek and telling her not to be long. Alix looked after him, a hand on her chest. To this day, it still seemed surreal that she had ended up in a romantic relationship with the crown prince, something that she couldn't have imagined a year ago. Not only because of their differences in station, but also that when they first met, she thought him the most obnoxious person she ever encountered.

Yet she fell in love with him. And Theo, notorious for his hatred of women, felt the same. If it weren't for the trolls, they might be married by now. On the other hand, it was the threat of trolls that brought them together.

The courtyard was mostly empty. Usually it was a flurry of activity, with vehicles and people waiting and talking, but today it was quiet. The carts and carriages stood in the wide open space, no one in sight.

"Lady?"

A boy's voice. She recognized him—Jacques, who sometimes drove Theo and Gerald to the city, where they picked up defensive spells and weapons at shady stores.

"Good morning," she returned with a nod and smile. It felt strange, being called "Lady." She wasn't even officially engaged to Theo, but everyone in the castle treated her as if she were the future queen.

Jacques smiled back, but it was a timid smile. She didn't

know him well, but she had seen him hanging around the court-yard and gardens, playing card games with the other boys in the castle employment.

"Are you going out?"

"Yes."

"I'll drive you," he said, before she even asked. "Where are you going?"

She gave him Fabio's address and climbed into the carriage.

The first time she rode in a carriage, she hid under the seat. So much had happened since her first carriage experience.

"Was it...did you see it happen last night?" Jacques said, after they crossed the moat. There was an opening in the carriage that allowed him to communicate with her. "I fell asleep in the stables and didn't hear a thing."

Lucky him. He was probably drinking and passed out in a stupor.

"I saw them," she said. There was no other way to diminish the effect—either there were trolls or not.

"And you saw them...kill people?"

"Not really. But it was enough." Alix shivered. She remembered the night before—of the screaming, the blood running down Selma's face, and worse, the blood splattered on the ground along with bits of nails and body parts. She had thrown up in a bush, unable to believe that a servant was gobbled up, only a short distance from Central Tower.

"When the queen said that there were trolls underground, I thought she was being deluded, yah know, like she used to be." His shoulders drooped. "And there are...more? More of them down there?"

She wanted to lie; it was obvious he was unsettled. But she couldn't lie to diminish his fear. "Yes."

Before she could answer, a yell split through the air. "If you leave now then you ain' coming back! Ever!"

She recognized the voice. Pulling aside the lacy curtains (the carriage must've belonged to a lady), Alix saw Gaspard walking down the street, a huge backpack slung over his shoulder. Pepe, his father, pelted him with balls of yarn. One bright orange ball struck Gaspard on the shoulder and bounced against the carriage.

Curious, yet not daring to intervene between father and son, Alix waited. A while later, Pepe stormed off. Gaspard stared at his father's retreating back. A tear leaked from his eye, but he didn't run after his father. He merely adjusted his backpack and continued walking.

Alix tapped on the wall. "Stop the carriage." She opened the door and hailed Gaspard, who turned around with wide eyes.

"Alix! How come you're here?"

"Hop on," she gestured. "I'll give you a ride."

Gaspard hesitated, but the weight of the backpack changed his mind. He clambered into the carriage and settled against the satin cushions.

"Where are you going?"

"Fabio's."

"That's also where I'm headed." Alix glanced at his backpack. She remembered Fabio talking of buying a house. "Are you going to move in with Fabio?"

"Move in?" Gaspard looked surprised. "Hasn't he told you? We're re-locating to Masaro."

"What?" She understood that they weren't keen on staying in the capital, where friends, family, and neighbors might not approve of their relationship, but Masaro was an ocean away.

"We've discussed our future. Anne-Marie offered Fabio a job in Masaro. None of the dressmakers over there are as satisfactory as him. The pay isn't as good as the Imperial Wardrobe, but we heard that Masaro people are more tolerant of people like us."

It made sense. It made a lot of sense. But it felt so sudden.

Fabio was still working with her at the Imperial Wardrobe weeks ago.

Alix put a hand to her forehead. How could she have missed it? She had been too focused on Theo and the troll problem, so focused that she didn't see the signs that Fabio planned to leave.

The carriage stopped at Fabio's house. Gaspard sprang off and made to the door, then stopped. He twisted his fingers and breathed deeply.

"I'll do it."

Alix knocked on the door. It swung open in a few seconds.

"You're here!"

The next second, she found herself swept up in a bone-crushing embrace with Gaspard.

"Papa has gone to engage a cart that will take us to the port. We'll be on the ship by afternoon." Fabio released them, beaming, but Alix retained his arm.

"You're really going to Masaro?"

"It's for the best, Aly." Rarely did he call her Aly since they grew beyond childhood. "We can't stay without incurring Pepe's wrath, and Anne-Marie promised to take care of us. Besides, Papa and Mama have enough to deal with. My uncles and aunts and cousins have been asking non-stop about the love of my life."

Gaspard blushed.

"But one thing is certain." Fabio gave her a familiar wink. "I'll come back to attend your wedding once you and Theo tie the knot. When is the mage Freja arriving with the countercurse?"

So he didn't know about the troll breakout yet. No need to tell him about it—best that he leave Savony in a cheerful mood. She didn't want him worrying about her, not when he had enough to deal with.

"We don't know yet. But it ought to be soon."

"Once she comes with the countercurse, she'll banish those remaining trolls and you'll be able to marry, right?"

Alix nodded, trying not to betray any sign of anxiety. She wasn't sure that Freja could successfully defeat the trolls without any more casualties.

"When we first came to the castle and you asked Theo for directions, I just knew he'd end up falling for you. I just knew you'd become the future queen of Savony."

Alix rolled her eyes, and he laughed.

"Send me a letter once you have the wedding date set," Fabio said. He hugged her again, and this time Alix couldn't help a sob. She wiped her tears on her sleeve immediately. Gaspard glimpsed her gesture, but said nothing. Perhaps he also sensed that it was best not to disturb Fabio's good mood.

"Of course." She made him promise to write her once he reached Masaro. "Goodbye. And take care!"

CHAPTER 7

There was a change in Alrik's look and behavior when he returned from Ulfred's last night. Clara also seemed rather secretive and nervous, as if...as if...did anything happen between the two of them yesterday? Perhaps there was a catalyst, like the object one added to a tracking spell, that caused the feelings between them to change and ripen into something more intensive. Gabi wondered if she should ask Clara, but she didn't have the nerve to ask right away.

She'd look for signs in Alrik when she administered the test.

When afternoon arrived, Gabi gathered her books and entered the main room. To her surprise, Alrik was already there. He wasn't even reviewing his book (the insolence! the nerve of him!), but instead had his long legs stretched out on the floor, a bored expression on his face, as if he was certain he'd have no problem passing the exam.

"What's been taking you so long?" he asked, pretending to give a giant yawn. "I've been waiting here since the chickens were fed and the cow milked."

"I have other chores to do," she snapped. She had mended his shirts, using a little magic when Clara wasn't nearby. "Now sit straight and prepare for the questions."

Gabi set her books on the table with a thud. She brought out a clay tablet so she could record his answers.

"When did King Tyrell ascend the throne?"

"Such a simple question," he drawled. "Thirty-one years ago, the same year that the treaty between Masaro and Arksar was drawn, regarding trade on olive oil and grapes."

"When was the first Arksan tribe settled?"

That took him a few seconds of contemplation. "The year of 651, when the Savon king Antoine was on the throne for fifteen years."

"Good. And what were the main exports of Arksar at the time?"

"Pine and spruce. Iron. Salmon..."

She couldn't believe it. Alrik, who always seemed nonchalant and lacking enthusiasm in class, actually did listen to her lessons. Surprised and delighted, she forgot why he offered to let her test him in the beginning. She forgot about making the questions too difficult or obscure. For that moment all she could think of was how pleased King Tyrell would be, as Alrik named all fourteen states of Arksar without hesitation. He had brains; he was just pretending he didn't have any.

When he answered the last question and reached for a drink of water, both were silent for a few seconds.

"Was I correct?" he asked.

Gabi nodded. "I didn't expect that."

"So now you can tell me." He rested his chin on his hands and stared at her. There was something distinctly disconcerting in his gaze that made her look away and wonder why he was acting so strangely. "Who's the person you're corresponding with?"

"Why are you so keen to know?"

"Why shouldn't I?"

"It's only an exchange of letters."

He rose from his chair and slowly approached her, pinning her with a piercing, intense gaze. She was trapped in the corner. And even if there was a door behind her, she was powerless unless she used magic to make him move out of her way. "You promised you'd tell me if I got all the questions right."

Unable to look at his face, she stared at his torso instead, and something about his sleeve made her blink. The sleeve that covered his right forearm seemed thicker.

"Eric, what is this?"

She grasped his arm and pushed his sleeve up. A strip of white bandage was wrapped around his forearm.

"You're hurt!" In an instant the world seemed to fall into pieces around her. "When? Where? How?"

"Calm down; it's nothing to get so worked up about," he said. "I got slashed by a knife yesterday at Ulfred's house, and the wound healed normally. That bleeding problem is probably only a childhood thing."

Alarm seized her heart. "How did you get slashed?"

"Rolf's father came to the house and wanted to take him back to Kardi. The nerve of him, abandoning his wife and son for years, and now he wants his son back. When Rolf refused to leave with him, I tried to stop him. That's when he brought out a knife."

"You idiot," she said, fear creeping up her spine. "Why couldn't you have let him take Rolf, and run for help instead? Where was Ulfred at that time?"

"He was in the woods, hunting for game. Gabi, do you think I could've just stood there and done nothing?"

"Ulfred and Rolf wouldn't want you risking your life. You're lucky that the knife only caught you on the arm. If he was violent or drunk, you could've been seriously injured."

"Well, I'm fine now," he said stubbornly. "And thanks to that wound, now I know my hemophilia is cured."

"Don't be so sure."

Freja stood in the doorway. When she had appeared, Gabi had no idea. But then, as an experienced and powerful mage, Freja had the uncanny ability to listen in when their voices were low, and to appear undetected when least expected.

"Aunt Freja." Alrik spared her a bored glance. "Evening. How's the new heating spell coming along?"

She ignored his question. "Eric, did you say you got slashed by a knife yesterday?"

He raised his arm, showing her the bandage. "The bleeding problem has gone. My wound yesterday healed just as fast as any normal man."

Freja took a step forward. For that moment she shed any pretense of looking like an ordinary peasant woman. Her eyes glowed with fury, and she seemed to have grown a few inches taller as she approached the future king of Arksar.

"You think that the slash you got yesterday was a mere scratch? You thought you healed normally, but that's only because we have kept you safe from bleeding for years." Freja poked a finger at his chest. "Why do you think I sent you to Ulfred? You were a thin, weak boy when I raised you, and I had to make you toughen up, or your bleeding problem would prove to be fatal. Now, you've succeeded in growing stronger, so the first or second injury is healing well. But just because you're not as vulnerable as when you were a child doesn't mean that the problem will never turn up. You still need to be careful. A prick here, a cut there, and you could still be in danger."

She finished her speech with a decisive huff. "Promise me, Eric. Don't you ever take your bleeding problem lightly."

Alrik met her gaze squarely. Then, after a moment, he shrugged. "All right."

Gabi watched the exchange, feeling wary. Alrik might have given in this time, but she sensed that the seeds of suspicion were already planted in his mind. They would have to be very, very careful in the coming few weeks.

Perhaps on the day of his twenty-first birthday, she'd have to tie him up and stuff him in a closet.

* * *

RONNIE CAME to the village next week and brought his bride-to-be with him. Everyone gathered at old Johan's house. Johan was Ronnie's father; he could've gone to Kardi but chose to stay behind. All his life he knew only about farm work and there was no decent job to be had at town. But he was getting older, and when Gabi congratulated him on his son's marriage, he grinned and said he might move when this year's harvest was over.

"This back of mine's been aching dreadfully these years," he said, making a grimace. "Ain' fit for work much longer, so I might as well go. Wouldn't mind helping 'em look after the children."

Marianne was blushing like a wild rose as she stood by Ronnie's side. She was so beautiful that Gabi had to wonder why Alrik wasn't drawn to her. Years ago, Freja soon noticed the young woman's beauty and had considered making her a "candidate" for bestowing the true love's kiss, but then they learned Marianne had a fiancé. About a year ago, the fiancé died at sea. Ronnie, in his last years of apprenticeship, gained confidence and swooped in. Miraculously, he won the fair maiden's heart, beating quite a few others who were also captives of Marianne's smile. Perhaps Ronnie happened to be the type Marianne fancied. After all, he was honest and hardworking, and for many women, that was more than they could ask for.

"We've set the wedding for next week," Ronnie said, his grin almost as wide as his face. "Eric, you'd better get a new suit for the occasion or I'll find another best man. Gab—you'll see that he dresses well, eh?"

"I sure will." Gabi smiled.

"Can't do without her nagging." Alrik pulled a face. "Guess what—she was so worried about me that she even considered forbidding me from coming."

Ronnie's jaw dropped. "But why?"

"That old blood problem of mine."

"Oh, surely it isn't anything to worry about!" Ronnie shook his head, incredulous. "It's a wedding, not war. Eric won't come to any harm. He's twenty-one, Gab."

"Almost twenty-one," she automatically said.

"How 'bout you, Eric?" Johan said, approaching them with a giant mug. "Haven't heard of anythin' from you. Is that why Freja hired her?" He sent a not-so-subtle glance at Clara, who was talking to Matthias's wife.

Alrik shrugged. "Don't know. But I promise you'll be the first to know when I do."

Gabi frowned. This was the Alrik she knew—friendly, even flirtatious, to girls, but never serious. Would he ever fall in love with Clara?

A while later, Ronnie was half-drunk and had to be carried to his bedroom. This was a signal for the guests to leave. Gabi limped to the kitchen, wondering if there was any help needed with cleaning up.

The door was half-closed. A flash of color caught her eye—Clara wore pink today. And there was a voice coming through, a voice that sounded petulant.

"I don't think he likes me."

Instantly she stopped. There was a large grandfather's clock standing against the wall. Looking around, Gabi made certain that no one was close by. She took a deep breath and made blue-white sparks glow at her fingers. With a few magical words, she sent the sparks to the bottom of the clock, making it levitate a few inches off the ground and shift aside, leaving a space behind the wall. She crouched behind the clock and strained to listen to the conversation.

"But I like him better than the boys we've met. Rianne, I don't want to stay here anymore."

"You've only been there for a week," Marianne said in a soothing voice. "That's too short to tell."

"Rianne, he only has eyes for Gabi."

Her heart jumped. It couldn't be true.

"I've been around him a lot. But the most he's done is say I'm pretty and I cook splendidly. But he doesn't even try to touch me. D'you think I'm not the kind he fancies?"

"It can't be," Marianne said. "Look at all the boys who were hankering after you since Mother let you wear your hair down."

"They were interested, I could tell. Hank got into a fight with his brother 'cause I didn't want to walk home with him. I don't think Eric'll get into any fight over me."

"You need to give him time. Eric seems the type to be popular with girls. Wait a few weeks, and if he still isn't interested, then give him up. But it's too early to tell now."

"I don't think he'll change," Clara said sulkily. "He mayn't have realized it, but he cares more for Gabi. He bickers with her, oh yes, but he seems to enjoy it. And last time she got a letter, he was all hung up about who it was from. He was upset 'cause she wouldn't tell him."

Gabi's heart pounded.

"Well…" Marianne sounded hesitant. "If he truly cared for Gabi, why did Freja invite you down here? She could've easily got a working woman for a cheaper price."

"No idea," Clara said. There was a clatter, sounding like dishes being put away in the cupboard. "How many people are you inviting for the wedding?"

The conversation drifted toward wedding preparations.

"Who moved the clock?" Johan's voice boomed. "Who

is...hello! Gabi, I thought you'd gone home already. What're you doing there? Eric's looking for you."

Gabi limped into the main room, nearly bumping into Ulfred. Clara's words echoed in her mind about how Alrik felt for her. It was sweet, yet impossible, but she wanted to believe it —even if it meant that eventually she must bid him farewell.

CHAPTER 8

*G*abi's disgruntled voice floated from her bedroom. "Do we have to arrive a day before the wedding?"

Alrik, who was hauling firewood from the shed, couldn't help pausing in the main room.

"Don't you want to get dressed and be prepared for the wedding?" Clara said.

"I don't see how it's necessary," Gabi said. "For the bride, yes, but I'm only a guest."

"The bride happens to be my sister and she'll need all the help she requires to look beautiful on the big day."

"Marianne's lovely," Gabi said. "She doesn't need a ton of ornaments or cosmetics to look beautiful. Ronnie's crazy about her already—you can see it in his eyes."

"Sure, but it's still better that we show up early." There was a faint rustle of silk. "Now take off that hideous apron and try this on."

Alrik forced himself to leave the cottage. Heat filled his mind when he imagined Gabi taking her clothes off and dressing herself in an elaborate gown for the wedding. Despite living with her for several years, it was rare that she wore nice dresses.

When he moved to Linberg and took up that assistant clerk's job, he planned to buy her a new gown once he received his first paycheck...

If his blood problem was truly cured. He couldn't wait until they arrived at Kardi. If the doctor said there wasn't anything wrong with him, he could finally go for what he truly wanted.

"Eric?"

Freja was behind him. There was a wariness in her gaze, as though she could see through his mind.

"Where are you going?" she said.

"I...I just came to deliver firewood," he said, suddenly unable to speak smoothly in her presence. For some reason, he had grown more wary of Freja now. The things she had told him—the things she forbade him—now that he had the time and chance to think about them, he was getting more suspicious about how she had raised him. But he wasn't going to confront her, yet. He'd get answers from the Kardi doctor first.

"About the wedding," Freja began, then paused. Her blue eyes, serene yet firm, rested on his face. "I want you to be extra careful."

"Why? Am I a five-year-old who cannot be trusted in a big event?"

"I meant that blood problem of yours," she said severely. "Although you healed fast from that slash at Ulfred's, there's no telling if it might return. Don't take your situation lightly."

Somehow, he had the feeling that Freja wasn't telling all she knew. But all he did was shrug his shoulders. "As you say, Aunt."

* * *

KARDI WAS A PRETTY TOWN. Not as pretty as some Savon or Masaro cities—those were renowned for hanging baskets of flowers, whimsical ironwork, and colorful walls—but for Arksan standards, it was pretty. The houses were quaint, if not the colors slightly mundane—brown and white. There were no flowers, as the Arksan climate was too cold most of the time, but there were carved patterns in the woodwork on the door and windows. Everything was neat, planned, and well-constructed, just like how a typical Arksan would behave.

Alrik always enjoyed visits to Kardi. Brek was small, and they lived in the outskirts of the village. He was, after all, an outgoing person and enjoyed social events. The few bars in Kardi afforded him the pleasure to sit down with his friends with tankards of beer, and talk about various matters from farmwork to current gossip. Gabi didn't seem to enjoy the visits as much as he did, though she did take interest in shopping for magical ingredients.

Right now she regarded her surroundings with a watchful eye, while Clara was all smiles and chattering away as if it were her own wedding.

"I wonder how many guests Marianne has invited," she said, counting with her fingers. "Mother likes a big crowd, but Marianne's worried there won't be enough space in the house. Do you know how to do a country dance, Gabi?"

"Gabi can't dance," Alrik said.

Clara's hand flew to her mouth. "Oh, I'm so sorry, I forgot. You act so much like everyone who's normal, I thought you'd know about dancing."

"Don't worry about it," Gabi said, managing a wan smile. "I expect I'll have just as much fun without dancing. Perhaps I'll get enough fun from watching him—" she jerked a thumb at Alrik "—tripping over his feet."

"I'll teach him," Clara immediately said, casting a bright smile in Alrik's direction. "It's so much fun, Eric. The music's lively, and everyone joins hands and claps to the rhythm. You won't want to stop until you're out of breath."

Alrik meant to smile right back, but a glance at Gabi made him sober down. "I suppose," he said shortly.

Clara knotted her brows. "What's wrong with the two of you? It's Ronnie's wedding tomorrow and both of you aren't acting happy at all!"

Gabi quickly broke into a smile. "I'm happy, of course. Ronnie's an old friend. Just feeling a bit tired from working long hours, I guess."

Clara glanced at her, then at Alrik. "Is there something going on between the two of you?"

"Nothing," Alrik said. So did Gabi.

"Aha!" Clara stabbed a finger in their direction. "I don't know what it is, but you two had better kiss and make up before the wedding. Marianne doesn't need to see grumpy faces when she's married."

Alrik felt a tinge of desire when Clara said "kiss and make up," even though she made it sound perfectly normal, almost like school kids making up after a quarrel. But Gabi merely seemed surprised.

"It's got nothing to do with him," she insisted. "Not in the way you're thinking."

Alrik would've given anything to know what was running through her head. Did she still feel anything more than friendship toward him? Was it too late? Was she already turning her attention to her letter correspondent?

He clenched his fists for a second and let go.

"Here we are," Clara said, as the wagon pulled up in front of a large house. "Come on, we've got a lot to do."

* * *

ALRIK DIDN'T EXPECT that his clothes-fitting would take as long as Gabi's, but it did. Ronnie, who wouldn't blink if he wore his shirt inside-out, was actually lecturing him on his best-man's suit.

"No one wears this shade of brown anymore," he said,

65

frowning when Alrik changed into his suit. "Unless you're from the last century."

"What, isn't this face of mine enough?" Alrik said, with a jest in his tone and a raise of his eyebrows. "I'm sure I can charm any woman even if I wore a sack."

"It's not the face that matters," Ronnie snapped. "When you accompany me to the altar, it's what you're wearing that catches everyone's attention. D'you think you can walk down the aisle in rags? You're at a wedding, not a tavern."

"So what can I do?" Alrik threw up his arms. "You got a suit I can borrow?"

"Naw, even if I can spare you something, you're...taller than me." Ronnie looked at Alrik's height with a tinge of irritation, as if he were annoyed Alrik was so tall. "We'll have to buy you something from the shop."

"What?" An image of him prodded and measured rose in Alrik's mind. "I'm not going to get a brand new set of clothes."

"If you're only a guest I wouldn't bother, but since you're my best man—" Ronnie slapped his arm "—you'd better do justice to the event. Look, it won't take long. The tailor I know has plenty of suits finished already; he'll only need to adjust the clothes for your size."

Alrik felt reluctant, but then a brilliant idea hit him. This could be a perfect chance to visit the doctor's without Gabi knowing.

"All right," he said. "But could Marianne spare you? Surely there are things you need to look over in the last minute."

"Marianne has her mother, my mother, and her sister, not to mention plenty of aunts," Ronnie said with total confidence. "Come on, let's not waste any more time."

* * *

ALRIK COULDN'T BELIEVE his luck when he and Ronnie were out

in the streets. When he mentioned that Ronnie wanted him to replace his "disreputable" suit of clothes, Gabi had looked surprised but said she would accompany him. Clara pulled her back.

"We're not done here," she said. "Let Ronnie take him clothes shopping. It won't take much time."

Gabi glanced at Alrik's wrist for a split second. On his wrist was a plain silver bracelet—a tracking charm he was made to wear since he was a child. Freja had told him it was for good luck, but from the occasions she appeared when he got lost in the woods or stayed over too long at friends' places, he soon deduced that it was a device that kept her informed of his location. He had confronted Freja, demanding that she remove the bracelet, but she had lectured him on how his parents died saving him from a burning house, and as his guardian, she had responsibility to see him grow into adulthood.

"Don't be too long," she said.

"So what is it between you and Gabi at the moment?" Ronnie demanded, once they were in the streets. "I thought you liked her."

"I..." Alrik opened his mouth, but he didn't finish. "It's complicated."

"Eric, you've lived with her for years. Years. Look at me—I had to trudge all the way from this edge of the town to the other end, every day, just to make Marianne laugh. You have all the advantages in the world and yet you're not together? I'm disappointed in you. Unless there's someone else she's interested in?"

A flash of that mysterious letter correspondent entered his mind. He still hadn't had the chance to ask Gabi about him.

"I don't know."

Ronnie groaned. "Or is it Clara? Have you fallen in love with her instead?"

Alrik immediately shook his head. His feelings for Gabi were convoluted, but he was certain that Clara and him could never be a couple.

"Then you'd better hurry up, man. You're almost twenty-one. Sure, a lot of us can get married after twenty-five, but by then most of the good ones are gone."

He didn't want anyone but Gabi.

"Where's the tailor?" he asked instead. "Let's get this clothes business over with as soon as possible."

After half an hour getting poked and primped, Alrik and Ronnie emerged from the shop.

"Want to grab a beer?" Ronnie asked, looking around. "There should be a tavern a few streets away..."

"No, I need to run another errand." Alrik clapped his friend's back. "I'll tell you all about it later."

Ronnie frowned, but when Alrik insisted, his best friend shrugged and headed back.

* * *

THE DOCTOR SEEMED SURPRISED to see Alrik walk into his clinic. After giving Alrik an assessing gaze, he said, "You seem in excellent health. What's been ailing you, lad?"

Alrik explained. The doctor listened, a finger on his chin, and when Alrik finished, he shook his head.

"Did you say that the blood didn't stop when you were a child?"

Alrik nodded.

"But when you were cut a few days ago, the wound healed quickly?"

"Is it possible that I 'outgrew' the illness?" Alrik said. Hope started to bubble in his chest.

The doctor pinched his chin and drew his brows together. "Either you have it, or you do not. This is a hereditary disease and cannot be treated. The only way is to be careful and not to get wounded deeply, or you'd bleed to death. Give me your hand, please."

Alrik obliged. The doctor brought out a glass vial, containing a light pink liquid. He poured the liquid on Alrik's palm and rubbed the liquid over his skin.

"This is a small but complicated spell," he explained. "A friend of mine invented it, back in Linberg. There was an old, wealthy family who had the blood problem, and they spent an extraordinary amount of ducats to find a cure. There is no cure, but my friend had at least discovered a way to show if the person is afflicted."

Alrik looked at his palm. He looked again. There was no trace of the pink liquid—it seemed to have entirely dissolved into his skin.

Alarmed, he pointed at his palm. "So do I have this disease or not?"

The doctor pushed at his spectacles and squinted. "Congratulations. If the color is the same as your skin, then it means you don't have it. If your skin turns blood red, you have the disease."

"Really?" He couldn't believe his ears. "Really, truly?"

The doctor rolled his eyes. "Haven't you proof enough when your wound healed normally?"

Alrik felt as if the weight of a mountain was lifted from his shoulders. All his life he had been worrying, worrying that he could never marry because he didn't want to pass on his disease to his children. But if the doctor was right...

"However," the doctor added. "As this is a newly invented spell, there could be errors. Did your parents have this disease?"

"They died when I was a baby."

"Well, can you find your relatives and ask them?"

Alrik blinked. He never knew if he had any relatives. He had asked Freja before, when he was a child, but she gave him vague answers such as they lived too far or were not interested in him.

But now that the doctor mentioned his relatives, hope was re-kindled. Perhaps, if he found a clue...

"But I'd put a very good chance that you're unaffected. Possibly it was only a mistake when you thought you had the disease."

Alrik hesitated. He did have hemophilia when he was a child —the memory of blood flowing from his wound was imprinted on his mind like carvings on wood.

Still, it was true that he had healed quickly at Ulfred's house. To be on the safe side, he should seek out his relatives, but he was fairly sure that he no longer had hemophilia.

Which meant he could court Gabi. He felt like floating as he rose from his chair, feeling like all his burdens were removed.

"I'd better be heading back," he said. "Thank you for your time, doctor."

CHAPTER 9

*B*ack in the castle, Alix was immediately summoned to the throne room.

"His Highness needs you to attend a meeting," the servant told her.

Duchess Claudia was already seated on the throne, arms crossed, with a grim expression. The twins were also there, along with Julian and Ferdinand. Since the curse was broken, Julian had been more agreeable. He scowled frequently and didn't always agree with Theo, but he no longer went to taverns and got drunk. The twins gave her a cheery wave in unison, their bright smiles doing nothing to indicate that they were going to have a serious meeting.

There were also two people Alix had never seen before: a lanky young man wearing glasses and the tallest young woman she had ever seen. The woman was dressed provocatively in a low-cut dress, and her fingernails were purplish-pink. Something in their demeanor made Alix guess that they weren't ordinary.

Theo gestured at a chair next to him. "Sit."

No sooner had she taken her place than the door opened and

a young man of extraordinary beauty entered the room. The woman with purple fingernails gasped out loud.

"Gerald!" Theo rose and strode to his brother, embracing him. As the second eldest prince, Gerald was also the closest to Theo. Before the curse was broken, they'd work together and devise methods to stay alive. "Welcome home."

There was also something different with Gerald that Alix couldn't quite place her finger on. He was beautiful, no doubt, still the most dazzling person she had ever seen. He had his spectacles. There was something more mature about him, like the journey he'd spent away from the castle had opened his eyes and made him older and wiser. Then, when she looked down, she saw it: a ring, glittering with tiny diamonds.

Her hand flew to her mouth. Did he get married?

"I had to come as soon as I got your message." Gerald looked troubled. "Is it true? About the trolls who broke loose and appeared on the grounds?"

Pain flashed through Theo's face. "A scullery maid was eaten; we have arranged for her funeral and compensation for her family. Selma was wounded, but she's in the healer's ward. Her life is not in danger."

Gerald exhaled. "I must see her. Well, after this meeting." He spotted her and held out his hand. "Hello, Alix. Hope you've been keeping my brother in a more tolerable mood."

"He's been a pain but I've been doing my best." Alix darted a curious glance at the two strangers. "Will you introduce us?"

"Ah...yes, I forgot, both of you haven't met them yet." Gerald indicated the man and woman to come forward. "This is Morkel." He pointed at the lanky man with glasses. "And this is Tamarka. They are mages who used to live in the south of our kingdom. They're two of the seven mages that Freja had invited to help us fight the trolls."

"Welcome," Theo said, extending his hand. There was evident relief in his face. Help from mages was what they needed at the moment. "We're honored and pleased that you have come."

Tamarka shook his hand and fluttered her eyelashes at him. Alix had a sudden urge to pull Theo away, but he merely slipped his hand out of her grasp and turned to Morkel. Tamarka looked a bit disappointed, but she stepped back. Her gaze fell on Alix and she tilted her head. Alix gave her an uncertain smile.

"Ah, so you're the little shoe cobbler who charmed the prince!" Tamarka swooped upon her like a mother hen. Up close, Alix noticed the mage had kohl on her eyelids. "You have pluck, breaking the curse. How'd you do it?"

Alix answered the best she could. Tamarka oohed and aahed in a way that reminded her of Fabio. "An invisibility cloak! That's so exciting. Can you show us how to disappear?"

Morkel shook Theo's hand. "Since two trolls have showed up at the castle, what defenses have you employed?"

Theo gave a list of spells. Morkel listened, nodding, but then he shook his head. "That won't be enough against two hundred trolls. We'll come and help you strengthen the wall until the countercurse is completed."

"Do you know when Freja will be done with the counter-curse?" Theo asked. "Anything that we can do to help her speed up? With the trolls breaking out sooner than expected, I'm concerned there will be more destruction if she doesn't complete it soon."

"She's doing her best," Tamarka said, "but you need to understand that she's hindered by the number of trolls."

'What do you mean?" Alix asked.

Tamarka settled down on a chair and crossed her legs. Although she was dressed fully from head to toe, there was a sultriness in her posture that felt seductive anyway. "Hasn't Freja told you the details? She's weaving two hundred magic collars—one for each troll. So it's not going to be quick. Besides, the witch Moira has returned with her sister. Freja needs to worry about the witches as well."

Gerald bit his lip. "I saw the witches, in fact." He launched into an account of the adventure he had when he was abducted by Moira. As he explained, he kept mentioning the name Sybil. By the time he finished, Alix had a good idea who Sybil was.

"Is Sybil the girl you married?" she asked.

Gerald blushed. "We're just engaged," he said. "I wanted to marry her, but she couldn't consent without having her servants present. So we decided to opt for an engagement instead."

"We can make it a double wedding," Theo said, glancing at Alix. Her cheeks warmed. Although he was adamant that they couldn't officially marry until the trolls were banished from Savony, he was firm that he would wed her.

"It's all Gerald's fault," Enzo spoke up sullenly. "Getting to the most beautiful lady in the kingdom before any of us had a chance."

"If only we got his compass, we'd be able to win Sybil's heart," Ethan said, with a disgruntled glare at Gerald.

The second eldest prince rolled his eyes. "If you met Sybil in her beast form, you'd have avoided her as much as possible, much less fall in love with her."

Tamarka cleared her throat. "Don't be devastated," she said, blowing a kiss at Enzo. "There are plenty of women who'd be happy to have you."

To Alix's surprise, the twins actually looked scared, as if Tamarka was brandishing a knife instead of blowing a kiss. Their reaction puzzled her. Tamarka was taller than most women, but she was undoubtedly gorgeous. It was the first time that she saw the twins shy away from a beautiful woman.

"Anyway," Tamarka continued, "we ought to discuss a way to keep the trolls at bay until Freja is done with the collars."

"How does the countercurse work?" Theo asked.

Tamarka reached into her pocket and extracted a loop-shaped piece of leather. "This is what the countercurse looks like. Urdu, the most powerful mage alive, invented it. With the power from the enchantment, even the strongest magical creature can be conquered."

"So how do you use it?" Alix asked. The others looked on with curiosity in their eyes. The leather looked fairly normal—similar to the collars they used on dogs and horses.

Tamarka smirked. Magical sparks glittered on her fingertips —the leather strap rose into midair. "Using this collar and the true name of the victim, I can make a person or creature do anything of my own bidding."

She flicked her fingers; the collar flew toward Morkel and wound round his neck.

"I command that Morkel, the wearer of this collar, raise both hands in the air."

Alix watched. Morkel's fingers twitched, as if he was trying to fight the power from the collar, but then he slowly raised his hands in surrender.

"I command thee, Morkel, to walk toward the window," Tamarka continued.

In jerky movements, Morkel crossed the room to the window.

"Amazing," Gerald said in an awestruck tone. Alix was reminded that the second eldest prince was a competent magic user—he used to create the spells that enabled the princes to defend themselves in the battles with trolls. "So when this collar is thrown onto the troll, all you need is to mutter his true name and he will do whatever you ask?"

"Anything."

"I command thee, Morkel, to hop on your right foot thrice," Ethan said suddenly.

Morkel made a face. He raised his foot, but then stopped. "Did you think that Tamarka used my real name?"

"Wait, was that only for show?"

"Any magical being would guard its true name like a nation's secret," Tamarka explained. "None of us dares to reveal our true name. Knowledge of our names means that one can control us —utterly, completely."

"Fantastic." Enzo rubbed his hands. "We'll just ask them to chop off their own heads."

"Freja advised that we send the trolls back to where they come from." Morkel adjusted his glasses. "Trolls are extremely difficult to kill, and their ability to recuperate is amazingly resilient. To this day, there's no foolproof method to judge whether they are truly dead. You might drive a stake through its heart, but it may still be tethered to life."

"Indeed," Duchess Claudia said. "That was how the late king died. He didn't expect the troll he defeated was still alive, and the troll delivered a fatal blow that killed him."

Alix drew in a deep breath. It was the first time she had heard how Theo's father passed away.

Morkel continued. "I found a story recorded way back in King Antoine's time. A group of villagers believed they had killed a troll. There wasn't any heartbeat or pulse. They dug a hole and buried the troll. A few days later, the troll broke out from the earth and gobbled up a group of children. Eventually they did kill the troll, this time inflicting multiple wounds, trussing up its body, and hammering it in a heavy coffin."

Alix caught Theo's arm. "Beatrice and Odeon have the trolls' corpses. We must take precautions."

"I'll tell the soldiers to tie up the trolls' bodies," Claudia said. She stood up and left the room.

A tense silence fell over the room for a while.

"In that case, it's equally risky to send the trolls back to where they came from," Theo said, frowning. "They could return and terrorize us again."

"Chances are much smaller for their return," Morkel said. "The region lies far north of Arksar, with the autonomous land of Sisu between, as well as a vast ocean. Trolls cannot swim."

"How did they come to Savony, then?"

"The ocean didn't exist at that time. Nor did Sisu. The trolls crossed to Arksar, which was sparsely populated at that time, so they headed south to Savony. Many Arksans and Savons fled west to the kingdom we now call Masaro."

The frown on Theo's face relaxed slightly, and he said no more. Alix slipped her hand into his, though he didn't notice until she squeezed his fingers. He returned the gesture, but his gaze remained fixed on Morkel and Tamarka.

Theo cleared his throat. "So how do we send the trolls back?"

"We have two options," Morkel said. "We can extract the names of the trolls and weave their names into the collars. Or we can wait for the trolls to come out, extract their names, and perform the spell to transport them back."

"The second option won't work," Tamarka said, rolling her eyes. "Do you think the trolls will hang around like dumb fools while we extract their names? By the time we get their names, they'd be close enough to kill us. There won't be time to perform the spell to send them back to their land."

Morkel shrugged. "Then we only have the first option."

"How do you extract the names?" Gerald asked.

"Tamarka and I will sneak into their underground lair, find a place to hide, and perform a name-revealing spell."

"What if the trolls notice?"

"They won't," Tamarka said, ignoring an alarmed look from Morkel. "Any decent mage should be able to perform magic without attracting attention."

Theo also noticed Morkel's lack of confidence. "Can't we wait until Freja arrives? I wrote her this morning; she should arrive with the collars soon."

"Freja has enough to worry about," Tamarka said, waving her

hand. Jeweled rings glittered on her fingers. "And she's far enough that even if she starts out today, it'll take days before she arrives. We might as well do something productive." She glanced at Alix. "Might we borrow your invisibility cloak when we go underground? We can turn ourselves invisible, but that'll cost magical energy."

"Of course, but…"

"Then it's settled." Tamarka beamed. "Morkel, how about you work with Theo and figure out how to leave an opening for us to enter the trolls' lair, while I try on the cloak?"

CHAPTER 10

Gabi pulled on her neckline, uncomfortable with how low it was. She had a necklace, but it was shaped like a collar. A good amount of her olive skin showed. The skirt, however, was quite long, the hems brushing across the floor. Was it the trend to have low necklines and long skirts? So uncomfortable and inconvenient. But when she looked into the mirror, she admitted that she did look pretty. More than pretty —the cut and design of the dress made her look desirable.

But the confident glow she gained from looking elegant disappeared once she twirled around. The effect was ruined by her crippled foot. No matter how beautifully she was dressed, she would never be graceful.

Briefly she entertained the notion of using magic. If she poured enough energy into her leg, she would be able to glide over the room like a dancer. NO, the voice in her head instantly replied. Everyone knew she was lame. Besides, she'd waste valuable energy. Just in case the witches suddenly showed up at the wedding, ha ha.

Someone rapped on the door. Gabi checked the mirror one

last time and went to the door. To her surprise, it was Alrik standing outside.

"It's almost time for the ceremony."

"Then shouldn't you be at the altar with Ronnie?"

"You hadn't showed up, so I was worried."

His gaze took in the sight of her in the dress, and his eyes darkened. Her insides started to flutter. It wasn't the first time she wore a nice dress, but it was the first time he blatantly showed appreciation.

"By the magi, you look lovely."

Gabi could feel a blush spreading over her face. "Thank you."

"Shall we?" Alrik offered his arm. She stared at his elbow. "You need help getting down the stairs. The skirt is so long that I can't see your shoes."

Giving in, Gabi placed her hand under his elbow. He smelled of soap and pine trees. When they descended the stairs, it felt like they were a couple.

Downstairs, the aroma from the wedding spread wafted through the air, even though the food was laid in a different room. Relatives and friends bustled around, carrying trays of cakes and jellies.

"You look so pretty!" Aunt Irma, Ronnie's favorite aunt, said with an admiring look.

Gabi blushed and was about to say thank you, when she noticed that Aunt Irma wasn't looking at her. Behind them, Clara was approaching in a dainty bridesmaid dress trimmed with lace. Her hair was done in pink ribbons, and a pink rose was pinned on her front. She was so pretty that even Alrik stared, his mouth half open.

If Clara noticed Alrik's slack-jawed look, she didn't acknowledge it. "We've got to go to the orchard now. Ronnie's already there and he's fussing over the decorations."

As old custom dictated that the bridesmaid and best man

enter the ceremony together, Alrik held out his arm. Smiling, Clara laid her hand in the crook of his elbow.

The aunts began to coo and gush.

"The two of you look so perfect together!"

"What a fine-looking pair you make!"

Alrik coughed and glanced at Gabi. She shrugged.

Outside, sunshine illuminated the orchard, turning parts of the trees and bushes into red and gold. As the sunlight struck her face, Gabi realized how much she missed good weather in Arksar. As a northern country, their summers were short. When this was over, she decided she was going to return to Masaro, where they had sunny weather all around. She wanted to spend more time in the place she was born. It was now a distant memory, but she could still remember visions of yellow brick houses, sparkling blue waters, and sun-dried tomatoes.

While occupied in thought, she tripped. Without Alrik by her side, Gabi reached out to grab onto a chair, but somehow she caught the arm of a young man nearby.

"I'm sorry!"

"Not a problem," the young man said, smiling. "Do you need to sit down? Let me escort you. Where are you sitting?"

"The bridegroom's section, please," Gabi said gratefully.

He led her to an empty chair on the right side and sat down next to her. She noted that he was probably the best-dressed man in the ceremony, with his black velvet waistcoat stitched with gold thread. "I'm Thom. May I ask your name?"

"Gabriella, but you can call me Gabi."

"Are you a cousin of the groom?"

"A friend." She wondered who he was—she hadn't heard of Ronnie mentioning Thom. "How about you?"

"I'm a second-removed cousin of Ronnie's."

"A pleasure to meet you."

Thom smoothed his waistcoat. "It's been a long time since

I've visited Kardi. I spent most of my time in Linberg, where I work as a barrister."

"It must be stressful but interesting to work in the capital."

"Indeed it is," he agreed. "But it's challenging and I like it. Have you ever been to Linberg?"

She had passed through the capital when Freja brought her back from Masaro, but Gabi was unwilling to tell the truth. "No. But I'd like to visit one day."

"I'll be happy to take you on a tour."

"We'd love to," Alrik interrupted, settling himself in the chair on Gabi's other side.

"By the magi." Thom's eyes widened. He pointed a shaking finger at Alrik. "You look just like the king!"

Warning bells clanged in her mind. "That's not unusual," Gabi quickly said. "Most people in Arksar have blue eyes and blonde hair."

"I attended Princess Iliana's birthday celebration and happened to see the king up close when he was heading to the skating rink. I swear that the shape of his aquiline nose is the same as yours, and the shade of color of his eyes are the same, too. You look exactly like a younger version of him."

Alrik laughed, as if it were a good joke. "I never knew my parents. Maybe I could be related to the king!"

"Isn't it time that you take your place at the altar?" Gabi pushed at his arm. "The violinists are already tuning their instruments."

Alrik stood up, but he cast Thom a warning look, as if to say that the latter wasn't to mess with Gabi.

Music started to drift through the air. Everyone took their places. Ulfred came and sat down next to her.

"Freja decided not to come," he whispered. "She's almost done with the collars and wanted to complete them as soon as possible."

Gabi nodded. She considered telling him what Thom had

said about Alrik's resemblance to the king, then decided against it. Thom was still sitting on her other side. Instead, she focused on the altar, willing for the ceremony to be over soon.

Ronnie stood in his best suit, his chest thrust out and his grin stretched wide. Anyone could see he was bursting with happiness, and with good reason. Of the twenty years she had lived, Gabi had yet to see any woman to rival Marianne's beauty, whether in Masaro or Arksar.

The song came to an end. The violinists began to play another song. When the third song ended, the guests were whispering with frowns on their faces.

The bride hadn't appeared.

Clara, who had been smiling for so long that her smile seemed frozen on her face, stepped down the altar and whispered to her mother. The older woman stood up and disappeared into the house, presumably to look for her elder daughter.

Gabi remembered a story about Marianne. Ronnie wasn't her first lover—she was previously in a relationship with a young man who became a sailor, but he never returned from the sea. As improbable as it might seem, could the man have returned just when Marianne was getting married? But she had seen Marianne the day before. The bride-to-be seemed happy and eager—no indication that she might stage an eloping.

A pretty young woman entered the orchard. Everyone swiveled in their seats, but it wasn't Marianne. She sat down on the bride's side, just behind Aunt Irma.

"Who are you?" Aunt Irma said.

"My name is Sorcha," the woman said, revealing large front teeth. "I came in place of Annalisa. The journey was too far for her old bones."

Annalisa was Marianne and Clara's grandmother. She was said to be a great beauty in her youth, which was why both girls were stunningly beautiful. However, Gabi had never seen her.

The old woman lived in Tybalt, a smaller town in the south of Arksar.

Music resumed. Marianne appeared, a dazzling picture in her misty white bridal gown, carrying a sheaf of crimson roses. Ronnie looked visibly relieved, and so did the guests. They'd never know why the bride was delayed, but it didn't matter. She was here, and she looked ready to continue with the ceremony.

On her father's arm, Marianne walked slowly down the aisle. When she reached Ronnie, she glanced at Alrik. For a moment, she froze. It lasted only for a few seconds, but it was long enough to make Gabi confused.

Did Marianne also notice that Alrik resembled the king? But she had met Alrik long ago. She shouldn't be surprised by his appearance.

Next to her, Thom let out a whistle. "Ronnie is a lucky man."

CHAPTER 11

“*I*’m not going back to Brek,” Clara announced.

“Freja needs you,” Gabi said, but it was a half-hearted plea.

“She doesn’t,” Clara said, wiping the table clean of tea stains and cake crumbs. “I’d much rather stay here in Kardi than living at a place where I have to walk twenty minutes to see another living soul.”

Two hours had passed since they saw Ronnie and Marianne drive off to their honeymoon. They planned for a trip to a small mountain resort in central Arksar; it must’ve cost Ronnie a tidy sum, but he didn’t blink twice when mentioning it.

“It’s only going to be once in a lifetime,” he said, when Alrik joked to him about him treating Marianne as if she were Princess Iliana. “Marianne’s parents had their honeymoon in the Loviska mountains, so she always hoped she could go there for her own wedding. You’d do the same for the woman you love.”

Gabi sighed. She had hoped that Clara would be able to attract Alrik, yet there was a curious sense of relief which she felt ashamed of. Hadn't she always told herself that Alrik's life mattered most?

"Besides." Clara tossed her hair. "The only reason I wanted to come was for Eric. Since he isn't interested in me, I don't want him anymore."

Gabi didn't know what to reply. In a way she also appreciated the girl's frankness.

"Eric only has eyes for you," Clara said, rather grudgingly. "He complains and nags, but most of the time I can see that he cares for you."

"I'm sorry," Gabi said. In a way she felt like remorse, but on the other hand, another thought lingered. Alrik seemed more attentive to her at the wedding. She couldn't forget the occasional glances he cast in her direction—they seemed to be filled with longing. If he cared, if he truly cared…

"Don't you feel pity for me," Clara said with an affronted glare. "I can have my pick of men—they're all hanging after me like they did to Rianne. Besides, I don't fancy Eric as much as I thought. Now Thom, he's a better catch. Much more sophisticated." Having finished cleaning the tables, she removed her apron and hung it on a nail on the wall. "Be confident, Gabi. You're pretty enough—you ought let your hair down more instead of braiding it. And you're smart. Just go and tell Eric that…"

"Tell me what?"

Alrik was leaning against the door frame of the kitchen. A twinkle in his eye made Gabi wonder how much he heard.

"That you've been taking ages to get out of that best man's suit and I was thinking of going home without you," she quickly said.

"Oh." He shrugged. "As a matter of fact, I was waylaid by a couple of charming young ladies and couldn't extract myself until I promised to come to Kardi again. Can't help being popular, you know."

Gabi rolled her eyes. Typical Alrik.

"Anyway, I got to hitch up the sorrel mare and get us back to Brek. It's going to be real dark if we don't leave soon."

"I'm not going," Clara said promptly. "I'm going to tell Freja that she can hire someone else. Farm life isn't for me."

Alrik raised his eyebrows. "What, aren't my charms enough for you?"

"It's not me that your charms are useful for," she said, with a shrug. "I don't fancy smelling like cow dung every morning. Or horse dung. Or like chickens."

He argued a bit more, but Gabi could tell that he wasn't that keen to make Clara return with them. In the end, the younger girl went off to find her mother, while Gabi accompanied Alrik to the wagon.

* * *

Freja was disappointed when Gabi and Alrik returned without Clara.

"Did you quarrel with her?" she asked Alrik.

He held up his hands. "Of course not. I treat her like a princess."

Freja pursed her lips and exchanged a look with Gabi. Reluctantly, Gabi repeated what Clara had said: she wasn't made for farm life.

Alrik went off to his cabin, declaring he was exhausted. When he was out of sight, Freja put a hand on her temple. "What are we to do? I've been doing everything I can to make the lad fall in love."

"Don't blame yourself, Auntie." Gabi put a hand on the older mage's arm. "After all, it's unlikely he'll meet with harm on his birthday. We'll be with him all day and ensure that he doesn't get hurt."

Freja sighed. "I suppose you're right. Well, I should be getting back to the basement. Just two more to go."

* * *

"I'VE FINISHED THE COLLARS," Freja announced the next day. She entered the kitchen, yawning, where Gabi was peeling potatoes.

"Congratulations!" Gabi started to reach for the water pitcher, but Freja held up a hand. With a flick of her fingers, the cup and pitcher rose from the top of the side table and floated toward her. She poured a full cup and gulped down the water, releasing a sigh.

"Are you going to send them to Savony?"

"I could, but I should deliver them in person. Tamarka and Morkel know the theory of the countercurse, but since I am the one who made the collars, to achieve the best results, I have to explain the workings to them. It's one of the most complicated spells I have ever produced, and if any detail is missed, the spell could backfire. The collar might be useless, or in the worst-case scenario, it could explode."

Gabi considered the issue. She had seen one of the collars that Freja wove. The markings on the collar were like a mass of wildly grown ivy, intricate and entwined. Anyone who had a basic understanding of magic knew that the more complicated the markings on a spell, the more powerful it was.

"How about asking Julong or Lorenza to deliver them for you? We can ask them to come to Brek; you can explain the workings to them, and they can travel to Savony."

"What are you talking about?"

Alrik sauntered into the kitchen. Gabi dropped her peeling knife. If Freja wasn't exhausted, or if she wasn't concerned about getting the collars to Savony, either of them would have sensed Alrik approaching. It was humiliating, to be honest, that a mage failed to notice a human nearby.

"Nothing important," she said, making her tone light and casual. "Freja is talking about visiting a friend."

"The friend you've been corresponding with?" he drawled. He perched himself on the side of the table and stretched with the languidness of a sleepy kitten. "You still haven't told me who he is."

"Sit properly," Freja said severely. "The way you sit, one would think you were ten years old."

"What does it matter? It's not as if I am nobility. No one will care about my posture."

Gabi muffled a cough.

Freja glared. Alrik sighed and caved in. He rarely openly defied Freja. She had adopted a strict, no-nonsense attitude since he was a child.

"Why're you back so early?"

"Because it looked like rain." Alrik jerked a finger at the window. Outside, dark gray clouds blotted out the sky. Earlier in the morning it was sunny, but it hadn't lasted. "So I herded the cows back to the barn. Here, let me help you with the peeling."

He reached out for the knife, but Freja laid a detaining hand on his wrist. "Have you forgotten your hemophilia?"

Alrik shrugged. "It can't be that bad. I saw a doctor in Kardi, and he assured me there isn't anything wrong with me."

"Eric," Freja said in a don't-argue-with-me tone. "We've been through this already."

"You can shell the peas." Gabi seized on the more welcome alternative and pushed the bowl toward him. "I'm almost done with the potatoes anyway."

Alrik looked like he wanted to argue, but Freja didn't move her hand until he took the bowl.

"Are my parents truly from Linberg?"

"Yes," Freja said calmly, though a twitch of her fingers betrayed that she was not completely at ease. Gabi arranged the potatoes in the baking pan and steeled herself to remain unruffled. The last time Alrik asked about his parents was when he was fifteen—almost six years ago.

"And is it true that I have no living relatives?"

Freja shifted uncomfortably. "I couldn't find any," she said carefully. "I told you, Eric, that I happened to be neighbors with your parents for only a few weeks. They didn't tell me about their own families. The fire was so sudden; I didn't have a chance to find if you had other relatives to take you in. And when my father left me this farm, I decided it was a good opportunity. Linberg was getting too expensive for me to live in."

"Where was their house? I should like to visit the place."

"The house is burned down. There's nothing to see, and possibly a new house is built in its place."

"But there are other neighbors," he said, strangely persistent. "Surely there has to be a clue somewhere."

Freja laid her elbows on the table. "Why do you want to know?"

"I'd like to go to Linberg. Soon. Since you've been telling me about that government job, it won't matter if I arrive a bit early. I could look around for accommodation, get used to the city..."

"You will not," Freja said firmly, as if he were a wayward child demanding candy from a jar. "There is absolutely no need for you to arrive at Linberg early."

"But why?" Alrik countered. "I should like to celebrate my birthday in Linberg."

"Why're you so keen to leave early?" Gabi intervened. "Why not wait until you're twenty-one?" In Arksar, a man came of age when he was twenty-one.

"I don't see how a couple weeks earlier is going to make any difference. If I start the job, I won't have much free time to go around asking about my heritage."

"Eric." Freja put her hands on her hips. "Be patient. When the time comes, you will know."

It was a rather quiet meal. Alrik looked like he was bursting with questions, but knew too well he'd get no answers. Gabi had burned the potatoes—the tops were charred—but for once he didn't make fun of her cooking. Freja was eating as if it were her last meal. Gabi suspected that the energy she spent on making the collars made the older mage ravenous.

Less than two weeks until his birthday. Finally, they would be able to tell him the truth.

By the time the meal was finished, rain was falling in torrents, accompanied by strong winds. Gabi had never ventured outside in weather like this. But as she cleared the dishes from the table, wondering how to lessen Alrik's suspicions about his hemophilia and curiosity about his parents, she noticed a figure coming toward their house.

Ulfred was trudging toward their cottage with a determined expression. He was soaked from head to toe. Not surprising, as he once said that umbrellas were for sissies.

"Eric," she called. "Get the door."

Freja took one look at the window, and her eyes widened.

"What is he thinking, coming in a storm like this?" She exchanged a look with Gabi, both of them thinking the same thing. It was a twenty-minute walk from Ulfred's house. If he had walked all the way to see them, in the rain, he must have something important to say. It couldn't be that he locked himself out of his own house. Whatever it was, Gabi felt that his objective for coming wasn't anything optimistic.

Alrik sprang up and opened the door. "Is everything all right? Where's Rolf?"

"He's staying over with Matthias." Ulfred wiped his muddy boots on the doormat, took the towel that Freja handed to him, and dried his hair. "Sorry that I came up here in a hurry," he said gruffly. "But the news couldn't wait."

"I'll get you a change of clothes," Gabi said. "We did laundry yesterday—there're plenty of clean shirts."

"Aw, this wouldn't kill me."

Freja rolled her eyes. "Remember you're nearly sixty. Think how much trouble you'll cause us if you catch cold."

Reluctantly, Ulfred agreed. When he emerged into the living room, in Alrik's largest shirt, he drew out a thickly wrapped package from his wet clothes. Like peeling an onion, he unwrapped the package, which consisted of several layers of oiled cloths.

"I got a letter from the king yesterday," he said, holding out a large white envelope sealed with crimson wax. "He wants Alrik back."

"Who?" Alrik said.

"You. You're the prince of Arksar."

Gabi heard herself gasp.

"Gabi, brew him a cup of hot tea," Freja said sharply. She looked furious—Ulfred had said the words so fast that she didn't have time to stop him. "He doesn't know what he's talking about."

Ulfred slapped a huge hand on his knee. "There's only two weeks left, Freja. Better let him know the truth. He's going to know it anyway, because the king is sending Lorenza and Julong over. They'll be here in a few days and accompany him to Linberg."

Freja snatched the letter and read the contents. She shook her head slowly. "I can't believe it...why did he change his mind?"

"Wait." Alrik held up his hands. He stared at Ulfred as if the latter had gone insane. "Someone needs to explain this to me. There's no prince of Arksar—there's only Princess Iliana."

"Because you were supposed to be dead." Ulfred took a step toward him. "Your life was in danger. That's why Freja brought you away—the enemy couldn't find you in a remote village like this."

Alrik looked toward Freja. "Tell me that he's lying."

"He's…"

"Remember that man at Ronnie's wedding?" Ulfred said loudly. "That man—Thom, was it? He came from Linberg. He said that Alrik looked like the king. I swear, Alrik, you look *exactly* like Tyrell. Do you know why Freja wouldn't let you go to Linberg until you came of age? If anyone who had seen the king saw you, they'd be suspicious. No one can look at you and believe you aren't related."

Alrik went white. He looked toward Gabi. She shook her head, unable to form words.

"You don't seem surprised. You've known it all along—all of you," he whispered. "This can't…this can't be true."

He turned and went out, ignoring the rain pouring outside.

"Alrik!" Gabi exclaimed. "I have to go after him."

"Wait." Freja lifted her hands—sparks sped toward Gabi's mouth. By instinct she opened her lips, and a cooling sensation filled her throat. The silencing charm that prevented her from speaking about the curse was lifted.

Alrik had locked himself in his cabin. However, she had no problem opening the door. Making golden sparks dance on her fingers, she directed the sparks toward the lock. In a few seconds, the door creaked open.

Inside, Alrik was huddled near the window, gazing out at the pouring rain. If he was surprised that she entered his cabin without a key, he gave no sign of it.

"Alrik?"

No answer.

Years ago, when he was in a petulant mood, Gabi would yell at him. This time, she dared not. Limping toward him, she repeated in a soft voice,

"Alrik."

"I don't know who that is," he said without looking at her. "My name is Eric."

"I'm sorry," Gabi said. Since the truth was out, there was no use denying it anymore. "Freja decided to change your name. Everyone knows that the prince's name is Alrik."

"But why?"

"We had to protect you. The witches want you dead. Moira wanted revenge on your father for rejecting her. She set a curse on you when you were a baby, cursing you to die on your twenty-first birthday."

Gabi went on to describe the details. He listened with a stony face. By the time she finished, she was half-regretting telling him the whole story. Why couldn't King Tyrell have waited? Why did Ulfred have to blab the truth?

But, a voice in her head reasoned, *Alrik would have reacted the same way even if they had waited.*

"So that is the whole story," he said dryly. "So that's the government job you have been talking about."

"You're not pleased?"

"What, am I supposed to be delighted that there are witches after me?"

"I meant the discovery that you're the prince of the kingdom. That you're going to be king of Savony when Tyrell steps down."

Finally he turned. There was resentment mingled with hurt in his eyes.

"I don't know. All I know is that you and Freja kept this a secret from me."

"I'm sorry," she said, tears in her eyes. No matter how they used to bicker and quarrel, he trusted her. The pain on his face showed how her lies had wounded him. "But if you knew it in the beginning, you'd be worried. Stressed. And the word would get out—the witches would find you."

He said nothing. Through the window, lightning flashed, followed by a roll of thunder.

"Leave me alone."

Gabi stumbled outside. She was soaked when she returned to the cottage. Freja was sitting with Ulfred in the living room; her "aunt" looked calmer, resigned to the fact that Alrik would have to return to the palace earlier than expected.

"Child!" Freja waved her hands; sparks burst from her fingers and settled over Gabi's body. Warmth engulfed her; in a twinkling the rain evaporated from her clothes. Some drops of water remained on her face, but it was nothing a quick swipe couldn't fix.

"How did he take it?" Ulfred said.

"Not well," Gabi admitted. "He's still upset that we lied to him."

A brief look of remorse from Ulfred, but he shrugged his huge shoulders. "There'll be a lot of trouble far worse than this when he becomes king. You have spoiled him too much. A little toughening in the spirit would do him good in the long run."

Gabi felt an odd sense of rebellion. Theoretically she agreed, but after seeing the broken expression on Alrik's face, she hated Ulfred for blurting the truth outright. Alrik had trusted her. Even if she had lied to protect him, it had come at great cost.

"By the way, I almost forgot." Ulfred handed her another letter. It was smaller than the king's, with a simple seal of glue. "From your admirer."

Gabi made a face. Morkel hadn't even seen her, and nothing in his letters indicated anything more than friendship. But she didn't bother to argue with Ulfred.

Ripping the envelope, she drew out a thin sheet of parchment paper. A quick scan made her spirits drop.

"What is it?" Freja said. "Bad news? Have more trolls broken out?"

"No, but Morkel and Tamarka are going underground to

gather the trolls' names." Gabi put a hand on her forehead. "They want to get the names before weaving them into the collars."

"But that's suicide! Two hundred trolls are down there—one is bound to sense them sooner or later."

"You've got to go to Savony," Gabi found herself saying. "The collars are finished, and you said you had to explain the workings to them in person. Even the most powerful mage alive has no chance against two hundred trolls. I'll stay here and accompany Alrik to Linberg."

Freja looked doubtful. "I made Tyrell a promise."

"Lorenza and Julong will be coming as well. Surely the three of us won't have any problem escorting Alrik to Linberg."

"Four of us," Ulfred said, placing a hand on his chest.

"I'll guard Alrik with my life," Gabi said, her tone strong and confident. "You can count on me on that."

Freja shut her eyes for a second. When she opened them, she gazed at Gabi.

"There're forty-nine defensive spells in a box under my bed. Take them, make Alrik learn how to use them. When I come back, I'm coming straight to the palace."

Gabi nodded. "Come as soon as you can."

CHAPTER 12

*S*woosh! The arrow flashed through the air, landing on the grass just inches away from a red-tailed fox, who scampered off and disappeared in a clump of bushes.

Sybil lowered her bow, irritated. When she was in beast form, not only could she hit a target at first try, she could make a clean kill with a shot through the jugular. Luckily it was spring, meaning that even if she came home empty-handed, they could buy enough food from the village across the river.

She took a swig from her water skin and wiped her brow. Her eagle-like eyesight was reduced, but at least human hands made it less likely for her to prick a hole in the leather, or rake scratches on her skin.

Sybil counted her catch—just a few rabbits. Normally she could bring back a deer. Maybe, when she saw Gerald again, she'd ask him for the ingredients of a strength-enhancement spell. He had told her about various spells he concocted to aid their fights with the trolls, from boots that enabled them to sprint faster and shields that were impenetrable.

She pulled off her hunting gloves, revealing the engagement ring. By the magi, how she missed Gerald. Years of solitude living at the manor didn't equip her better to endure loneliness. Every time she conjured a memory of his eyes, his smile, a painful longing would engulf her and she'd wonder what he was doing at the moment. She received a letter from him a week earlier, detailing how they dealt with the aftermath of the trolls breaking out. Although he assured her there was nothing to worry about, the fact he needed to reassure her made her concerned nevertheless.

Sybil strode back to the manor. A tall, middle-aged man with silver streaks in his hair opened the door.

"Welcome back."

Hugo bowed and stepped aside to let her in. He was a new manservant they had hired recently. Most of their servants had already left—Sybil wanted them to experience life in the world outside, after being trapped in the curse for decades.

"Let me take your cloak, milady."

Sybil unfastened the clasp. Was it her imagination, or did his gaze linger on her skin? Divested of her cloak, the gleam of her throat and collarbone, white as marble, was plain in the hall mirror.

Surely Hugo wasn't having untoward thoughts. Laurent had interviewed everyone thoroughly, but she couldn't shake off old memories—from fifty years ago but which remained etched in her mind—of the lecherous gazes that followed her when she was once belle of the court; of the nudges and winks and grins between men of high ranking, their conversations focused on dissecting her body parts as if she were a piece of juicy beef; of the slack-jawed, wide-eyed stares that made her distinctly uncomfortable and even fearful. What if someone intoxicated or insane should attack her?

A strong, delightful aroma reached her nose. Hugo bowed and disappeared, much to her relief.

"Milady?" Laurent paused in the dining room, a silver chocolate pot gleaming on the tray he carried. "Would you care for some hot chocolate?"

"Just lay the tray on the table. Laurent, I thought you were packing? Both you and Margot?"

Her footman—soon to be former footman—shrugged. "We don't have much to carry, milady. And Margot's concerned that the new cook won't be able to make food to your liking, so she insisted on preparing every meal before we leave."

Margot had been devastated since Sybil returned and told her that her daughter, Victoire, was dead. But with Laurent and Flavien comforting her, Margot gradually stopped her endless weeping and began to consider leaving the manor. She had begged Sybil to let her stay. But Sybil knew that it was better for Margot to go to Linberg with Laurent. The manor held too many painful memories for her, and she needed to start a new life with the man she loved. They had been attracted to each other for ages, but couldn't act upon their desire because of the curse.

As if on cue, Margot appeared. Her expression was filled with motherly concern, as if Sybil were a child. Flavien followed, rubbing his forearms. Sybil suspected that Margot had made him sweep and scrub the entire kitchen.

"You ain' thinking of going to Savon Castle, lady?" Margot demanded.

"Prince Gerald would want you to stay safe," Laurent added earnestly. "You can come with us."

"I can't wait until this troll problem is over and the two of you marry," Flavien said. He glanced at the silver engagement ring she wore. "Maybe I'll meet some lovely lady at your wedding."

He was making an effort to be lighthearted. Sybil smiled. "Maybe you will marry sooner than I, Flavien. Don't you fancy Arksan girls?"

"He'll be lucky if anyone can stand his laziness." Margot slapped her son's back lightly.

"Mama!" Flavien flushed, embarrassed at being treated like a child in front of Sybil.

"You sure you're going to stay here alone, milady?"

"I have some company," Sybil said. She had an idea brewing in her mind, but she wasn't going to mention it until she found what she needed.

"But they're all new. You sure you'll be all right?"

"Bernardin's staying." Sybil sighed. "No matter what I tell him, he refuses to leave."

"The boy is afraid of the world out there," Margot said with a shrug. "I know he ought to learn to be independent, but I don't think it's a good idea to send him out on his own. Give him a little more time, lady."

Sybil nodded. While she believed Bernardin should leave the manor and find his own way in the world, her heart was glad that he chose to stay. At least she had one of her faithful servants—one who had also lived through the curse—remain with her.

"Have you made arrangements with your family?"

"Margot will be staying with my nephew's daughter, who has recently gave birth to twins. Her husband works long hours at a store, so he'll be glad for an extra pair of helping hands. He's also offered Flavien a position at the store."

"Perfect." Everything was going well with her old servants. If only the same could happen for Gerald…

Just then, footsteps approached the room. Hugo appeared, holding out a thick, leather-bound book.

"The book you asked for, milady. The cover was quite dusty, so I've cleaned it with a dry cloth."

"Thank you." Sybil took the book; it was titled *Anecdotes in Pre-Medieval Arksar*. She ran a finger down the table of contents, found the chapter she was looking for, and her face lit up.

"So the spell does exist."

"A spell?" Laurent asked.

"What's it you're reading?" Margot said.

"Many years ago, I read about trolls invading a small Arksan village. They came from the north, so they passed through Arksar before arriving in Savony. The village, called Otani, managed to hold off the trolls with a simple freezing spell, using local ingredients of stone and ice. But Gerald said he never heard of the spell, so I had to look it up."

"If it's that simple, why hadn't the princes heard about it?" Flavien asked.

"Otani soon disappeared from Arksar's map. Most young men died in the battle, and the elderly didn't have many years left either. Of the few who survived, one told the village's story to a wandering tin peddler, who in turn narrated the story to an Arksan writer collecting local folk tales. Because it was so long ago, Gerald never even heard that the book existed, and even if he did, he wouldn't expect a collection of Arksan folk tales would contain a spell that could impede the trolls."

"So how does this spell work?"

Sybil squinted. "The villagers created the spell by mixing ice and stone in a cauldron. They dissolved the ingredients in water, and tossed the water over the trolls. The water turned into ice immediately, trapping the trolls inside, which gave them an opportunity to kill them."

"Sounds fairly straightforward." Laurent nodded. "So you will send a message to Prince Gerald and let him know about the spell?"

Sybil stood up. The sunlight streaming in through the window passed one side of her face, illuminating her exquisite features. "More than that. I'm going to travel to the capital."

"No," Laurent said.

"Don't," Margot said.

Flavien blinked. "Why must you go?"

"I need to see him." The moment the words were out did she realize the acuteness of her pain. She missed Gerald, missed him with a fierce longing that made forty years of loneliness as a beast seem paltry. "He told me to stay away, but I don't have to be in the front lines. I can create spells for him, spells that could help him and his brothers defeat the trolls."

"It's not safe for you to travel alone, milady," Margot said in a stern tone that she usually reserved for Flavien.

"I've traveled to Arksar. To Finsoor."

"But you had company at that time, and you nearly came to death in Finsoor," Laurent said.

Margot gasped. "She nearly lost her life in Finsoor? Why didn't you tell me?"

Sybil took a deep breath. "Laurent, it's only going to be a few days' journey. I have defensive spells I can use. I can't stay here any longer, waiting for Gerald's letters. If anything happens to him..." She didn't want to finish the sentence. She couldn't imagine a life without him.

"I'll go with her," Bernardin spoke. He stood in the entrance to the dining room.

"You?" Flavien echoed. "But you haven't even been out of the village for all these years!"

"I'll go with her," Bernardin repeated. He might not be able to argue eloquently, but when he made a decision, nothing short of moving mountains would sway him.

"Better have some company than none," Laurent said, recognizing the iron in Bernardin's tone. "But both of you must be careful. Don't attract attention. Stay to the main roads. And don't talk to anyone if you can—let Bernardin do the talking."

"I'll wear my veil," Sybil said. It had been useful when she was a beast, and it also served her well during her trip back to the manor. "If the freezing spell can help him..." Her heart soared at the prospect. "All the effort will be worth it."

Margot and Flavien still looked anxious, but they didn't try to argue any further. When Sybil and Laurent aligned in opinion, there was little they could do.

* * *

DESPITE HER PROTESTS that she'd be fine, Sybil nevertheless felt a pang of loneliness when she watched her servants' carriage roll through the manor grounds, out the iron gates, and disappear from sight.

It's what's best for them, she told herself fiercely. They couldn't stay with her forever. No matter how much they felt like family, they weren't true family. Her future belonged with Gerald.

Gerald. The thought of him cheered her up slightly, reminding her that she had her own path to travel—her own mission to achieve. Turning away from the window, Sybil directed her attention to half-filled trunks on the floor. Cloaks, gowns, handkerchiefs, scarves, stockings...various items were strewn across the bed. Jars of defensive spells sat on the tables, yet to be labeled, sorted, and packed. She should've been done long ago, but she was used to having Victoire pack everything for her. On her own, it was a tiresome but necessary task.

The thought of Victoire made her mind wander briefly to a newly erected slab of stone standing in a tiny graveyard behind the manor. Since they were frozen in time under the curse, the graveyard had been rarely used—weeds had grown thick over the low wall and over the tombstones. Sybil couldn't remember the last time she visited the graveyard as they cleared the weeds to make space for Victoire. There was no body, so they buried a box containing her clothes and possessions, except for a precious few that Margot insisted on keeping.

Tears sprang in Sybil's eyes. One day, she vowed, one day she and Gerald would find the witches. They'd persuade the mages they met in Linberg to help them. She'd kill Sorcha, who had taken Victoire's body for her own, and bury it where the box was. Should Margot ever meet Sorcha in the streets one day...Sybil didn't even want to imagine how Margot would react. The witch had to die.

"Milady?"

A gentle knock on the door. Hugo stood outside, bearing a steaming pot of hot chocolate.

"Laurent told me to keep you supplied with chocolate when he left." Hugo gave her a grin. "My culinary skills are far from Margot's level, but I did my best."

The aroma of cinnamon and hazelnuts wafted in the air. Smiling, Sybil waved a hand at a table near her bed.

"Thank you, Hugo. I'm sure I'll enjoy it."

"Better drink it while it's still hot." Hugo's gaze roved over her trunks. "Are you sure you don't need any help packing, milady?"

"Perfectly sure."

"Then at least allow me to carry your luggage to the first floor when you're done."

"That would be much appreciated. Can you check on Bernardin for me? See if the horses are fed and groomed for travel. We plan to leave shortly after lunch."

"As you wish, milady." Hugo bowed and left.

As she reached for a jar containing a spell that could produce a small fire for cooking, Sybil did a mental calculation. After discharging most of her servants, she had more than enough left for the journey and for Hugo's wages. He came with stellar recommendations—he had served at an old family in Calois, but after thirty years of service, he preferred to live the rest of his life quietly in the country. She should be able to trust him while she was away.

By the time she finished labeling her spells, the aroma of chocolate was too hard to ignore, so she poured herself a cup. It wasn't as rich and creamy as how Margot used to make it, but decent enough that she poured a second cup.

Sybil resumed packing. She was almost done—just her cloak remained. It was mid-spring—or was it mid-summer? No matter what, she needed the cloak in case of rain. She was feeling surprisingly drowsy, yawning every now and then. Did she rise too early that morning? She sometimes got sleepy around noon if she didn't sleep well the night before. But still, the weight of sleep pressed so powerfully on her head that it didn't seem normal.

The cloak fluttered to the ground. Her last conscious thought was that she had been drugged, just as her eyes closed at the same time she crashed to the floor.

CHAPTER 13

"*A*lix, you've got to come. Now."

Alix looked up. She had been cobbling a pair of sturdy boots for one of the soldiers guarding North Tower. The stink was intolerable, but there were worse things in the world than a pair of smelly boots.

She was in a private room in Central Tower, just a few rooms away from the queen's chamber (far enough to keep away from the queen's various herbal teas, but close enough that she could visit the queen anytime), and a floor above Theo and Gerald's room. Since the trolls broke out, the princes had left North Tower. The younger ones were forced to leave for Calois, under strict orders from both Queen Marguerite and Theo. She missed the younger princes and prayed for the day when they could return.

"What is it?"

Gerald sighed. "Theo hasn't slept last night. Or if he had, he's doing a very poor job of convincing us he did. He's in his usual irate temper—well, more irate than usual; lack of sleep makes him even more intolerable. We need you to come and make him go to bed. He rarely listens to anyone."

Despite her worry for Theo, Alix couldn't help a tiny surge of pride in her chest. The future king of Savony, who wouldn't even listen to his own brothers, might listen to *her*, a young woman who couldn't even make ends meet just months ago.

But then the tiny flare of elation disappeared. This was no time to dwell on her relationship with Theo.

"So he's at North Tower, yelling at the soldiers?" Alix set aside the boots and went to the door. Since she hadn't any magic, nor fighting or healing skills, she did what she was able to do—mending shoes.

"My mother's ability as a seer must have rubbed off on you." Gerald sent her a wry grin. "He was bad enough when the curse bound us to troll battles every fortnight, but this is worse. Possibly because it's the first time he saw trolls attack and kill innocent people. He snaps at anyone who tries to tell him about the castle's situation, and insists on guarding North Tower all the time."

Alix rolled her eyes. Typical Theo. But then, if one day he started acting patient and sweet-tempered, peppering her with flirtatious terms like the twins used to do, she'd be weirded out.

She laid the boots aside and followed him outside. "Tell me about your fiancée. All we know is that she's incredibly beautiful. How did she capture your heart?"

Instantly the worried lines on his face relaxed, replaced by a mellow glow. Alix hadn't plenty of experience with men, but she knew that Gerald was deeply in love—his affection for his lady was more powerful than mere appreciation for her beauty.

"She was cursed when I met her," he said. "Under the curse, she was far from what was typically considered attractive, but she was such a singular young woman that I couldn't help falling in love with her. She read extensively. She could hunt like a man. She didn't see me just for my face—we were able to have long, stimulating conversations. It was when our lives were threatened that I discovered I couldn't imagine my world without her. I proposed, and that broke her curse."

"Sounds like a far more attractive method to break a curse."

Gerald grinned, but soon grew sober. "I wish I could see her now, but it's better that she stay away. In fact, I told her—made her—stay away. She was nearly killed by the witches in Finsoor; I don't want her risking her life."

Yet here he was, risking his life. Alix pursed her lips. Theo had tried to make her leave when the trolls broke out, but she refused point-blank. She had the invisibility cloak. She was far too involved, too deep in the situation now. And like Gerald, she couldn't imagine her world without Theo in it.

By this time, they had reached North Tower. It had changed much since she first laid eyes on it. A wall, seven feet high, surrounded the tower. A blue-white hue glowed on top of the wall, indicating it was fortified by magic. Soldiers in full armor, carrying swords and maces, were stationed around the wall.

Alix heard Theo's shout before she saw him. Dark patches were below his eyes, and there was a wildness in his stare as he whirled around.

"What are you doing here?" he barked.

Alix put her hands on her hips. To avoid a prolonged shouting match, she decided to go for the unexpected.

"I've come to take you to bed."

More than one soldier choked. Gerald averted his gaze, but his shoulders were shaking. Theo was as scarlet as the crimson tunic he wore. Really, the princes were incredibly sheltered when it came to the opposite sex.

"Don't..." Theo growled. "You're being ridiculous."

"Compared to someone who didn't even sleep last night, I think I'm being perfectly reasonable." Alix stared at him, her gaze unflinching. "How are you going to protect your people if you don't take care of yourself?"

"I'll watch over the tower for you," Gerald said, stepping to

Theo's side. "I promise I won't even bat an eyelash. You know you can trust me. Always."

"Come along, darling." Alix slipped her hand under his arm. "The trolls will wait."

Amid muffled laughter from the soldiers, she led him away.

Theo behaved like a lamb, surprisingly, as she steered him back to Central Tower. When going up the stairs, they ran into the queen, who merely smiled sweetly and told Alix she was doing a fine job. When they reached Theo's chamber—a temporary room that he shared with Gerald—Alix made to close the door but he protested.

"This is the farthest you can go." He stood in front of her, arms crossed. "Go back to your room."

"And what promise do I have that you won't sneak out once I turn my back on you?"

He growled. "Dang it, woman, have you so little faith in me?"

"Not a whit."

Alix shut the door before he could stop her, knowing that in his sleep-deprived state he was more vulnerable.

"Take your clothes off."

His eyebrows rose alarmingly close to his forehead. "What did they teach you before you came to the castle?"

"Loads of shocking stuff." Alix made a clucking sound. Though he was nearly ten years her senior, at the moment she felt like a matronly, experienced woman. "Theo, you stink. I'm going to draw you a bath. Then you're going to sleep like a baby until I come for you."

"I can take care of myself."

"Right, you're doing a remarkable job of it. Now get out of those clothes and I'll get you a tub of hot water."

Alix slipped out of the chamber. It took her two flights of stairs and three corridors before she found a manservant who could help her heat up water and carry buckets to Theo's room. The near-silence in the building made her wonder how many servants had left. Peering out of the window, she noted how bare the grounds were. When she first entered the castle as a dressmaker's apprentice and shoe cobbler, it was difficult to move around without running into someone. The castle was essentially a self-contained, self-reliant unit on its own. Now she wasn't so sure.

It took an hour, longer than expected, but finally Theo was bathed and changed.

"Thank you." She handed the manservant a gold ducat, half for the extra service, half as gratitude for not abandoning the castle. The servant bowed and left, hauling the tub of dirty water with him.

Heaving a sigh of relief, Alix wiped sweat from her forehead. "Now you can go to bed. Don't you wake up for at least three hours."

She wiped her hands on her apron and started to the door, when two sturdy arms wrapped around her body.

"Alix, stay." Somehow he had changed his mind about propriety. Maybe it was the bath that altered his thoughts. The air was damp and warm, smelling of soap. It was a world of difference from the tension outside North Tower.

"You're the one who needs rest," she managed to squeak out. Where was the brazen flippancy she displayed an hour ago? Though she wasn't a shy, bashful maiden, Theo's embrace nevertheless made her heartbeat speed up.

"I want you to stay."

She gave in. The truth be told, she hadn't been sleeping well either. And she enjoyed his embrace, as well as the knowledge that he needed her.

Climbing into bed, she settled in the crook of Theo's arm with a sigh of content. After his bath, he smelled good—of soap, and something distinctly masculine. She rubbed her head against his chin like a kitten, and he tightened his arm around her shoulders.

"Mine..." he slurred.

She would've preferred a sweet proclamation of undying devotion, but considering Theo was the least romantic person she knew, that single possessive word was probably equal to a marriage vow.

"Mine," she whispered back, feeling his drowsiness infect her like wind. For that moment she forgot about the life-threatening threat lurking underground, forgot that they might not survive to wed. At that moment she felt firmly bound to him, like they were one half of a whole. Nothing was sweeter than snuggling in your beloved's arms.

Alix closed her eyes, a smile on her lips.

* * *

She woke up to a heavy pounding on the door. Theo's arm was still around her, but she easily pushed him off when she sprang out of bed. He must have been extremely sleep-deprived, to be able to sleep through the noise outside, and not noticing that she was up.

Opening the door, she found Julian. His mouth fell open as he took in her wrinkled dress and apron, her hair tumbling in untidy locks on her shoulders. But he asked no questions—for that she was grateful. If it were the twins, she'd hear no end of their teasing.

"The mage Freja has arrived. With collars."

* * *

The bag Freja carried seemed barely large enough to fit a dog, but she kept pulling out collars as if her bag were a live creature that could produce magical collars from its intestines. When she extracted the last one, there was a small mountain of leather piled on the carpeted floor.

"Here are the collars. Two hundred of them."

Gerald examined a collar with the eye of a competent magic user. "This seems different from what Tamarka and Morkel showed us."

"What does their collar look like?"

Gerald gave a brief description. Freja scoffed.

"No doubt it was only for the purpose of demonstration. A collar that size can only control a creature the size of a dog. Trolls are at least six feet tall; some can reach the height of eight or nine." She pointed at a row of metal spikes embedded on the leather. "These were added for extra magical control. With the spikes, the power in the collar is strengthened. This is the minimum magic needed to subdue a troll."

"Excellent," Theo said. He only slept for two hours, but looked fully awake, perhaps buoyed by Freja's arrival. Alix knew that he hadn't anticipated that Freja would actually come; they already had Tamarka and Morkel, so it was more likely that she'd send instructions through the bracelets. But here she was, with the weapons they needed to conquer the trolls. "What should we do now? Everything is at your disposal, lady."

"I'll stay for a few days to teach Tamarka and Morkel how to operate the collars, then I must be heading back. My other duties are equally important."

Her other duties must be about dealing with the witches. Alix felt resentment and despair. Why did the disasters have to happen at the same time?

"Don't worry, Urdu will be here soon. He was in bad shape when we rescued him in Finsoor, but he is well taken care of in Linberg palace." Freja paused, looking around. "Why aren't Tamarka and Morkel here yet? What're they doing?"

"They're gathering the trolls' names," Gerald said.

"They're still down there?" Freja stood up. She usually seemed calm and collected—this gesture made Alix alarmed. "What if a troll senses them? What if they get caught and are surrounded by dozens of trolls? Not even Urdu in his prime can take on more than ten trolls single-handedly. That's why Antoine had to make the arrangement with the trolls—there was no way he could defeat them on sheer power!"

"They said it would be more convenient to get the trolls' names and weave them into the collars," Gerald explained, though his brow was furrowed. "Tamarka was concerned there wouldn't be enough time to get the trolls' names and perform the countercurse at the same time."

"Which is why I said we needed seven mages in the least to defeat the trolls," Freja said, pacing around the room. "With the seven of us, we could create power that's enough to get the trolls' names when we confront them, then weave the names into the collars. Yes, we could be pressed for time, but it's less of a risk than seeking the trolls in the beginning! How long have they been gone?"

"This morning," Gerald said, looking toward Theo. "When was the exact hour they went underground?"

Theo blinked. In his overworked state, his memory was failing him. "No more than three or four hours earlier from now, I believe."

"And how long do they usually take with every trip?"

"No more than half a day."

"Then it ought be a couple of hours till they emerge. I suggest we put the time into good use. Show me the wall you've constructed around the tower."

CHAPTER 14

To Gabi's surprise, Alrik seemed to have completely recovered from his dejection by the next day. Considering how hurt he looked, huddled in his cabin, she thought it'd take days for him to regain his sunny mood. And a normal person, she assumed, would be at least worried, and to a larger extent, fearful of his life, knowing that there were two powerful witches who wanted him dead. He was aware that he could fall into permanent slumber if he pricked his finger on his twenty-first birthday. But Alrik greeted her with a sunny smile the next day, and didn't even make fun of her burnt bacon or runny eggs.

Maybe it had to do with Freja, who departed at the crack of dawn. Alrik was usually more carefree when Freja was away.

"Lovely morning," he said, plunking down on a stool beside the rickety wooden table. He grabbed the fork and started eating with gusto. Gabi glanced outside. The storm had passed last night, and the sky was clear, but still she didn't understand why he was so cheerful. He was rarely affected by the weather, unless it did harm to the garden or animals.

Maybe he finally realized the advantages of being a prince?

He was already an attractive prospect when he was merely an ordinary farmer from a distant village. Clara might have clung to him if she weren't certain that Alrik's heart already belonged to someone else. Once he became king—he could have his pick of any woman in the kingdom. The thought of him on the throne with a beautiful, elegantly arrayed noble woman sitting on his side, made her insides churn.

"Gab?" Alrik waved a hand in front of her face. "What's gotten into you?"

Gabi blinked. "Wha...what?"

"You've been staring at your mug for an entire minute. What's so fascinating about the contents of the mug? Or has a mouse drowned in the milk? Geez, I knew your cooking's terrible, but to mess up even a cup of milk—"

Gabi poked his ribs, making him yelp.

"We shouldn't waste any more time," she said.

His face lightened up. "Now you're talking."

"The mages should arrive in a few days, but it doesn't mean we should sit around idly."

"For once, I am in complete agreement with what you're saying." He leaned close, light shining in his eyes. "What do you say that we—"

"There's a bunch of defensive spells that Freja left for you," Gabi said, remembering what the older woman had told her the night before. "I need you to familiarize yourself with the spells. The other mages and I will protect you, but it's always better to be well prepared."

His face fell. "Defensive spells?"

"Of course. Why else did she send you to Ulfred? Freja wanted you to be a decent fighter, always ready to defend yourself from assault. Your ancestors were great warriors. You ought do them proud."

He passed a hand over his forehead. "As you say."

Gabi limped toward the basement. The door wasn't magically locked this time. She entered Freja's room and re-emerged with her arms filled with corked jars.

Alrik, who was slumped on a chair in the main room, sat up.

"All the time Freja was talking about making mundane housework spells, she was working on this?"

"Not exactly. She got many of these spells from the Savony princes. They were cursed to fight trolls every fortnight, and until they broke the curse, they had to rely on defensive spells to protect themselves. When Freja traveled to Savony, she asked to have a look at some of their spells, and decided they could also be of use to you."

Gabi set the jars on the table. Alrik eyed the assortment with keen interest. There were no two jars that looked exactly the same. Some were large, some were small; some were fat, while others were tall. But every jar had a tag attached around the lid, with a brief description of the spell within the glass enclosure.

"We can use this one right away," Gabi said, pulling out a round, fat jar filled with a peculiar purple ointment. "Rub the ointment on the soles of your boots, and they will go faster when you run."

Alrik uncorked the jar and sniffed. He grimaced and put the lid on the jar. "This smells worse than cow and horse dung on a rainy day. And what about that one? Is it empty?"

The jar was transparent, and there wasn't any ointment or colored substance inside.

Gabi laughed. "If it weren't for the tag, I might've thought it was empty, but actually it contains a spell of invisibility. Once you uncork the stopper, a transparent mist will engulf your body and guarantee you ten minutes of invisibility."

"Only ten minutes?"

"Staying invisible isn't simple magic," she said. "Smaller spells can enhance a certain quality, like enabling a fire to burn brighter, or an ice box to stay cool. But it requires big magic to make a person invisible to the world, so a small spell like this could only last ten minutes. In fact, this is a rare spell that Freja acquired. Usually, you can only make yourself invisible either if you're a mage, or if you possess an invisibility cloak."

"Most impressive," Alrik commented. "But isn't there anything that can cause damage and destruction? What am I to do if the witches chase me into an alley with a dead end? Speed-enhanced boots and invisibility wouldn't be much help if the enemy has me trapped."

While she highly doubted the chances of that scenario (a powerful witch could simply summon ropes and tie Alrik up long before he could escape into any dead-end alley), Gabi rummaged through the assortment. "Here." She held out her hand. A tiny white pearl—actually half pearl, as one side was flat —lay on her palm.

"What's this?" Alrik drew his brows together. "Poison? Does this mean I need to work on my seduction skills and make the witches drink wine tampered with this white substance?"

Gabi rolled her eyes. "It's an explosive. You need to be extra cautious handing it."

"Explain, sweetheart." He leaned forward, a smile playing on his lips. Just a few inches nearer, and he could've kissed her.

Privately thinking he didn't need any work on seducing women, Gabi ignored the blush that she felt sure was creeping up her face.

"This can be attached to your teeth. No one will ever discover you're carrying a spell in your mouth. When you need to create a diversion, yank the pearl off your tooth, and throw it hard at a spot at least thirty feet away. It will create an explosion."

Alrik whistled. "I have a new respect for Freja. Not that I didn't respect her in the beginning, but if she created these spells—" he shook his head "—she deserves better than hiding in this tiny place."

"She owed the king a huge debt," Gabi said. "I don't know

how it came to be, but that's why she's willing to risk her life to protect you."

As was I, she thought. Because Freja saved her life, she owed it to Freja to protect Alrik. But now she realized, even if the older mage didn't make her promise to do it, she would've willingly sacrifice everything to ensure Alrik was alive.

As if he could read her thoughts, Alrik pounced on the subject.

"How about you, Gabi?"

"What are you talking about?"

"This risky, life-threatening business of making sure that the future king of Arksar doesn't die," he said. "Did Freja tell you that you had to sacrifice everything to protect me?"

She couldn't speak. He was approaching her with a ferocious light in his eyes. She wasn't sure how to handle this unusual side of him.

"Don't," he said harshly. "I don't want you to sacrifice even a drop of blood for me, Gabi. I'm not worth it."

"That's not for you to decide. I *want* to protect you, Alrik. Ever since we first met and I fell in love..."

His hands were on her shoulders in an instant. "Say that again."

"Take your hands away from me."

He didn't budge. "I want to hear you finish that sentence."

When she still remained mute, he sighed. "Fine. Would it help if I order you to say that again? As the future monarch, you know."

She couldn't help a giggle. "Why are you so keen to hear that?"

"Because it matters to me." Alrik kissed the top of her head. "Because I want to affirm that my feelings for you are mutual."

Joy washed over her in waves—it felt as if she had jumped into a lagoon with steam rising from the surface. So she wasn't imagining things. He did love her. Freja's wish had come true after all.

"It is mutual," she said in a low voice, suddenly feeling bashful. It was easier to banter with him than admit that she loved him.

Raising her face, she was both startled and gratified by the explosion of joy that lit up his face like a huge lantern.

"I've been waiting six years to hear you say that," he said, and lifted her right off the chair, into the air. She couldn't help smiling at his exuberance. He was so happy that she loved him, it was almost painful to imagine the future when they had to part ways.

"I can almost forgive you for lying to me about hemophilia. If I didn't believe any of that crap, I could've had you in my arms much sooner."

Gabi blinked. "Wait...what?"

"All these years I've been repressing my feelings for you. I wanted you, Gabi, ever since you arrived in Brek, but because I was afraid that our children would be afflicted, I held back. So yes, I'm mad that you deceived me, but I can't stay mad long because it means I'm free to make you mine."

So that was why he didn't seem anxious or worried about the witches—the joy of discovering he could have children with her blotted out other risks.

Surprise, mingled with sympathy and affection, flowed through her. She always assumed he was being frivolous when flirting with girls and never taking them seriously. Now she knew: it was because he didn't dare to act on his true desire. The selflessness of his motives made her love him even more.

He set her down, the laughter still glowing in his eyes. Gabi didn't want him to let go; she pulled his head down to hers and kissed him. He responded with enthusiasm, kissing her so thoroughly that when they broke apart, both of them were panting for breath.

"That wasn't your first kiss," she said. She felt by instinct that he had to have some experience to kiss her in that passionate manner.

"Well, there were a few girls in Kardi who took advantage of me," he admitted. "But that was the best kiss I had. So far," he quickly added. "You can bet I plan on kissing you a lot more."

She blushed. For a moment she wished that they had told him the truth earlier. It was cruel that they could only enjoy their time together for less than two weeks.

"Once the witches are taken care of and I have to return to Linberg, you're coming with me. As my bride."

When she didn't answer, he pressed on.

"You'll come with me, surely? I don't know if I'll make a good king, if I'll ever become used to living in a palace, but I know for sure that I can't do without you."

Gabi bit her lip. What could she say? Tell him that yes, she'd happily accept his proposal and marry him when he became king? But she couldn't. She was disabled; she was a liability.

"It mightn't be met with approval," she started, and pointed at her foot. "Imagine a queen greeting her subjects while limping."

He rolled his eyes. "If anyone dares ridicule you because of your foot, I'll have them banished from court."

"It isn't that simple," she said. "You can't make orders simply because you don't like it. Besides..."

"Then we'll figure out something, because I am for certain not going to let you go," he said fiercely. "Not after all these years."

Gabi opened her mouth, but decided not to argue.

Remember the curse, her mind whispered. In order for the true love's kiss to work, she had to play along. Any difficulties that lay in the path of becoming queen could be set aside.

So she gave in to her secret desire. Leaning forward, she wrapped her arms around him and let out a small sigh. His arms slid around her, gathering her close, as if she were a dream and might disappear if he weren't careful.

"Promise me that no matter what happens, you won't run away from me," he whispered. "Prince or not, I'm still Alrik. That will never change."

Gabi didn't answer. But she tightened her arms around his body, savoring the warmth. It was easy for him to declare his affection and vow he'd never change. For now, she'd give in to her desire, but she knew that it wouldn't—couldn't—last.

CHAPTER 15

*S*ybil opened her eyes. Her vision was hazy; she blinked, and made out the interior of a carriage. Her carriage. It lurched to the side, causing strands of inky black hair to tumble in front of her face.

But she couldn't brush her hair away. Her hands were bound tightly on her lap, and when she wiggled her feet, she discovered her ankles were tied as well. Something was stuffed into her mouth—it tasted like a bunch of cloths. She couldn't even scream, just make a noise of helpless protest.

The only part she could move was her neck. She turned her head to the right, meeting the window with a heavy curtain drawn over it. She turned to the left. Hugo was sitting with a tight, determined expression. As if sensing her gaze on him, he looked at her.

"My apologies, lady," he said calmly. "But I did what I had to do."

Sybil made a noise through her gag. He shook his head and sighed.

"I didn't want to abduct you. But I have no choice, since you are Gerald's fiancée."

Her eyebrows shot up. What did Gerald have to do with his kidnapping her?

"My young mistress, Lucie de la Motte, suffers from a melancholy longing for the prince. Since she saw him in the capital a year ago, she lost her heart. She didn't eat for days, until my mistress forced her with a spell. She eats now, but she refuses to marry. Every day she sighs over the prince's picture, saying that she will never be good enough for him." He bit his lip and glared at Sybil, as if she was responsible for Lucie de la Motte's unrequited longing.

Among the countless books she read, Sybil had come across a few volumes of poetry. The troubadours wrote of unrequited love for women they admired, but could never have. Some described their burning passion like illness. Perhaps Lucie was the female version of these troubadours.

"I've cared for my young mistress since she was a toddler. I cannot bear to see her suffer so much. I thought Gerald never meant to marry, or he was interested in men. But since you are his fiancée, this proves he is not impervious to women. So I came up with this plan." Hugo folded his arms. "In exchange for your life, the prince must marry my young mistress. She'd die of a broken heart without him."

Sybil again made a noise of protest, muffled by her gag. Hugo ignored her; he went on talking of his plan as if he were a general devising the best strategy for a battle.

"He will marry her in a great public ceremony, in front of thousands of people in Savony and abroad. Rose petals will shower on the carpet they walk on. There will be dancing and singing, followed by a banquet fit for a king. It is the only way that she can be cured from her sorrow."

Tears glistened in his eyes; he spoke as if he were in a trance. Sybil sensed there was no point arguing with him; in fact, she couldn't argue even if he were reasonable, thanks to the gag.

She was better off keeping quiet. Better to stay calm and devise a plan to escape.

Hugo continued outlining his grandiose plan of marrying Lucie off to Gerald. Sybil barely listened as she pondered on her chances. Without spells, she was powerless against him. She had to wait until they arrived at their destination.

The carriage came to a halt. Hugo yelled at the driver, who yelled back that the horses needed to rest.

Grumbling, Hugo opened the door.

"Looks like a village," he said. Sybil glimpsed part of a thatched roof from over his back. "Stay here while I get some food. If you try to escape—" he slashed a hand across his face "—I'll give you a scar so bad that Prince Gerald will be disgusted at the sight of you."

Knowing how Gerald fell in love with her in her beast form, Sybil considered it an empty threat, but still it was impossible to escape from the carriage while she was bound and gagged. She edged toward the door and bumped against the solid wood, but it didn't budge.

She tried moving the handle by jamming her elbow against it. Nothing happened. She tried again, but only received soreness from her efforts.

A low hiss came from somewhere close by. Horrified, she realized it was a snake—a large one with yellow-and-brown patterns, and it reared a triangular head, showing a forked tongue.

The snake's body was like a glistening rope, and there was a rattling sound as it slithered across the floor.

Sybil hastily raised her feet and folded them under her lap, so she was sitting completely on the seat. It was tough, considering her wrists and ankles were bound, but sometimes when desperate measures were called, the human body could do desperate things.

The snake, possibly deciding that the inside of the carriage was a warmer, more welcoming habitat than the cold, dewy landscape outside, coiled itself on the floor. Still, the snake was large enough that it could reach her if it raised its arrow-sized head.

Sybil thought about the books she read. There was one book that mentioned snakes and other reptiles. What was written about snakes?

Don't provoke them. Even nonpoisonous snakes could inflict considerable harm with their bites. Without proper treatment, there could be dangerous infections.

Her heart pounded. She was going to stay calm. She was going to pretend she had turned to stone.

She also wished Hugo would come back. Getting kidnapped by an obsessed footman was bad, but her chances of survival were much larger than being trapped inside a carriage with a snake that could be poisonous.

Time seemed to pass slower than a snail crawling. Her feet became numb; when she thought she regained feeling in her feet, she tried to wiggle her toes.

Suddenly, the snake reared its head.

Sybil screamed. Her foot shot out—somehow the bindings were loosened when she folded her legs on the seat—it hit the front of the carriage with a thud. The snake lunged forward and clamped its jaws over her ankle. She was wearing stockings, but she could still feel its jaws puncturing her skin.

Sybil fainted away.

CHAPTER 16

Alrik was whistling as he left the house and headed to the barn. Yesterday was the happiest day of his life, and today looked like it was going to be just as good, or even better. Finally. He had been waiting for years to confess his feelings to Gabi. And now to discover that he had been free to do it all along!

Just this morning at breakfast, he had surprised her by wrapping his arms around her waist and nuzzling the softness of her cheek. She was startled, but soon relaxed in his embrace, while muttering that he was little better than a caveman. But the rosy bloom in her cheeks and the light scent of coffee and cream from her dress were worth making his day.

"Think about it," he whispered. "You and me, waking up together every day. I want that, whether I become king or not."

"That'd be lovely," she sighed. But a few seconds later, she retreated into her more reserved exterior and gently pushed him away. "Lorenza and Julong will be arriving the day after tomorrow. Let's hope that it'll be a smooth, uneventful journey."

"We'll be heading straight to the palace?"

She nodded.

It felt surreal. In a week, he'd be in Linberg. He'd be meeting his parents—the king and queen. It seemed simply incredible. He had heard snippets about King Tyrell and Queen Ingrid and Princess Iliana. He heard that Iliana was a beauty; Ronnie and he used to talk about visiting Linberg and catching a glimpse of the famous princess who was notoriously shy. And now it turned out that Iliana was his sister.

He knew that Gabi felt insecure—normally, anyone would. But surely his parents would not object to a mage as a future queen. No matter what, he wouldn't give her up.

He sauntered into the barn, welcoming even the stink of cow dung and other unpleasant smells. Opening the door, he shooed the cows outside, coaxing them to head to the pasture. It was cloudy, but didn't look like another thunderstorm would be coming up.

As he followed the cows, Alrik noticed something amiss. They kept five cows; Freja was supposed to have brought another one from Matthias, so that should be six cows in total.

Where was the sixth cow?

I must have missed her when going back to the house yesterday, he thought. When Ulfred told him about his heritage, he forgot all about the cows. Alarm came over him—it was his fault that he didn't count the cows when shepherding them back to the barn. The sixth cow might be injured, starving, or even dead, knowing how the storm raged yesterday.

Alrik unfastened the latch of the fence bordering the pasture and shooed the five cows inside. Locking the fence behind him, he set off across the pasture, looking for the sixth cow. It probably wouldn't matter if he didn't find the cow—they were going to leave once the mages arrive—but he was disinclined to leave the cow out there alone.

The cows ambled around him, apparently glad to be out and roaming in the wide, open space. Beyond the pasture ran a sparkling river flanked by slender trees and wild bushes, and across the river rose a large grassy hill.

He cut across the pasture, reaching the river, calling for the cow. He hoped that it wasn't lying somewhere, mooing in pain. A tree was struck by lightning from the storm yesterday, and its branches were buried deep in the water. Seeing the broken tree made Alrik uneasy.

The wind blew across his face, lifting his straw hat off and carrying away behind him. Alrik looked for his hat. It was lying at the foot of the hill. He waded across the river to retrieve it, when a voice spoke.

"There he is."

Startled, he looked up. And his jaw dropped.

"Marianne?"

It was indeed the gorgeous young woman. She was dressed in an elegant lavender dress, her hair adorned with white ribbons, and in her hands she carried his hat. A little way off stood another girl, who could've been pretty if she didn't have rather large bunny teeth. A locket dangled in front of her dress.

"Aren't you supposed to be in the Loviska mountains?" Alrik said, astonished. "And where's Ronnie?" Fear, swift and sudden, gripped his heart like a vise. "Has anything happened to Ronnie?"

"Ronnie?" Marianne repeated, as if it were the first time she heard the name. "Oh, him. He's currently...very ill. He sent me to take you to him."

"He fell sick in the mountains?"

Marianne nodded and held out her hand. "Come. Let me take you to him."

He stared at her hand. Marianne...offering to take his hand? If it were Clara, it mightn't be that surprising, but he knew Marianne was so shy that she wouldn't touch a man of her own volition. Not even if he were Ronnie's best friend. And why was she accompanied by a girl he never saw before? Wait, he *had* seen the girl—she was at the wedding—wasn't she friends with Marianne's grandmother?

"Who is she?" he said, stepping back instead.

Marianne looked back. "A friend of Annalisa. Ronnie's friends couldn't come with me; she offered. Now come—we don't have much time."

Suspicion started to gnaw at his mind. Something was wrong, but he was unsure how to deal with it.

"Fine," he said, though he made to turn away. "I'll call Gabi, and we'll go together. Is he in Kardi?"

"She needn't come," the bunny-teeth girl spoke. "Ronnie wants to see you alone."

"It'll be real quick," Marianne added.

"I can't go without telling Gabi," Alrik said. He turned to leave, wondering if Marianne was lying, and if she did, why? Then he froze.

Thick cords wrapped around his body. His first instinct was to struggle, but the more he tried to break free, the tighter the bonds grew.

Shock filled his mind. Marianne was looking at him with the most bizarre expression he had ever seen. Usually she was demure and shy, keeping her beautiful features less conspicuous. Now, her rosebud lips were twisted into a sneer, and there was a ferocity in her eyes that reminded him of a wild hound who found an intruder trespassing his territory. She was still undeniably stunning, but in a frightening way.

"I cannot afford to let you go running back to your little friend," she said, and her voice was icier than winter snow gathered on the roof. "We must leave now."

"You can't be Marianne," he stated. "You're...you're..."

"You may call me Moira," the woman who looked like Marianne said. "I'm tired of others using this pathetic name—anyone called Marianne must be a sniveling idiot. And she—" Moira jerked her chin toward the girl with bunny teeth "—is Sorcha—my sister."

The revelation struck him like waves crashing around him. Moira and Sorcha. The witches that Freja and Gabi had been talking about. The witches who wanted him dead since he was born. They had found him—despite all the efforts that Freja had attempted these years.

"How did you find me?"

Moira gave an eerie, high-pitched giggle. Alrik looked away, unable to bear that twisted look on the young woman he once knew. And where was Ronnie? Was he dead or alive? And how did Moira manage to assume Marianne's appearance?

"Ronnie told me," Moira said. "When I asked him about you, he told me the name of this village. I left him in the mountains and came here straight away." She stepped closer and caressed his cheek. Alrik wanted to spit in her face, but repressed the urge. He had to stall until Gabi arrived. "Since I possessed the body of Annalisa's granddaughter, I've been seeking for a man who'd suit my taste. There was that prince of Savony, but he's too far away. Besides, his looks were too feminine. But when I saw you at the wedding, I knew I must have you." Her voice dropped to a sultry whisper. "You resemble a man I once knew —the man who should have married me."

King Tyrell. So after all these years, she hadn't forgotten him. For a moment Alrik felt a wave of pity, but as the bonds cut into his skin, any pity was soon vanished and replaced by fury.

"So you're using me as a substitute?"

"You should consider it an honor," Sorcha said. "My sister has powers you can never imagine. She can bestow you with riches that you could never attain in this run-down place. All you need to do is to obey her command."

Something else struck him as weird. Wasn't Moira keen on killing him? And then another thought hit him: the witch didn't even know he was Tyrell's son. She only saw the resemblance, but assumed that it was a coincidence. She didn't make the connection between him, a poor peasant farmer, and the son of Tyrell.

The realization was reassuring, but only slight. Were Moira to discover that he *was* the prince she cursed long ago, or if he were to prick his finger by accident...

"Sister," Sorcha prompted. "You're wasting time. We don't want to wait for someone to show up and find he's bound."

Moira tilted her head. "Indeed. We can continue our chat once we're on the way, my dear boy. Let's go."

Panic swept through him. Gabi still hadn't come looking for him. Alrik opened his mouth to shout, but the witches had anticipated his move. An invisible hand clamped over his mouth, muffling his voice. Moreover, there was no telling his shout could be heard, for the pasture was far from the house.

Moira held up her hands. Ice-blue sparks appeared from a dagger strapped to her waist, and glowed around her body. With a few muttered words, the sparks flew around her. Half of the sparks headed to Alrik. The sparks converged into a whirl-wind—he felt his feet leave the ground—and then everything surrounding him was a blue-whitish blur, the wind whistling by his ears. It didn't matter if he could shout. No one could hear him.

The last thing Alrik thought about before he closed his eyes was Gabi's face. Her cheeks were rosy, her eyes sparkling after his embrace.

At least, he thought, if he were to die, he had done what he had longed and yearned for all these years.

CHAPTER 17

Freja inspected the wall surrounding North Tower. She ran her hands on the smooth stones, knocking occasionally, teasing the spells that Theo and Gerald had installed within. When she came to a loose stone she turned.

"Why isn't this stone attached to the others?"

"We needed to leave an opening for the mages."

"It's akin to a sleeping giant," Freja said severely, as if Theo were three years old. "What if a troll discovered the opening when Tamarka and Morkel weren't looking?"

Theo drew his eyebrows together. Usually if someone chastised him in a tone like this, he'd retort with heat, but this was Freja, whom they desperately needed.

"We'd be ready for it."

"Hmph." Freja folded her arms. "Once they return, I'll give them a good talking to. Tamarka and Morkel are decent mages, but they're young and inexperienced. They haven't seen the world like I did. They never met foes like Moira and Sorcha. Yes, princeling, I understand there isn't a perfect solution that would allow us to gather the names and perform the transportation spell. But their method bodes for more risk, mark my words."

Theo nodded.

"But so far you've done a good job of fortifying this wall," Freja said. "Except for this opening. Now, I'd like to take a look at the two trolls that are now dead. I have never seen a troll—everything I knew about them is based on historical records. Examining a troll might give me ideas for additional elements to weave into the collars."

"Right." Theo signaled to Alix. "Can you take Lady Freja to the healer's ward? I want to keep an eye on the tower."

Alix wanted him to go back to rest, but at this moment, she knew that nothing would make Theo budge. She let her shoulders sag. "Of course."

"I'll go as well," Gerald offered. "I'd like to know if there's anything concerning spells that I can help with."

"Very well," Freja replied. "Let's go. Inform me immediately when Tamarka and Morkel return."

At the healer's ward, the familiar scent of herbs in the air greeted them. A few months earlier, Alix was used to seeing Beatrice's slender figure along with Odeon's crooked one. Recently, there was the addition of a tall, broad-shouldered young man. Prince Ferdinand, the fifth eldest prince, looked rather comical as he wore a homespun apron, sleeves rolled up, standing near Beatrice and following what she told him to do.

Back when the Savony princes were cursed, Theo had strictly forbidden his brothers to associate with any woman, fearing that an attachment would only lead to tragedy, since the princes might be dead any time. Their lives were still in danger, but he had relaxed the "rule." Since then, Ferdinand had been paying frequent visits to the healer's ward. Beatrice confessed to Alix that they want to make the most of their time together.

When she entered the ward, she noticed Ferdinand sitting by the window, while Beatrice leaned over him.

"You need to rest," she was saying, while dabbing at his forehead with a handkerchief. "I can get someone to carry the new supplies upstairs. Didn't Theo ask you to stand guard at North Tower?"

Hearing Beatrice speak was a novelty that Alix was still getting used to. Years ago, Beatrice had followed the princes underground, and the sight of trolls was so traumatic that she lost the ability to speak. Not until the curse was broken did she begin to speak again. Her words were still uttered slowly, and she lacked intonation, but it was already huge progress from when she was communicating with hand gestures and writing on paper.

"There are soldiers who could do that," Ferdinand murmured, grasping her wrist. Beatrice blushed rosy red, but didn't pull away. "Odeon isn't getting any younger. I'd rather stay here and provide help when I can."

If this were any other time, Alix would've slipped away and come back later, not wanting to disturb the moment. But Freja was only going to be here for a few days. Time was more precious than a sack of gold ducats.

She coughed. Beatrice jumped away from Ferdinand, a guilty expression on her face.

"Lady Freja, the mage who's creating the countercurse to banish the trolls, has arrived," Gerald said, apparently deciding that going straight to business would make Beatrice forget about her embarrassment. "She'd like to take a look at the two trolls' corpses and analyze if there's an effective method to control them through magic."

"Ye...yes, of co—course," Beatrice stammered, making a wobbly curtsy. "They're kept in the basement. This way, please, lady mage. Your Highness."

She led the mage and Gerald to the stairs, Ferdinand following close behind. Alix declined to accompany them; she wanted to visit Selma.

In a larger room, where beds and cots were lined up against the wall, Selma was sewing while sitting in bed, looking grumpy.

"Hello," Alix said, approaching the older woman. "How're you feeling today?"

Selma grunted. "Awful. That chit wouldn't let me out of the ward. I've been bored out of my mind."

"Can you walk properly?"

Another grunt. "I can walk if she'll give me crutches. But she insists that I need to be watched as if I were a babe."

Privately, Alix thought that Beatrice's insistence was based on concern for the princes. If Selma was hanging around, limping on her crutches, it would distract the princes. All of them had great affection and respect for her.

"Are they all right?" Selma asked. There was no need to clarify the "they" she meant.

Alix gave an account of the princes, except for the younger set, who had been forced to leave for Calois. She downplayed Theo's refusal to rest, though Selma wasn't fooled.

"You tell him that he needs his beauty sleep, or when I get out of the ward he'll have to deal with me."

"I'll do that," Alix promised, unable to suppress a grin.

Selma leaned back on the pillows propped against the wall. "Didn' think you'd be the one for him, but seems that he's made the right choice. Loads o' other girls would've fled when they saw those trolls."

"Thank you."

"The girl Gerald found had better be good enough for him. He's too soft-hearted, that boy. Did ya know that the girl actually proposed to him?"

Alix laughed. "It must have taken her a lot of courage to ask him."

"Well, I just hope that the one Julian finds won' be in it for his money," Selma said. "With a temper like his, the girl has to be a saint to put up with him."

"Has Julian found a girl?"

"No, but he's been talkin'..."

A low rumble sounded. Alix fell back against the bed; Selma grabbed her arm.

"They're coming!" Her voice was shrill with terror. "Quick! Get the mage!"

She needed no second bidding. Alix flew down the stairs, and almost collided with Gerald.

"We heard," he said simply, steadying her with a hand. "We're going to North Tower now. Stay behind, Alix; you don't have the cloak."

Alix hesitated. She was nervous for Theo, but also knew that she was useless when it came to fighting. Biting down a noise of frustration, Alix returned to the ward. Beatrice watched Ferdinand race outside with an expression that made her heart break.

Alix took her hand. "They'll be fine," she said firmly, making sure to inject confidence in her tone. "They've tons of experience battling the trolls, and we have three mages now. One of them brought a weapon that will control the trolls."

Beatrice nodded, but her lip quivered. "I...I don't want to watch. Is that terrible of me?"

"Not at all," Alix said. To be honest, she was afraid as well. But she had been underground three times, and she had watched the princes battle trolls. She could stuff her fingers in her ears and close her eyes, but then she thought of Theo and she walked to the window.

The opening left for Tamarka and Morkel was completely torn down. Stones lay scattered on the ground. Alix watched, horrified, as an enormous green leg covered with hair emerged from the opening. A huge, hulking troll appeared, his eyes blood red, and his mouth as large as her own head (meaning he could gobble her up in one swallow). His tongue lolled around; saliva dripped down his chin. On his shoulder he carried a mace. The spikes on the mace glinted in the sun.

"Get him!" Theo shouted.

The soldiers were roused from their positions. Arrows were fired at the troll; most bounced off its thick skin, but one hit it in the cheek. Enraged, the troll pulled out the arrow and hurled it at the soldier nearest him. The arrow pierced the soldier straight through the chest—and such was its force that after running through the soldier's flesh, it flew on and hit the ground, completely stained in blood.

Alix put her hands on her mouth. The other soldiers, shocked by the swiftness of their comrade's death, were either frozen or retreating, terror in their eyes.

Morkel was carrying Tamarka on his back, a trail of blood left in the wake. In one arm he clutched her invisibility cloak. Tamarka seemed to be yelling at him, but he ignored her and set her beneath a tree close to Central Tower. Then he ran toward North Tower, sparks shimmering on his fingers.

"Get his name!"

The shout came from Freja. Morkel's hands paused in the air —the coal-black sparks on his fingers changed into a blue-white glow—and he sent the magic toward the troll's head.

The troll ducked. Morkel made a noise of frustration and shot the blue-white magic at the troll again—this time he succeeded. The troll's head was engulfed in the blue-white glow. A second later, letters appeared on the troll's forehead, showing its name: *Saukrin*.

Freja, who had appeared behind Morkel, held up a large, metal-studded collar. She uttered a string of sentences—Alix was too far to hear her chanting—but just before Saukrin attacked, she threw the collar at him.

The collar spun through the air, the leather spread out like arms, and fastened around the troll's neck. Saukrin howled and tried to pry the collar off, but his hands slammed on the metal spikes and he let out a cry of pain. Blood dripped down his fingers.

Meanwhile, Freja was chanting a second string of sentences. Saukrin gradually stopped struggling; he froze as the collar's magic bound him until he was like a cocoon.

"BEGONE!" Freja thundered.

And before Alix's eyes, Saukrin disappeared with a popping sound.

So that was the transportation spell Freja was talking about. No throwing punches with the troll, no sweat and blood, no fuss.

Theo and his brothers, along with the other soldiers, cheered. But Freja and Morkel shouted something at them; Freja was gesturing at the torn opening in the wall.

"NO!"

Alix felt a weight press into her shoulder; Selma had risen from the bed and was leaning on her for support. Her face was terror-stricken as she pointed a shaking finger at the tower.

From a window on the second floor, a large troll emerged, grinning like a madman. Then it leaped.

CHAPTER 18

Gabi hummed a tune as she cleaned up the main room. A wave of her hand, and the dust on the tables and chairs disappeared. Another flick of her fingers, and the broom started sweeping the floor by itself. Now that Alrik knew she was a mage, she didn't bother hiding her magic. She'd still feel tired after using magical energy, but it sure was better than getting on the floor on her knees and scrubbing away the dirt and stains.

But what made her even happier was Alrik's confession that he loved her. She kept reliving it; it was sweet to know that after all these years, Alrik did hold a strong affection for her—stronger than she suspected.

It wouldn't last—she was the only young woman he truly knew, but it was lovely to know that he had cared. She'd treasure the warmth of his embrace always.

By the time she finished cleaning, she looked up, expecting Alrik to enter through the back door. He usually liked to stay at the pasture, lying on the grass and gazing at the sky, especially when the weather was pleasant, but after he admitted his feelings for her, she had an instinct that he would return to the house as soon as he dumped the cows in the pasture and locked the fence.

Gabi headed to the barn. No Alrik gathering eggs. She went to the gardens. No Alrik pulling up weeds or watering the cabbages. Was he still in the pasture? Or had he gone to the woods? It was possible—he might want to surprise her with a batch of freshly caught trout or a bunch of wild spring flowers.

She turned, considering going back to the house, when she paused. Freja had left her in charge; she assumed sole responsibility of Alrik's safety until the mages arrived—or even until he was in the palace.

She limped to the fence dividing the garden and pasture. A few cows were grazing peacefully; there was no sign of Alrik's checkered shirt. She opened the gate and entered the pasture, scanning for any sign of him.

Hating how her wooden foot couldn't enable her to run, Gabi combed the pasture. No Alrik. She went down to the river and looked around. Still, no sign of him.

"Alrik!" she yelled. "Where are you? Come out this instant!"

No answer. By this time her anxiety was growing. Surely— the unthinkable couldn't have happened. The mages would be arriving the next day—Alrik couldn't disappear at this moment.

But when she called again, nothing replied except a faint echo of her voice across the hill. Gabi tapped her bracelet, activating a tracking spell designed for Alrik, but there was nothing but a hazy resistance.

Alarm struck.

If the tracking spell didn't work...Alrik must have run into someone who possessed magic—someone who actively suppressed the tracking spell. And it had to be someone whose magic was strong enough to suppress the magic Freja and Gabi had created together.

Then something caught her eye. Alrik's hat was floating in the river. As quick as she could make it with her wooden leg,

Gabi reached the river and waded in the water. It was shallow enough that she needn't worry about drowning, though she had to go slowly in case of tripping over the rocks on the bottom. Carefully, she picked up the hat, then headed back to the house as fast as she could.

The main room was littered with the spells that she unearthed from Freja's basement. Rummaging through the numerous pots and jars, she found a vial containing a tracking spell, everything completed sans the catalyst, and a brand new compass.

With a few muttered words and a lot of crimson sparks, she heated up the liquid in the vial. An ordinary person would have to make a fire or use a heating spell, but as a mage, Gabi could simply produce heat by hand.

Once the magical liquid started bubbling, she ripped off the brim of Alrik's hat and fed it to the spell. When the liquid turned into a glue-like substance, she took a brush and coated the spell on the compass.

Gabi tapped the compass and it spun, pointing north. The color of the compass's tip was dark orange, indicating that Alrik was already at least a hundred miles away.

"NO!"

She vented her frustration by landing a fist on the table, which helped her feelings, but did little except giving her hand pain. How could Alrik be so far away, when she just saw him off this morning? He only had one hour—two at most—to have gone that far.

It had to be Moira. With Sorcha, along with the infinite power from the Peerless Knife, it wasn't impossible that they'd have the power to transport Alrik that far.

Setting aside the question on how Moira came to discover Alrik, Gabi pondered what she could do. Why did Moira take Alrik up north? Arksar was known for its cold climate. Brek was already situated northeast—farther up north would be the place known as the Sisu region—a sparsely populated area where some places were permanently covered in snow.

"When Lorenza and Julong found the witches, they were hiding in Finsoor," Freja had told her, "where they kept their own father, locked and trapped, and siphoned magic from him for their own personal use."

It looked like the witches planned to do something similar to Alrik. The reason that he wasn't dead was probably that they wanted to torture him, or maybe hold him hostage and make demands to Tyrell. At any rate, Gabi had to save him before Moira decided to kill him.

Gabi swallowed. She had to act. Fingers trembling, she tapped the bracelet and sent a verbal message to Lorenza and Julong, alerting them that Alrik was already gone, possibly taken by Moira and Sorcha. She considered sending Freja a message as well, but decided against it. If Freja knew that Alrik was kidnapped, she wouldn't be able to deal with the trolls.

The replies from the mages were instantaneous.

Lorenza's voice came through the bracelet, with a recognizable Masaro accent. "We'll come straight away."

A wave of mixed emotions swept through her. Gabi had lost her own distinct Masaro accent after staying in Brek for so many years.

A masculine voice followed Lorenza's. "Stay where you are." The accent was even stronger—it had to be Julong. "Don't try to go after the witches on your own. Wait for us; we shall be in Brek soon."

Gabi shut down the bracelet. The compass on the table was still pointing north. The color of the tip was darker—meaning that Alrik was even farther away. The witches were traveling fast. But at least there was color. If Alrik were dead, the compass wouldn't even move.

She had to start packing. Lifting her hands, she uttered a simple summoning spell. Within seconds, a large burlap sack came zooming out of Freja's room and straight into her waiting hands. She shoved the pots and jars into the sack—she was going to need a lot of magic on the way.

It was going to be a long, difficult, dangerous journey. She detested the icy chill from colder weather up north, hated dragging her wooden foot when traveling, dreaded meeting an adversary who was much stronger than she, without Freja's presence. But when she thought about Alrik's smile, and chances that she'd never see his smile again, Gabi hardened her resolve.

Time to save a prince.

CHAPTER 19

*lrik opened his eyes, finding himself bundled up in a large sled. A warm, fur-lined cloak was wrapped over his body, and a scarf tied around his neck. Was he dreaming? It was already spring, yet he was dressed as if it were late autumn or even for a mild winter. Tipping his head back, he looked up into a dull gray sky. A few snowflakes fluttered down, alighting on his face.

"So you're awake." The voice came from a young woman sitting across him. His gaze snapped back to focus on her face—her large front teeth told him that it was Sorcha.

What happened before he passed out came rushing back. A quick check informed him that his feet were bound, though the rest of his body was free.

"Where are we going?"

Someone laughed: Marianne—no, Moira, the witch who wanted him dead. "A place where you will forget all about your past."

"How long have we been traveling?" Alrik looked around. There was nothing but flat lands, half of the area covered in snow.

"Two days," Sorcha said. "It was a hassle, getting away from eastern Arksar as fast as possible, but we're far enough now. Don't even think of escaping; you'll either die from our hands or perish in the coldness."

"I wasn't even thinking of escaping," he said. "I swear. I wouldn't even dare."

Moira smirked.

But Alrik didn't tell her why he wasn't planning on escaping. It was more important to stay alive until Gabi came to rescue him.

Eight ferocious wolves were pulling the sled. If the witches were able to make wolves pull for them, Alrik was certain he wouldn't be able to escape their clutches.

"Though there is something that has been puzzling," Moira said, taking his hand. Alrik felt like recoiling at her touch, no matter that she appeared to be a beautiful young woman. "Why do you have a tracking spell on you? An ordinary farmer from a village shouldn't have this. Even if Arksans can make decent spells, I fail to see the need."

"Why me?" he said instead. "Why did you pick an ordinary farmer like me?"

"I'm asking the questions," she snapped. "I could toss you off this sled and leave you to starve to death."

Don't provoke her, he told himself. As much as his nature rebelled against being a subservient slave, he had to remember that staying alive was the most important thing of all. "My aunt is worried about me. I have a bad sense of direction and often can't find my way home, so she made this charm, just in case I got lost in the woods or were stuck in a snowstorm. It almost happened, twice, and…"

"An ordinary village woman couldn't create a complicated spell like this," Moira snapped. She traced the patterns on his bracelet. "The workings are so complex that I had to use the

Peerless Knife to break the connection. This is the work of a mage, not an accomplished magic user."

"Who's your aunt?" Sorcha said.

"No one. She's just incredibly talented at magic and spells. We couldn't have survived on that tiny farm if it weren't for her creations."

Moira's lip curled; for a moment she reminded him of a wild cat. He wondered how she came to resemble Marianne. "Do you take me for a fool? The workings on this bracelet are fashioned from pure magic, not magical ingredients. Tell me who it is that made this bracelet for you."

"I told you already, it's my aunt."

"You're not a mage or half mage," Sorcha said.

"I didn't say she was my aunt by blood relation."

Moira's nails dug into his skin, drawing blood.

"I want no impertinence, young man," she hissed. "If you keep up this attitude, I can—and I will—make you regret it."

Reluctantly, he told the truth. "Her name's Freja."

At the mention of the name, both Moira and Sorcha exchanged a look of alarm.

"Freja?" Moira whispered. "That annoying old hag who kept messing up my plans with Tyrell?"

Gabi had mentioned that Moira preyed on young, beautiful women because she was too ugly, yet wished for handsome partners like Tyrell and Prince Gerald.

"If Freja's your adopted aunt..."

"I've been thinking the same thing, sister," Sorcha said.

"Are you Tyrell's son?" Moira demanded. Her long white fingers curled around Alrik's wrist, making him shiver. She was made of flesh and blood, but her skin felt as cold as ice. "Tell me now, or I'll force you to say the words."

"You don't want her using magic. Trust me," Sorcha said.

"I have no idea," Alrik lied. "Freja always brushed me off when I tried to ask her about my parents. She said they were ordinary folk living in Linberg." That part, at least, was the truth for most of his life.

Moira glared. For a moment Alrik wondered if she'd attempt something like a truth-revealing spell (if that existed), but then she loosened her grip.

"He must be Tyrell's son," Sorcha said. "The resemblance is too striking. I had my suspicions when I saw him at the wedding. And if Freja adopted him, she must've saved him from your magic."

"True. Though I wonder how that old hag managed to counter my curse," Moira muttered with venom in her tone. "She's powerful, but I used the most complicated curse imaginable. She couldn't have reversed it."

Alrik kept silent. He wasn't going to let Moira know that Freja only modified the curse. Let her remain in suspicion—it would buy him some time.

"It doesn't matter anymore," Moira finally said, stroking his cheek. Her fingernails felt like the sharp edge of a knife— he told himself it was his imagination speaking. "If I can't have Tyrell, his son is just as good a replacement. Imagine his reaction if he knows his son became my consort." She gave a nasty laugh. "Fitting retribution for what he did to me."

"What did he do?" Alrik said.

Moira glared at him, as if he were responsible for his father's actions.

"More than twenty years ago, I met your father. I didn't care much for him—a spineless youngster who couldn't stand up to his parents, but he was the best-looking man I had seen, and he was going to be the king of Arksar. I had ruled over Sisu, but what is that land of ice and snow compared to a kingdom with real culture and development? So I extended my hand to Tyrell. I tried to convince him that our union would make the entire kingdom, including Sisu, flourish and prosper. In the beginning he seemed interested, but then his snobbish old mother intervened."

"How well I remember her, sister," Sorcha put in. "Sweeping around with her nose in the air, as if she were the only woman in Arksar."

"Tyrell's mother claimed a Sisu, queen or not, was not good enough for her precious son. No matter how Arksans pretend that Sisus are their equals, in their hearts they look down on the region in the north. Only pure Arksan blood is acceptable. Only Arksan women who are from noble families, who adhere to decorum and propriety, and who have no blemishes, can have the privilege of being chosen as the future queen."

"Blemishes?" Alrik said, thinking of Gabi.

"There was a woman that Tyrell's elder cousin was courting, but she was rejected because she had a scar on her upper arm. Ha! As if anyone would notice that—she can't even reveal her upper arm in those sleeves long enough to reach the floor. Were she as beautiful as this—" she ran a finger down the face that was once Marianne's "—he would have defied his parents and married her right away."

Alrik bit his lip. If his father's cousin couldn't marry a woman with a scar, then what would they say when he announced he wanted someone with a crippled foot?

He thought everything would be resolved when it turned out he didn't have hemophilia. But it looked like there were going to be a lot more hurdles.

But, he reasoned cynically, those hurdles wouldn't matter if Moira decided to get rid of him.

The sled slowed down. Sorcha uttered a faint cry.

Ahead were a dozen giant moose. Most of them had antlers so large that they wouldn't look out of place on trees. Alrik didn't know much about moose, but based on his experience taking care of horses and cows, he sensed that the moose they ran into weren't a friendly bunch. The nearest one had its hackles raised on the back of its brown neck, and another one let out a roar.

"Why're there so many?" Moira demanded, her eyes flashing. "They're supposed to be lone creatures!"

"One of them is female, I think," Sorcha said, leaning a bit out of the sled. As much as he resented the witch for luring and abducting him, Alrik was impressed that she showed little fear. "The few times moose will gather together is when the males are fighting for a female's attention."

"How do you know that?" Alrik asked.

"I used to live up north," Sorcha said, surprisingly amenable to his question. Even a witch couldn't help being smug sometimes.

"Well, get rid of them as soon as possible," Moira said irritably. "I want to reach Sisu by nightfall."

"As you say, sister. But I'll need some help."

Moira frowned, but she reluctantly dipped her hand into a side pocket and withdrew a dagger. It wasn't particularly long or curved or flashy, but what made Alrik notice were the carvings on the hilt. Twisted and entwined in complicated patterns, the carvings reminded him of a mass of crawling ivy draped over a wealthy Kardi man's house.

"The more complex the patterns are, the more magic the spell possesses," Freja had said. Which meant Moira's dagger must be...

The sled suddenly gave a violent jolt. A moose had delivered a powerful kick—Alrik couldn't help a bit of surprise mingled with alarm. He had thought the moose would charge with their antlers, but apparently they could kick as well. Another rammed into the sled. To his amazement, the wolves didn't growl or snarl or snap—one let out a whimper and tried to run.

"Cowards," Moira said with disdain. To Sorcha, she made an impatient gesture. "Hurry up and finish them off. The wolves can't pull in the dark."

"It's spring now; it doesn't get dark soon," she replied, but unsheathed the knife. The blade's color was unusual—a shiny black.

Aiming at the first moose, Sorcha struck out with the knife. Alrik held his breath in mixed fear and anticipation. He was torn with the desire to see the moose attack the witches, yet also was afraid that if the witches were seriously injured, his chances of surviving would be even lower.

Was it too much to hope for the moose and the witches to end up battered and bruised, leaving him free to leave? But then, would he be able to drive a sled pulled by wolves?

The knife glowed. Silver light became visible from the intricate carvings on the hilt—Sorcha uttered a few incomprehensible words, and the light slashed through the air in a blazing arc.

Like a spinning sickle, the silver arc slashed through the nearest moose. Then it went through the other one, then another. The three teetered for a second, before sinking to the ground. Blood trickled down their necks. The knife's magic had severed their heads from their necks so cleanly that the neck wounds were as thin as needle threads.

"Not bad on your first try," Moira said. "But I expected you'd do better than take down three moose."

"You had the knife for most of the time," Sorcha said, sounding irritated. "I didn't have enough time to engage with its magical capabilities as you had."

"If you possessed half the brains I inherited from Father, you'd have found a way to gain possession of the knife." Moira sounded contemptuous. "Stand back, sis. This is how you eliminate whatever blocks your way."

The other moose were backing away. Whether it was the alarming flash of light or the sight of their fellow moose falling dead within seconds, they sensed that the knife-wielding witches were terrifying.

Moira, however, had no compassion. She stepped forward, crimson robes flapping in the icy wind, and held the knife high. Magic, like a storm, burst from the tip and rushed toward the remaining moose. Alrik wanted to shut his eyes, but morbidly, he didn't. All the remaining moose—eleven of them, he noted with typical Arksan accuracy—were slashed through the neck and crumpled to the ground.

Moira sheathed the knife, gave her sister a taunting glance, as if to say that this was the way to kill moose properly. Returning to the sled, she sat down with the air of a warrior general.

"You needn't have done that." The words came out of Alrik's mouth without thinking.

The witch turned to him, an eyebrow raised, as if she couldn't believe her captive had the audacity to question her.

"Done what?"

"Killing all the moose. The rest weren't planning to attack us."

Moira now looked as if he stuck a thorn on her face. "You dare criticize me? I saved your life, little prince. If I didn't kill those moose, you'd be dead by now."

"I wouldn't even have met those moose if you didn't kidnap me."

She slapped him. It came so fast that he didn't have time to avoid her hand. So much for the training from Ulfred.

"Keep talking like that and I'll use the same magic I just did on the moose," she hissed. "I don't need a man to tell me what to do."

Alrik said nothing. He regretted the outburst; no matter how he thought of her cruelty, the first and foremost objective was to stay alive.

He looked down on his bare wrist. A few hours in the journey, Moira and Sorcha had discovered he was wearing a tracking spell. Sorcha ripped the bracelet away, while Moira placed a cool hand on his head. Magic wove around him like a spider's web, making it difficult to breathe, before fading away.

"This will wipe any trace of your scent," Moira said. "If Freja tries to track you down with an object you possess, she won't be able to find a clue."

If what Moira said was true...how was Gabi going to find him? And if she did, would she have any chance against the Peerless Knife?

Alrik swallowed. Conflicted emotions battled in his mind. After seeing Moira demonstrate her power, he began to have doubts. He wanted to escape, of course, but if it meant that Gabi might be seriously injured while trying to save him, he'd rather that she never found him.

Something cold brushed on his nose. Snow was falling again, indicating that they were in the far north of Arksar, where winter was permanent for most of the year.

CHAPTER 20

*I*t was a nightmare come true.

Alix stood frozen, Selma's fingers digging into her shoulders. The troll landed on top of the wall, its claw-like hands gripping the stones like a bird might cling on a branch.

The new troll was different from Saukrin. It was like a mountain cat as it landed on the ground on all fours with a screech, characterized more by lithe movements than brute strength.

It sprang and caught an unlucky soldier, ripping off the poor man's arm as easily as if it was plucking an apple from a tree. The soldier screamed, blood gushing from his wound in a crimson stream.

Alix closed her eyes for a second, wishing that what happened wasn't real. But the screams and yells in her ears continued, making her cold with dread and worry.

Arrows rained on the leaping troll, but none made permanent damage. The troll evaded most—even caught two arrows with both hands. It bounded and rolled on the ground and twisted with alarming agility, as if it were a monkey trapped in a troll's body.

Morkel was trying to get its name; he shot blue-white sparks now and then, but the troll was too slippery.

Then another shout broke through the air. "There's more! Watch out!"

And indeed, from the torn opening in the wall stepped several menacing trolls, their feet thudding on the ground. Alix counted eight of them. Plus the leaping troll, they had nine trolls to deal with.

The princes, soldiers, and mages froze on spot for a moment. The new trolls were all well over eight feet, some hairy, some bald, one with only one gigantic eye, another with three arms. But what made them similar was the predatory glint in their eyes as they advanced on the humans.

Blue-white sparks flew toward the three trolls who came out first. It was Tamarka—unknown to the others, she had limped from her place under the tree, a makeshift bandage torn from her gown tied around her thigh.

Three names appeared on their foreheads.

"NOW!" Tamarka screamed.

Freja acted immediately. Three collars were thrown, incantations muttered, and the first three trolls disappeared in the same way Saukrin did.

Alix breathed a sigh of relief. But she was so focused on Freja's collars that she didn't notice the other five trolls engaged in intense battle with the princes and soldiers. A few soldiers had fled, shocked and scared, preferring to run for their lives.

A low growl came from Theo. He staggered back, blood streaming down his left shoulder, but he didn't seem to notice. Gerald grabbed his right arm and jerked him out of the way, just when a hulking troll's club landed where Theo was standing, leaving a deep hole in the ground.

Alix felt as if her heart was going to jump out of her chest. Near her, Beatrice let out a whimper. Ferdinand was lying on the ground, motionless. Was he unconscious or dead? Alix felt her heart sink to the bottom of her stomach.

Wasn't there anything she could do? She couldn't stay there at the window, standing like a statue, unable to lend a hand. After all, she had helped the princes break the curse. Because she had felled the silver tree while wearing the invisibility cloak.

The cloak!

It was left under the tree, where Morkel had dragged Tamarka. Alix felt in her pocket; there was a poisoned dagger nestled among the silken material.

Beatrice had concocted a strong poison and coated the blade with it, drawing inspiration from that time Theo was poisoned by the trolls.

"It could be useful one day," Beatrice had said. "You don't know how to fight, you don't have the strength, but the poison will be able to kill ten men."

While Alix hoped that she would never have to use the dagger, she sensed this was the time.

Shaking off Selma's hand on her shoulder, Alix crept downstairs.

"Alix?" Selma and Beatrice cried at the same time.

Alix paid them no attention. She reached the tree, retrieved the cloak, and flung it around her shoulders.

Freja was chanting; two more trolls vanished. But one was bearing down on Ferdinand, who remained motionless. Theo and his brothers were still fighting the other trolls; all of them were injured. Blood splattered everywhere.

Alix crept toward the troll. It reached out a huge claw-like hand to grab Ferdinand—she crouched near the unconscious prince and pulled the poisoned dagger from her pocket, pointing it at the troll.

The troll, unable to see her, lunged for Ferdinand. Its hand met the blade of her dagger; the troll let out a grunt of pain and looked at its hand.

Furious, the troll swiped at Ferdinand, apparently under the belief that the prince had somehow regained consciousness and stabbed its palm. While swiping through the air, the troll's hand knocked off Alix's hood, revealing her head.

The troll let out a scream of rage. It knew she stabbed him in the palm. Then its fingers were around her throat, lifting her higher...

Alix screamed.

A flash of silver. Theo's sword chopped down on the troll's foot. A gust of blood flew into the air.

"Run, you idiot!" he bellowed.

Alix scrambled to her feet and ran, though not before draping her cloak around Ferdinand, hoping she could buy him some time.

Theo was engaged in battle with the troll. He parried, he struck, keeping his gaze firmly fixed on the troll's red eyes. But he was too close—without defensive spells, Theo couldn't match the speed of the troll.

A punch caught him in the stomach, and the crown prince staggered. The troll followed up with a kick to Theo's chest, and he flew backward, landing in a heap on the ground.

"Theo!" Gerald shouted.

Alix and Gerald raced toward the troll, who had grabbed Theo by the nape of his neck, and was raising him to its huge jaws...

Alix screamed.

Then the troll's grip slackened. Theo sank to the ground. The poison had finally worked its way through the wound on the troll's palm, spreading over its entire body.

Gerald took in a deep breath. He drew his sword and ran it through the troll's chest, and it crashed on the ground.

"You idiot," Theo croaked, blood dribbling down his side. He was badly hurt from the fall, but he had enough strength to grab Alix's wrist. "You almost got killed."

She was too tired to retort, "So did you." Instead, she reached up and put her arms around him. Never had she so appreciated being alive.

More pops. Alix looked around; all the trolls, except the one they killed, had vanished, leaving wisps of white mist behind.

Freja was wiping her forehead, her posture stooped. "We need to patch up the wall before more can enter. Right now."

Tamarka limped toward her, but Freja waved her off. "Stay there. If a troll comes out again, Morkel and I will be distracted while trying to protect you."

She disappeared through the wall's opening, Morkel following close at her heels.

Footsteps sounded behind them. Beatrice came flying out of the healer's ward, making a beeline for Ferdinand. She placed something under his nostrils, and gradually he stirred.

"Where...how...what?"

Beatrice let out a little cry of joy. In front of everyone, she kissed Ferdinand with a passion that she rarely displayed.

Theo struggled to his feet. Alix supported him the best she could.

"How many casualties?"

Gerald counted. Eleven soldiers were dead, all of their deaths brutally caused. But considering the number of trolls, and the suddenness of the attack, it could've been much worse.

Odeon and several assistants had arrived as well. Along with Beatrice, they tended to everyone's wounds.

"It's all my fault," Tamarka said, tears running down her face. "I thought it'd be quicker this way. But I got too carried away when I managed to extract ten names in one try. I made a sound, and they discovered us. If only I had stayed silent!"

Beatrice patted her shoulder. "Please don't blame yourself," she said softly. "You did your best."

Tamarka buried her face in Beatrice's side and sobbed like a baby.

"We'll have to build a taller wall," said Theo to Gerald. "And no more going underground for name-gathering, now that the trolls are able to come through the opening."

Just as Odeon was applying salve to Tamarka's ankle, Freja and Morkel returned.

"There's a hole through the wall you blocked over the fireplace," Freja said. "We've patched it up and used the furniture in the room to make a more secure obstruction. And we'll fix the opening in the wall. No more going underground—you've seen what happens."

"But how are we going to deal with the rest of the trolls?" Gerald said, rubbing his forehead. "If they all burst out at the same time, we won't be able to keep up. We had enough difficulty dealing with nine trolls."

Freja closed her eyes for a second. "I need time to think. But one thing's certain. We can't go down there for some time. We need more defensive spells, more armor, more weapons that can help us keep the trolls at bay."

Alix clenched her fists and let go. Her own neck was bruised and sore from where the troll wrapped his fingers. She shuddered; if Theo hadn't arrived in time, the troll would've squeezed the life from her body.

It was impossible to defeat the remaining trolls without casualties. But gazing at the soldiers' corpses and the injuries the others sustained, anxiety and frustration gnawed in her chest. Even if they could defeat the trolls, most of them would lose their lives. Was there an easier way that didn't require so much sacrifice?

"Anyway," Theo said, seeming determined to inject confidence when everyone was battered in spirit, "we'll figure out a way. We already broke the curse, and we have the collars. It won't be long until we'll be permanently rid of the trolls."

Freja looked toward Tamarka and Morkel. "Did any of you

take care of that leaping troll? It was moving so fast that I couldn't put a collar on it, and then I lost sight of it."

Tamarka and Morkel exchanged a look. Both of them shook their heads.

"Then the corpse must be lying somewhere."

But after a thorough search, there was only one troll corpse —the one Alix poisoned.

"It can't be…" Tamarka whispered.

Freja looked grim. "It's possible. If we don't find that troll's body…"

They all looked at each other; fear reflected in each other's eyes.

The troll had escaped into the castle grounds. It might even be on its way to the city.

Theo set his jaw. "Send out a search team. That leaping troll must be found and destroyed."

CHAPTER 21

*I*t was three in the morning when the mages arrived. The ungodly hour didn't matter, for Gabi was still wide awake at the time. She had performed another tracking spell, and much to her consternation, the compass barely twitched. The color didn't change. Which meant that either she created a faulty spell, or that on Alrik's end, a cloaking spell was performed to cover his tracks.

Since she was a mage and had reasonable confidence in her spell-making skills, it had to be the latter. And she had a sinking suspicion that Moira was the one who prevented Alrik from being found. That tracking spell planted by Freja was a powerful one; only another mage or witch would be able to nullify its effect.

It had been utterly quiet in the deep, dark night. Gabi was wringing her hands, longing to snatch the compass and hurl it against the wall, wishing that Freja was home and could offer some helpful suggestion. She lamented her ignorance—how could she let Alrik be kidnapped right in Brek? In her frustration she ran into the table, banged her knee against solid wood, and crumpled to the ground in a pitiful heap.

Then came a knock on the door.

Clinging to the table leg, Gabi pulled herself to a standing position and limped to the door. For a moment she allowed herself a wild hope—hope that Alrik had returned.

But it was an unusual group gathered at the door—Ulfred, tall and muscular, his red beard dirty and unkempt; Lorenza, whom she guessed from her olive skin and curly dark hair; Julong, who was easily identifiable from his lifeless eyes and smooth black hair. And finally—her gaze fell on an elderly man leaning on Ulfred's arm. This must be Urdu—Moira's father.

Known as the most powerful mage alive, Urdu was not what Gabi had imagined. His hair was snowy white, his skin covered with wrinkles, and while he moved with relative ease for an eighty-year-old human, he would be regarded as snail-like for an elderly mage. It seemed he hadn't fully recovered from his imprisonment in Finsoor.

"You weren't in bed," Ulfred said, peering at her closely. "Couldn't sleep because of Alrik?"

"The tracking spell was blocked," Gabi said, gesturing that they all come inside. "I can't find Alrik's location anymore."

"The witches must have blocked the tracking function," Lorenza said, stepping into the main room. Despite the long journey, both she and Julong maintained a tidy appearance— largely to do with magic, Gabi supposed. It didn't require a huge amount of magic to keep your hair combed or remove the wrinkles in your clothes. Ulfred, on the other hand, was scruffy, though he usually didn't bother with his appearance unless it was an occasion like Ronnie's wedding.

"You mentioned that you can't find his location anymore," Julong said. With Lorenza's guidance, he settled on a chair. "How much time has passed since you discovered his location in the north?"

"Yesterday afternoon, around three." Gabi summoned the

Arksan habit for precision. "Which makes it about twelve hours from now."

"And twelve hours earlier, where was Alrik?"

Gabi showed them the map, which she had pinned on the wall. The compass lay on a table beneath the map.

"I estimated he was here." She pointed at a dot in the far north of the kingdom. "But now I have no idea."

"Twelve hours isn't long enough to travel outside of the kingdom," Lorenza said. "Even if they were aided by magic, I don't think they're on the sea or crossing the desert to Lulan."

"Where could they go?" Julong asked.

"She must have taken him to her snow castle," Urdu said.

They all looked toward him.

"She has another place to hide?" Lorenza said, looking surprised. "Apart from Finsoor islands?"

Urdu sat down. Outside, a flash ripped through the dark night, followed by a roll of thunder.

Lorenza shuddered, a reaction that surprised Gabi. A mage afraid of thunder! But then, Lorenza was from Masaro, and Masaro was known for its year-long sunny climate.

"Nice weather," Julong commented.

"The road's going to be real smooth to travel on tomorrow," Ulfred said.

If Urdu heard them, he gave no sign of that he did. "Forty-three years ago," he began, with the air of an elderly grandfather telling bedtime stories to his grandchildren, "Moira discovered a way to make herself beautiful—through possessing the body of another. No one knew of this spell, but it goes without saying that it is forbidden. She made Sorcha practice it first—she had Sorcha scout a young, beautiful Arksan woman, and tested the magic. When Sorcha successfully took on the appearance of the woman, Moira decided to perform the spell on herself. She found a woman renowned for her beauty in Tybalt. I got wind of it and hurried to intervene. I was just in time to prevent her from committing this heinous crime. I put a seal on her magic and told her she was a disgrace to all mages."

"So how did she come back and imprison you in Finsoor?" Ulfred said.

Urdu held up a hand. "I will get to that later. After I sealed Moira's magic, I went back home. I lived in peace for nearly twenty years, until I learned that she broke through my seal and had taken over the northern region of Arksar, calling herself the queen of Sisu."

"How did she break the seal?" Gabi asked.

Urdu sighed. He looked old and frail. Looking at his thin face and sallow skin, it was difficult to imagine he was once the most powerful mage alive. "I can only guess," he said, after taking a sip of water. "She's familiar with my style of magic, and being exceptionally brilliant, she figured out a way with Sorcha's help. Were her magic sealed by another mage, it's possible that she would've taken longer, or might have never been able to break the seal."

"And how did she end up in Sisu?" Julong said quietly.

"Moira and Sorcha wanted a place where they could exercise their powers without being demanded to solve petty human problems. They searched far and wide, and finally decided on the northern, autonomous region of Arksar. Here they could rule like queens. Few people lived here; they wouldn't be much bothered even if they treated the local people like slaves. I believe they also found a way to harvest magic from certain local substances, which enabled them to exert control over the Sisu people." Urdu coughed. "Moira attempted to form a union with Tyrell, but he rejected her on the grounds that she isn't qualified to bear heirs for the Arksan royal family. Only daughters of aristocratic blood are considered candidates for queen."

"Not that I'm taking Moira's side," Lorenza said. "But that is a pretty rotten reason from Tyrell."

"It was an excuse," Ulfred intervened, his tone gruff. "Tyrell rejected Moira because she was too domineering. He wanted a wife who'd keep her head down, and frankly speaking, it's much less fuss that way…"

Lorenza snorted. It sounded like a noise of derision.

Gabi rolled her eyes. She used to think that Alrik was the same type—the kind that preferred a docile partner who'd rarely argue with him, who'd be content to play the role of a conventional wife. But when he confessed he loved her, she was glad he wasn't like his father. Was it because he was brought up in Brek, under Freja's tyranny, that made him this way? Would he become like Tyrell when he returned to the palace?

Assuming he'd make it through this alive. If he were in the clutches of Moira…Gabi pushed her pessimistic thoughts to the back of her mind.

"Moira was furious," Urdu said. "I've been trying to curb her vengeful streak since she was a child. When I admonished her by forbidding her to go out, she'd put thorns in my bed. She told Tyrell if he wanted pure-blooded heirs, she'd make sure he never had any. When the prince was a month old, she appeared in the palace and laid a curse on him."

"That witch," Ulfred growled. "I was there and couldn't stop her. She had taken the appearance of a hapless maiden. No one knew she was Moira. After she uttered the words, she took flight immediately. We were too late to do anything." He stood up and paced the room like a bear. "Freja spent weeks trying to reverse the curse, but she failed. Devastated in his grief, Tyrell ordered for Moira's head. Anyone who could bring her in, dead or alive, would be awarded a million gold ducats."

"It isn't a question of money," Julong remarked. "People may be willing to risk their lives, but no one is equipped to deal with Moira. Not even a mage—it takes at least two or three."

"Knowing that Moira and Sorcha could be formidable together, Freja also asked Tamarka and Morkel's parents to come, but they were unwilling to get mixed up in what they regarded as an Arksan matter. Then she sent for Julong. We searched high and low for the witches."

Gabi looked toward Julong. He wasn't young, but he didn't look over forty. Or maybe was it the Lulaners? Some of them could look ten years younger than their real age.

"You must have been very young when you came," Gabi ventured.

"I was eighteen," he said. "My parents knew Freja way back, but they weren't keen to make the journey across the desert. I was young and eager to see the world, though I didn't expect that Moira was so powerful. My flying daggers were unable to penetrate through her shield."

Ulfred was pacing, but he now stopped in front of Julong. He made a low bow. Despite his blindness, Julong rose and grasped Ulfred's arms, making the latter look up.

Impressive. If it wasn't obvious that there wasn't any life in his eyes, Gabi couldn't have believed Julong was blind.

"If it weren't for you, Moira would've killed me. Master Julong, I owe you a debt."

"I wish I were there," Lorenza said, with the air of a child missing out on the fun. She seemed to be in her late twenties, so of course she wasn't part of the hunt-Moira-down team. "How did you let Moira escape?"

"Sorcha arrived in the end," Julong said. "Moira was half-dead at that time; we didn't think she'd survive. Or if she did, she would never be strong enough to heal and retain her magic."

"It was my mistake," Urdu said with a sigh. "I vowed I was done with her. I washed my hands over where she was concerned. But when she went for years without any news, I began to feel concerned. Without magic, she was vulnerable. I worried that some of her enemies in the past might track her down and finish her off..."

Ulfred muttered something that sounded like, "Moira took

so many lives; if someone 'finished her off' she would have deserved it."

Urdu flushed, but he didn't refute. "I finally tracked her down in Finsoor. She was alive, but living miserably alone. I stayed for several days; I wanted to convince her to come home with me, but then she turned the tables on me. I was taken captive."

"How was she able to imprison you?" Lorenza said.

Gabi wondered the same thing. Wasn't Urdu supposed to be the most powerful mage alive?

"Sorcha appeared out of nowhere. I was completely off guard. She and Moira overpowered me. I learned that Moira was faking it—she did have magic. Before I could break free, Moira had set up the equipment that drained my magic. It was a strongly forbidden ancient method to draw power from another mage. I never expected she'd use it on her own father."

He coughed again, violently. Gabi summoned a pitcher from the kitchen and poured him a cup of water.

"So what are the chances of us against her?" Lorenza said.

"Very little." Urdu shook his head. "I have only recovered half of my magic, and now that she has the Peerless Knife, I don't know how anyone in the kingdom can defeat her."

"What is that?" Ulfred asked.

Urdu explained. Gabi heard everything about the knife from Freja, except for one thing that Urdu added. "The Savon princes were previously under an ancient curse, binding them to fight with trolls every fortnight. The power used to create this hereditary curse came from the knife."

"Which means," Urdu continued, "the knife has an infinite reservoir of magic. She can do anything with it—enslave the Sisu people again, take down an entire kingdom. Killing the Arksan prince would be like squashing an ant for her."

There was an uncomfortable silence that followed his speech.

"Great," Gabi said. Her stomach quivered at the thought of facing the witches, of seeing Alrik's lifeless body—he might be dead at this very moment. But she couldn't run away. If there was even the slightest chance of rescuing him, she had to take it. She raised her chin and put up a smile. Alrik had once said that when he saw her smile, he felt like anything was possible. "Then let's go and save him."

CHAPTER 22

Sybil blinked. She was lying on someone's lap—she struggled to get up, noticing that the bindings on her wrists and ankles were gone.

"Careful, lady." Margot laid a comforting hand on her shoulder. "It's all right now. We're with you."

Sitting across them were Laurent and Flavien. Laurent gave her a relieved smile, while Flavien beamed.

"How…" Sybil was at a loss for words.

"Bernardin found us," Flavien said. "He discovered that scumbag had kidnapped you, but he knew he couldn't go after you alone. When he found us, Laurent concocted a tracking spell. Took us a while to catch up with you. When we found you in the carriage and Hugo nowhere near, Bernardin took the reins and hurried off as soon as possible."

The carriage lurched; Sybil's elbow bumped against the wooden panel. It was real—her servants had come after her and freed her from Hugo's clutches. There was a sting in her ankle; she took off her boot and stocking. There were two marks, but no blood was visible. Fortunately, her stocking was thick enough that the snake's fangs did not puncture her skin.

"Where's the snake?"

"Laurent shot it dead," Margot answered. She put a hand to her heart. "Laws, but that was the scariest thing I've ever seen!" She reached out toward Laurent; their hands met in a brief squeeze.

"How did that scumbag kidnap you?"

Sybil ran her tongue along the side of her mouth. She could still taste the chocolate that Hugo brought her. The drug he used was as bland as water; she hadn't detected anything strange in the chocolate.

"He drugged me."

She related the story of Lucie de la Motte, and how Hugo wanted to use her to threaten Gerald.

Margot gasped. "How DARE he!"

"The nerve of that scumbag." Flavien scowled. "That Lucie de la Motte is pathetic. As if there's only one prince in the kingdom."

"Forgive me, lady," Laurent said, looking contrite. "I should've sensed something wrong in his character when I interviewed him. If anything happened to you, I could never forgive myself."

"Don't feel bad about it," Sybil quickly said. "How could any of us suspect he would kidnap me for the sake of his mistress? You saved me from that horrible snake."

"Which you wouldn't have met if I never let Hugo into the house."

"Enough." Margot bumped her knee against Laurent's leg. "What's happened has happened. We'll make it up by ensuring her lady's safe passage to the castle."

"We're going to the castle?"

"We aren't leaving until we see you safely delivered to Prince Gerald," Flavien said with a grin.

"It's not necessary," Sybil said.

"This is not up for discussion," Laurent said. "We're coming with you."

Sybil gave in. Though she didn't want her servants sacrificing their time to accompany her to the capital, she was relieved. "How much time do you estimate till we arrive, Laurent?"

Her footman consulted a large bronze pocket watch—an expensive gift from Sybil's father. Laurent had once saved his life when they went hunting in the mountains. "We passed La Salle thirty-seven minutes earlier. La Salle is about a four-hour drive to the capital. So we have three hours and twenty-three minutes remaining."

Sybil smiled. Laurent's answer perfectly demonstrated his Arksan precision.

But it turned out that they didn't take three hours and twenty-three minutes to reach the capital.

About an hour later, the carriage abruptly halted. Bernardin reported that one of the horses got a stone in his foot. They waited for help, but the people who passed by either rode on horses or didn't have room to carry them all. In the end, Laurent rode the other horse to the nearest town, Reine, and engaged a carriage. Flavien and Bernardin transferred their luggage to the new carriage. By the time they arrived at Reine, dusk was falling.

"We had better stop for one night," Laurent said. "It isn't safe to travel in the dark with our lady. Besides, the capital will be closed during the night. We may as well take a nice long rest and start off tomorrow refreshed."

"I agree," Flavien said. "I'm starving! Hadn't a decent meal since breakfast."

While Sybil wanted to see Gerald as soon as possible, she agreed. Margot was looking exhausted; her cook had never taken a journey longer than an hour. And Sybil herself was feeling hungry and in a desperate need for a bath.

"Let's find a place to stay."

Reine was a medium-sized town, judging from the number of houses lined across the streets, but few of the houses were lit. In the darkness, it was difficult to see the state of the houses, but Sybil sensed the town was not exactly prosperous or even decently run, despite its proximity to the capital. The road was so bumpy that Laurent decided they should get off, in case an accident occurred.

"I'll ask where's the closest place to stay," Flavien offered, pointing at the nearest house that had a light in the window.

The man who answered the door was thin and sickly. The smell of alcohol from his mouth was strong enough that Sybil, who was standing a little way off from Flavien, was able to smell it.

"An...inn?" He burst into laughter. "Who'd want to stay here?"

"Very sorry to bother you," Laurent said politely, laying a hand on Flavien's shoulder. Sybil noted that the man was clutching a bottle. "We'll ask somewhere else."

It took them two more houses before they found an inn. It was small and worn-looking, but the woman who greeted them was eager to please.

"Come in, come in," she said heartily, holding the door wide open. Her gaze strayed toward Sybil for a moment, and her mouth fell open. Sybil had used a spell to make her features plainer, but since she couldn't perform complicated magic, the most she could do was look pretty instead of downright stunning. "Are you a...a lady?"

"Only a minor one," Sybil said, deciding not to reveal that she was Gerald's fiancée. "We're traveling to the capital to visit relatives."

"Must be a long journey," the woman said, taking in their wrinkled clothes and weary faces. "I'm Pauline, by the way. My husband's the innkeeper, but he's gone to the port. We're thinking of relocating to Masaro; times have been getting rough here."

Sybil noted that the tables and chairs were old. The walls were moldy and needed a new coating of paint. There was a lingering odor of cooking oil in the room, suggesting that the ventilation of the inn was poor.

"But that's not to say...er, you're most welcome here, my lady," Pauline stammered, grasping the ends of her apron. "It's just a bit rare that I get so many guests. This way—your rooms are upstairs."

The stairs creaked as they trudged to their rooms. Margot sneezed twice. Laurent remained passive, though Sybil suspected that he was cringing inside. In addition to his precise nature, Laurent was very keen on cleanliness. Under his supervision, her manor was always neat and spotless, despite its size.

"There ain' any other guests, so you have the entire floor," Pauline said, opening a door. "Make yourself at home, dears. I'll heat up water for your bath and get supper ready."

Since there were only three rooms, Sybil decided that she would room with Margot. Laurent and Flavien would share the other, while Bernardin would take the smallest room. Margot protested, saying that Sybil ought to have a room to herself, but Sybil said that she'd rather have some company. In truth, Sybil knew Bernardin was used to sleeping alone, often in a small hut near the stables. He'd be terribly awkward sharing a room with Laurent and Flavien.

Once they brought their luggage inside and unpacked, Sybil went to the window. A thin layer of dust covered the sill; she ignored it and peered outside. There were a few houses near the inn, but all of them seemed run down and in need of repairs. One cottage looked like it had been through a fire, but no one had bothered to rebuild it.

A memory rose in her mind. Months ago, when they defeated Moira and sailed from Finsoor to Arksar, she had spent a lot of time with Gerald on the ship. There was little to do on the sea except to eat, sleep, and talk. Gerald had told her of his worries concerning his kingdom.

"Savony hasn't been well governed over these years," he had said, as they watched the white-tipped waves roll in the sea. "Mother was incapable of ruling; she spent all day drinking tea and making empty predictions. Theo was consumed in surviving the fights with the trolls and ending the curse. He attended the meetings, but his heart wasn't in them. Le Gris essentially was in charge of state affairs, but he didn't have the people's best interest at heart. I wished I could have done more, but it was easier to surround myself with books and work on producing defensive spells for my brothers."

She had read guilt and shame in his face. She had comforted him, told him that he had done his best under the circumstances.

"Lady?" Margot said. "Is everything all right? Your leg ain' hurting?"

Sybil turned and parted her lips into a reassuring smile. "I'm fine."

* * *

DINNER WAS AN UNCOMFORTABLE AFFAIR. Pauline kept apologizing for the simple fare of potatoes and beans. There were a few strips of bacon, hardly enough for them all. Sybil reassured the innkeeper's wife that it wasn't a problem. She had it worse when she was captured by Moira, though of course she couldn't bring it up.

Flavien tried to lighten the mood with some bad jokes, but in the end, Sybil was relieved when the meal was over.

As she rose from the table, hoping that tomorrow's journey would be a swift one, there came an urgent knocking on the door.

"Pauline! Pauline!"

The innkeeper's wife, who was clearing away the dishes, looked up in astonishment. She set a pile of dishes on the edge of the table and went to the door. Outside was a boy around Bernardin's age.

"Oliver! What brings you to the house at this hour?"

The boy swallowed, then stepped aside. He pointed at a donkey cart behind him. A blanket covered the top.

"He...you'd better take a look."

Frowning, Pauline went to the cart. A second later, she screamed and collapsed on the ground.

CHAPTER 23

*A*lrik considered himself a generally mild-mannered, easygoing man, but in the company of the witches, he found his temper frequently tested. Being under Moira's thumb was not just his burden to bear. She terrorized other people as well.

They had entered the autonomous region of the Sisu today. He recognized Sisu traits, thanks to the lessons from Gabi. They wore red caps rimmed with fur, and patterned scarves that were tucked high around their noses. Tents with wide bases were scattered here and there, covered with reindeer hides sewn together, and had smoke coming out of the top. The Sisu dwellings might be simple, but adequate even in extreme weather.

"Aren't we going to stop yet?" he asked. He had no idea how late it was in the morning, but it seemed hours since he last ate.

"Not now." Sorcha glanced at her sister. "These peasant tents won't satisfy her."

Alrik also glanced at Moira. Sitting upright in her furs, she was hauntingly beautiful. Yet what she had done—kidnapping him, killing a herd of moose, not to mention taking Marianne's body—hatred welled up like poison. No matter how breathtaking she looked, she was a viper.

After a while, a house came into sight. It looked far more impressive than the tents. It had a proper chimney, a fence, and a storage shed in the back. Two hounds were frisking in front of the house.

Moira held up a commanding hand.

"Stop."

Sorcha pulled on the reins. Alrik didn't know whether it was magic, or if she was an expert wolf trainer, but the sled slowed down instantly.

Moira lifted the ends of her gown and placed her other hand on Alrik's arm. Startled, he shifted away, but her fingers gripped on his arm like a raven's claw.

"Escort me," she said.

Nausea rose within him, even though she was wearing Marianne's face. *When Gabi arrives and defeats you*, he thought, *I'll tell her to tie you up and drop you in the ice-cold river we passed.*

But the thought of Gabi brought pain as well. She must be frantic, especially when she had been tasked the duty of protecting his life since fourteen. How he wished he could see her. But she hadn't even entered his dreams, despite his thinking about her constantly every day.

Trying to act as normally as possible, he helped Moira off the sled and accompanied her to the house.

A middle-aged man with a round face and kind eyes opened the door. Surprise flashed over his face, but he broke into a genial smile. "Kinna help you?"

"You may," Sorcha said. "We need a hot meal, plus food and water for our transport." She jerked a finger at the wolves, still tethered to the shed.

The man's gaze landed on Moira, and he turned into a deeper shade of crimson.

"Cer...certainly," he stammered. "Anything ye need, lady. Come in."

It was warm and cozy inside, thanks to a roaring fire in the end of the main room. An elderly woman, her hair completely white, sat in a chair covered with a patterned quilt, darning a pair of socks. Three children, all of them under the age of ten, were playing with wooden toys in front of the fireplace. A straw-haired middle-aged woman, who seemed to be the man's wife, entered the main room and stopped when she saw them. In a rather high-pitched voice, she spoke to the man in a language that Alrik couldn't understand. From the annoyed expression on Moira's face, she wasn't able to understand either.

The Sisu man talked to his wife. She frowned, but disappeared into a room in the rear of the house.

Moira swept over to the old woman. "Move," she demanded.

Alrik caught her sleeve. "What're you doing? There're other places you can sit."

She cast a contemptuous eye at the bare wooden bench. One of the kids was perched on the bench, but scampered off when he met her icy gaze.

"I want to sit here," she said. "Now get rid of this old hag or I'll remove her myself."

"Don't," Alrik quickly said. Having seen what Moira was capable of, he was worried what she might do.

He talked to the Sisu man, trying to convey that Moira was someone not to be crossed. But the man, with his heavily accented Arksan tongue, kept shaking his head and pointing at the older woman's foot.

"She can't," he said. "Cannot be moved."

Which meant that the old woman was lame, like Gabi. Blood rushed to Alrik's face; for a moment he was tempted to use one of the moves Ulfred taught him, and send Moira sprawling over the floor.

177

Sorcha snapped her fingers. Sparks burst forth, wound around the old woman, and lifted her into the air. A second later, the woman was placed on the bench.

Moira looked at her sister, with an irritated expression. "I could've taken care of that. With more precision."

"You needn't trouble yourself to perform a task like this, sis," Sorcha said, shrugging.

The Sisu man, his children, and the old woman all stared at Sorcha with amazement. One of the kids let out a whoop of excitement and bounded up to Sorcha, but she held up her hand, and he stumbled back with a cry.

"Did you hurt him?" Alrik said.

"If he bothers me again, I will."

It was one of the most humiliating moments of his life. In case the witches got offended at the slightest discomfort, Alrik had to play the role of pacifier and sycophant. He loathed every minute of it, but knowing that Moira could kill him anytime (in fact, he only had to prick himself and he'd fall into a permanent sleep) made him swallow his disgust. Perhaps it was just as well he was used to charming girls. If it were Ulfred in his place, the palace guard would've lost his temper and tried to pummel Moira into pulp.

When the Sisu woman served food, she was made to kneel and hold the tray over her head. She was indignant in the beginning, but a nudge and whisper from her husband made her yield with reluctance. To spare her from being humiliated for long, Alrik quickly took the tray and approached Moira.

"Would you like me to serve you?" he said, hating every word that came out of his mouth.

Moira glanced at the tray. "What's this stinking thing?" she sneered.

"Fish," the Sisu man said. "Freshly caught this morning, lady."

She looked disgusted. "This is unfit for my palette. And why isn't there any bread?"

Alrik remembered one of Gabi's lessons on the Sisu history. About two hundred years ago, a plague had raged through Arksar, taking thousands of lives, but the Sisu people were safe. After a thorough examination, doctors concluded that the plague came from flea that lived in wooden barrels containing wheat and rye. But since the Sisu didn't have wheat and rye in their diet, they weren't affected. It was also because of the plague that the Sisu were at their strongest—they were able to bargain with the Arksan army and demand autonomy.

"Take this away." Moira turned up her nose. "I demand a proper meal, not peasant fare."

The Sisu man had no choice but to kill one of his reindeer. His wife fried the meat in oil and sprinkled a bit of spice. Moira still ate with reluctance, but didn't complain this time.

When the meal was finally over, Moira rose. "Do you know who I am?"

The Sisu family cowered. They huddled together on the floor, looking scared. Alrik had an enticing vision of throwing Moira out of the window.

"More than twenty years ago, I lived at the snow castle," she said. "Is it still standing?"

The man and his wife glanced at each other. The wife nodded, and the man spoke.

"It...it is still there, lady."

"Very well." The corner of Moira's mouth quirked up. "I want you to spread the word. Every family must send a representative to the castle in three days to pay their respects to me. Except for yours." She curled her fingers; the youngest child crawled toward her, struggling and crying. The woman let out a cry and tried to pull her child back, but Sorcha prevented her with a sweeping gesture.

Moira looked down on the child, who cowered at her feet, looking terrified.

"Consider this your incentive," she said coldly. "Your child shall remain with me for the time being. If one single family fails to send a representative, she will be a servant at the castle forever."

CHAPTER 24

*G*abi felt a pain in her leg, the kind she usually got whenever it rained or the temperature took a dramatic dip. Today, both cases happened. After a heavy downpour last night, they started north. By afternoon, they had reached a town near the Loviska mountains—the resort where Ronnie and Marianne planned to spend their honeymoon. Clouds had gathered in the sky, thick and heavy and gray. Soon rain was falling. It turned into a tempest, battering over their heads so hard that they had no choice but to take shelter.

To save as much time as possible, Ulfred proposed riding. The horses couldn't travel much farther with the storm raging over their heads, so they had to stop and rest. They stopped at the largest house in the town—its roof jutted out from the walls, allowing shelter, though inadequate when the rain was so heavy. A lopsided sign hung over the door, indicating it was an inn.

Beside her, Lorenza and Ulfred dismounted. Urdu had gone back to Linberg to rest and recover, partly because he hadn't fully gained his magic, and partly because he couldn't face his daughters. He promised, however, that he would travel to Savony to aid with fighting the trolls once he was well.

Gabi slowly dismounted, though when she landed on the ground, her crippled foot still made her wobble. After all, she wasn't a dancer or acrobat who could remain perfectly upright on one foot. Someone slid a hand under her arm, lending a welcome support. It was Julong. How he detected her unstable state was remarkable, even for a mage.

"It's our training in Lulan," he said serenely, as though reading her mind. "Since losing my sight, I was motivated to train harder, to attune myself to the slightest sound. Your movement was not difficult to discern."

"Thanks," Gabi said. "Can a normal human attain your level of proficiency, even without possessing innate magic?"

"Some can, to a certain extent, but it definitely helps if you're a mage," he said.

"That sounds useful." A memory of Alrik, as sudden as the wind, breezed into her mind. Back at the farm, there were times when she rode on a horse with Alrik, often to visit Ulfred or Matthias. Freja had encouraged them to ride together, hoping that the shared intimacy would sow desire that would eventually lead to true love. But while Alrik joked and flirted, his behavior remained within the boundaries of a gentleman. When he helped her dismount, he'd withdraw as soon as she landed safely on both feet. She had thought he wasn't interested. Now she knew he was restraining himself.

"What's this?" Ulfred's voice, loud and filled with suspicion, arrested her attention.

A piece of paper, splattered from rain that was blown inside, was tacked on the wall. It depicted a crudely drawn picture of a young woman. Despite the simple lines, Gabi could tell it resembled Marianne. There were the braids she used to wear crisscrossed on top of her head, and the tiny heart-shaped birthmark on the left side of her throat.

Wasn't Marianne supposed to be on honeymoon with Ronnie?

"That's the bride of a young man who was here last week," a voice said. A middle-aged woman, plump and rosy-cheeked, came out of the house. "They were planning to go to the mountains but did not."

"What happened?" Gabi asked, feeling icy dread creep down her spine.

The woman shrugged. "They went out together to buy food, but the young man came back alone. Said that his bride disappeared. He looked like he was going into pieces, all white and shaken, and it took us hours to calm him down. My son had to go for the doctor for a tranquilizing spell."

"Marianne disappeared?" Ulfred said, looking utterly confused.

The woman's eyes widened. "You know her? Have you seen her? Oh, do say you have, 'cause it just broke our hearts seeing him break down like that."

"We haven't seen him," Gabi said. "We were at their wedding and saw them off. I thought they were back in Kardi by now."

The woman looked disappointed. "Still don't understand how she disappeared. The bride's the most stunning I've ever seen, but I still can't see how she could go missing in broad daylight. I've lived in this town for forty years, and the worst I heard of was a burglary." Letting out a sigh, the woman rubbed her hands against her apron. "You lot here for a night's stay?"

"Just for a while," Lorenza said. It was still raining, but it wasn't the downpour that threatened to drench them from head to toe. "We're in a hurry."

Ulfred produced a handful of ducats, and they had a quick lunch that disappeared within minutes. He also insisted on purchasing food for the journey, such as bread, nuts, and hard cheese. Mages could make themselves invisible or do forbidden magic like altering a human's memory, but they couldn't create food out of thin air.

Before leaving, Gabi had a sudden inspiration. "May I have

the drawing of Marianne? We could ask other people on the journey if they have seen her."

"Sure thing. It's been days; I don't reckon she'll turn up suddenly." The innkeeper tore off the drawing and handed it to her. "I really hope you'll find her, dearie." She gave Gabi's foot a brief glance, but eventually didn't say anything about it. "Safe travels, and stay warm. It's going to be real cold up there."

Gabi thanked her. The rain had stopped completely, which seemed like a good omen.

Once outside, Ulfred grasped her arm.

"Why'd you ask her for the drawing? You...you don't think..."

Gabi looked at him straight in the eye. "It's possible, Ulfred. It's possible that she has taken Marianne." Of course, it was also possible that Marianne was abducted by highwaymen, or she fell down a well. Whatever it was, things weren't looking good.

Moira is back.

Closing her eyes for a moment, Gabi prayed that Marianne was safe.

* * *

A FEW DAYS LATER, they reached the Sisu region. They had gone just a few days' travel, yet the land already looked a lot more different than the Arksan villages and towns that Gabi was used to seeing. A thin layer of snow covered the ground, though it was late spring already, and the houses—or rather dwellings—looked like large tents formed of reindeer hides. The people wore scarlet caps and patterned scarves. Not much hair was revealed, but their eyebrows were white-blond. The farther north, the lighter their hair color.

The dull ache in Gabi's leg returned. A chilly wind blew over her head, making her shiver. Years of living at Arksar hadn't equipped her with resistance to the cold; her body was still Masaro, where the climate was mostly sunny and dry. Gabi extracted a small jar from her cloak and activated the heating spell within. Warmth spread from the jar to her body; it was like she was sitting in front of a roaring fire. She could've used innate magic, as a mage, but she needed to save her energy in case they suddenly ran into Moira.

A hairy dog bounded across the snow, chasing a twig. But before it reached the twig, it saw them and started to bark.

This dog had pluck. There were five of them on horseback, and Ulfred alone towered like a monster.

"Chewy, down!" A Sisu boy of about eleven or twelve ran toward the dog.

Ulfred made to dismount, but Gabi held up a hand. Even if Ulfred was a doting grandfather, he was intimidating to strangers.

Gabi dismounted slowly. "Hello," she said, putting her hands on her knees and leaning down. "My name's Gabi. What's your name?"

"Dal," the boy mumbled, looking like he wanted to run, but curiosity kept him from doing it.

"Have you seen a young man this tall?" Gabi drew a hand in the air at Alrik's height. "With blond hair, blue eyes, and a friendly smile." Perhaps the last one was unnecessary. If Alrik *was* kidnapped, he mightn't be smiling.

"I haven't seen no one."

"How about this lady?" She brought out the drawing of Marianne.

He shook his head. Gabi knew the chances were slim, but she persisted anyway.

"Has any stranger arrived recently?"

Dal hesitated. "A man came to our house yesterday. He told us we have to send someone to the snow castle, 'cause the queen has returned."

"Moira," Ulfred growled.

"And was there a man with her?"

Dal shrugged.

"There was another woman with her," someone said behind Gabi's back. From his age and resemblance to Dal, she guessed he was the boy's father. "I was hunting for game and saw 'em pass. They traveled in a sled."

"Did she—the queen—look like her?" Gabi showed him Marianne.

His jaw dropped. "You've seen her before?"

Her heart dropped to the pit of her stomach. What she dreaded had come true. If the "queen" looked like Marianne, there was no explanation other than that Moira took her body. Marianne was no better than dead.

Gabi stumbled; Ulfred caught her arm.

"We'll find her," he growled. "Make her pay for all the deaths she caused."

She nodded, trying to collect her thoughts together. "We've got to save Alrik."

"Did you see a young man with them?" Ulfred questioned Dal's father.

He scratched his beard. "I did see someone else in the sled, but I couldn't see if it were male or female, young or old."

"No matter," Gabi said. "Where is this snow castle?"

"Wait," Julong said. "When I faced Moira twenty years ago, I plunged into battle without anticipating the consequences. Before charging into her residence, we should make a plan."

"Agreed." Urdu sounded reluctant, but he stepped forward. "She has the Peerless Knife. Do not underestimate the infinite power she can wield. Besides, she probably has control over the Sisu already."

They were right. Gabi wanted to ride straight to the castle and demand for Alrik's release, but it wouldn't work.

She unclenched her fists and took a deep breath. "Any suggestions?"

CHAPTER 25

During the years when she hunted in the forests, Sybil had seen a fair share of gruesome scenes. Wolves tearing into the carcass of a deer; mountain cats fighting over wild rabbits and rats, their sharp claws ripping the prey into pieces. But those were bodies of animals. She had never seen a human body treated like one of those animals—bloody and mutilated—under the hands of a ruthless predator.

It was night, but the moon shone brightly in the sky. Along with the light from the inn, they were able to see the body lying in the cart. Sybil gasped and turned away. Margot buried her head in Laurent's chest. Flavien also looked away, his shoulders shaking.

The man lying in the cart was barely recognizable. His right arm was missing, and so was his left foot and right leg up to the thigh. There were deep gashes on his chest, and half of his hair was ripped off with a good chunk of his head.

"The cart was left in the town square," Oliver said. He kept his gaze firmly fixed on his shoes. "The people who found the cart told Father, and we brought him home."

Sybil hastened back to the inn. She found a glass of water

and hurried back. She would have preferred a snuff box or smelling salts, but she didn't know where Pauline kept her things, so water was the best option.

She sloshed a bit of water over the innkeeper's wife, and gradually the woman stirred.

"Claude..." She sobbed. "Claude...it can't be...how? How?"

"We'd better get her in the house," Sybil said. "And the body...the body can be brought into the shed." She had seen a tool shed right behind the inn.

Oliver wheeled the donkey cart to the shed. Laurent and Flavien supported Pauline, carrying her to a low chair lined with cushions.

When Oliver returned, Sybil went to the boy. The way the man had died was so horrifying it was beyond belief. Who could have done something so terrible? Even if someone wanted his life, surely there was no need to tear the body apart like a wild animal.

"Did he have any enemies?"

Oliver shook his head. "No...no, I don't think so."

"It's a monster!" Pauline burst out, breaking down in a fit of weeping. "It's what they say in the stories, a monster must have caught him!"

Sybil and Margot did their best to comfort Pauline, and after making the innkeeper's wife go to bed, Sybil lay awake for a long time. Her thoughts turned toward Gerald. Could this be the work of a troll? Had more trolls broken out from underground? Was Gerald all right?

* * *

THEY BURIED Claude's body in the graveyard outside of town. Laurent and Flavien rolled up their sleeves and dug a hole. Oliver and his father got a coffin and laid Claude inside. Sybil and Margot supported Pauline as she staggered to the coffin for one last look. It seemed doubly tragic that her last look of her husband was of him in such a terrible state. Sybil was at a loss of words to comfort the woman, so she kept her arm firmly pressed on Pauline's shoulder. Margot did the same.

Several townsfolk dropped by to see Claude off. They asked questions in hushed tones—the death was so sudden.

"Robbers ambushed him," Oliver's father said in a low voice. He closed the lid on the coffin when Pauline drew away, tears streaming down her cheeks. He knew that if anyone saw Claude's body, they would be shocked and terrified.

When Claude was laid to rest, they returned to the inn. Since Pauline was still in a state of visible distress, Sybil didn't feel like leaving town at the moment.

"I'll brew some tea," Margot offered, going to the kitchen.

Pauline sat on a low chair. Sybil sat down across her. "Is there anything we can do for you?" she asked gently.

Pauline dried her tears on a handkerchief. "Did you say you're going to the capital?"

"Yes."

"My sister's living there with her husband and children. If it ain' too much trouble—can I travel with you?"

"Of course," Sybil said. "We'll hire two carriages."

Pauline put a hand over her face. "Thank you," she whispered. More tears trickled down her face. Sybil pressed another handkerchief in her hands.

Margot entered the main room. "There ain' any tea left," she said in a low voice. "Nor is there much stuff in the pantry; I reckon we ate most of it yesterday. I'd best get some food in town."

"There's a store in town," Pauline said. "I'll get some bread and cheese for the journey." She started to rise, but swayed on her feet. Sybil put her arms around Pauline's shoulders and made her sit down.

"Margot will go to the store," she said.

"Yeah, it won' be any problem," Margot said. "Don' you trouble yourself, dear. You rest well and I'll get up lunch for us all before we head to the capital."

Laurent offered to accompany her to the store, but Margot waved him off. "You've been tired digging all morning. I'll be back in a jiffy."

When Margot was gone, Sybil coaxed Pauline to lie down in her bedroom. But just when Pauline approached the room, a knock came on the door.

The knock was so soft that Sybil wondered if she imagined the noise. But then a second knock came, louder this time.

Sybil went to the door. Outside stood a bearded man in his forties. His eyes widened at the sight of her.

"Who are you?" He rubbed his eyes.

"I'm a guest at Pauline's inn," Sybil said. "I'm sorry, but she isn't currently taking any bookings. Her husband died yesterday."

The man wiped his forehead and looked down on the ground. "My name is Esteve," he said in a low voice. "I traveled to the capital with Claude. May I come in?"

"Esteve!" Pauline cried. She ran and grasped the front of his mud-splattered shirt. "Did you see what—who did this to him?"

"I'm sorry." Esteve made no attempt to push her away.

"Did you stand by and let him get killed?" Pauline's voice rose to a shriek. "How come you're alive and well when Claude is...is..." She slapped him across the cheek. "He's your best friend! You grew up together!"

Sybil grasped Pauline's arm. "Let him explain what happened. If he deserves a beating, I'll find you a cudgel."

"Agreed." Laurent had heard the commotion and came downstairs. "Let's sit down and hear what he has to say."

Pauline gave Esteve a withering glare, but she allowed Sybil to drag her away. Esteve looked like he was about to walk a plank that led to hungry sharks, but he sat down and stared fixedly at the table.

"Believe it or not, I couldn't have done anything." He shivered. "You have no idea what we met."

The fear in his eyes made Sybil uneasy. Pauline's cheeks were still red with anger, but curiosity took over.

"What happened?" she demanded.

Gripping his knees to stay calm, Esteve continued, "Claude and I were getting back to the village. The horses were tired, so we stopped to rest. The bread we carried was dry and tough, so I took our water skin. There was a stream not far away. I filled the skin and halfway on returning, I heard a scream."

Pauline's nails dug into her skirts. "What?"

"It was a monster," Esteve whispered. His shoulders trembled. "Laws, if I could forget it! A monster larger than any man, with green skin, black hair, and red eyes. It jumped on top of Claude and ripped his hair off. I couldn't move. Claude was trying to wrench the creature away, but then it landed on the ground, seized him by the shoulders and tore his arm off."

Pauline looked on the verge of fainting again. Sybil grabbed her hand and squeezed.

Esteve swallowed. "I should've helped him, but it happened so fast. Then the monster saw me. I took off running—it bounded after me—I thought my heart was going to jump out of my chest. I jumped into the stream and held my breath. It hit the water but didn't jump in. I could see its shadow hovering above on the bank."

Pauline's fingers gripped Sybil's wrist. Her mouth was half open, but no sound came out.

"When I couldn't hold my breath any longer, I came up but only let my nose bob out of the water. No way was I getting out of the stream when it was lurking on the bank. Don't know how long I stayed there, but finally the monster left. I waited longer —a long time after it left—and climbed out of the water."

It was likely a troll. Sybil remembered Gerald telling her how they broke the curse. A lake lay between the trolls' lair and the tunnel leading to the castle. The trolls could not cross the lake until a bridge was formed. Which meant that they couldn't swim.

"When I returned to our cart, the creature was gone. But Claude, poor Claude..." Esteve's voice became hoarse. "I scooped up his body, placed it in the cart, and started back, expecting that creature would jump out any moment. When I arrived back in Reine, I abandoned the cart in the town square and went back home. I was afraid that someone might see me and think I...I did this to Claude. But in the morning, I told myself I had to come." He took out a glass bead necklace from his pocket. "Claude bought this for you, Pauline. It's one of those necklaces they make in Masaro. He wanted you to have it. I'm so sorry he wasn't able to give it to you in person."

Pauline clutched the necklace to her chest. Tears dripped down her cheek. Sybil put her arm around the woman and let her cry into her shoulder.

Esteve hung his head. "I am so sorry that it happened, Pauline. Hit me if you want. But I couldn't have saved him. Only a mage could've taken care of that monster."

Pauline sniffed. "I'm not blaming you," she said brokenly. "But how...how could this happen? We never had a monster in this part of the kingdom."

Esteve put a hand over his heart. "I swear that I saw it with my eyes." He coughed and looked up. "Can I get some water?"

Sybil poured water from a pitcher. Glancing at the kitchen counter, which contained an empty tea canister, she realized Margot wasn't back yet.

She went upstairs. Margot wasn't in their room. Frowning, Sybil went to the room that the three men shared.

Flavien answered the door, yawning.

"Have you seen Margot?"

"Isn't she with you?"

Back downstairs, Laurent shook his head. "I looked at the clock before she went. It should be two hours and two minutes by now."

"Let's go and get her," Flavien said. "Maybe she got carried away with shopping."

Sybil had her doubts but she readily agreed. Bernardin was napping in the stables, so she set off with Laurent and Flavien.

Pauline told them there were several stores in town. The first store they visited claimed that they hadn't seen anyone that met Margot's description. The second one was closed. The third —a large, two-storied building in the town center—was surrounded by people.

Sybil found a woman with mild brown eyes, and tapped her shoulder. "Did anything happen in there?"

The woman jumped as if Sybil's hand was hot coal. "Didn' you know about Old Blair's store? I was getting a pound of flour, and then the most frightening creature came in!"

"Tell us more," Laurent said immediately.

The woman took out a handkerchief. "Laws, if I could ever forget! It was a huge green monster—it leaped on the counter, where Blair's cat was napping, and tore the poor thing into halves. We were scared out of our skins—we bolted for the door. Old Blair was last; he shut the door and locked it before the thing could get out. They're now deciding what to do."

Sybil scanned the crowd for Margot. Plenty of women in the square, but she didn't see her cook.

"Lady," Laurent said, his voice tense. He met her gaze, and she knew what he was thinking.

What if Margot was trapped inside?

CHAPTER 26

*D*espite his hatred for the witches, Alrik grudgingly admitted that the snow castle was a magnificent work of art. Formed of hard ice bricks and layers of snow, it sparkled like a giant diamond in the distance even before they reached it.

Not that it was perfect. The wall surrounding the castle had parts missing, and out of the dozen towers that formed the castle, more than half needed to be restored, whether it was crumbling walls or missing doors. The ice sculptures erected in the castle grounds were nebulous shapes; there was only one he recognized as a wolf. From the conversation between Moira and Sorcha, he knew that they left Sisu twenty years ago. No wonder the castle was in need of repair.

Moira's lip curled in disgust. "I did not expect they had the intelligence to maintain it, but I had expected that the castle would be sturdier when it was built."

"Patience, sis," Sorcha said. "It has been years since we left. All we need is a little time to restore it."

The tallest tower, which stood in the middle of the grounds, looked the most intact out of them all. Moira swept in through the entrance, her gown trailing across the ice-cut floor. A set of iron-clad double doors were left open. Through the iron doors, they entered the largest room that Alrik had ever seen. The ceiling was two stories high, and in the end was a raised platform with a tall, high-backed chair.

"Well," Sorcha said. "At least the throne room has remained intact."

Alrik remembered in one of Gabi's lessons, she had told him about King Tyrell receiving guests or commoners in the palace's throne room. It looked like Moira had created something similar.

Another thought rose in his mind. If he survived and became king, he would be sitting in a room like this, greeting people from Savony and other kingdoms, and listening to what his people had to say. While he was by no means an introvert, the prospect of holding imperial power in his hands was daunting. But if he had Gabi by his side, he felt he could endure anything difficult.

"One room out of a hundred," Moira said, sounding disgruntled. "This will not do. As queen of Sisu, I cannot live in a castle in ruins."

"Not for long, sister," Sorcha said soothingly. "Not for long."

Although for Alrik, even a minute spent in Moira's company felt like a year. They settled in the castle, with a dose of magical help from the Peerless Knife, and he was forced to sleep on a mattress on the floor, in the same room with Moira, as if he were a servant.

"We are to be husband and wife soon," she said sweetly, when he asked why he didn't have a room of his own. "It makes little difference since we're going to be sharing a room soon, so why not start from now?"

Alrik was tempted to be sarcastic and ask, "Then shouldn't

we share a bed now, since it's going to be soon?" but swallowed the words immediately. If she took him seriously, he'd be retching every morning.

The real reason, he knew, was that Moira wanted to keep an eye on him. The snow castle was large, and she hadn't acquired servants yet. She could plant a tracking spell on him, but if he escaped in the middle of the night, he'd have hours before she found him, and he sensed that she didn't want to waste either time or effort keeping a leash on him.

It was a relief when the Sisu arrived two days later. Each family sent a representative, and the throne room, which had seemed enormous in the beginning, became crowded and uncomfortable, with more than a hundred men and women crammed inside. He was surprised that Moira's throne of ice didn't melt. Probably the ice in the Sisu region was different, or there was magic at work.

Moira sat in the high chair made of ice and draped in reindeer hide. She was dazzlingly beautiful, but all he felt for her was disgust. She wore Marianne's face, yet her facial expressions were nothing like the Marianne he knew. The Peerless Knife's hilt was visible from her belt, and occasionally magic was visible, flowing in sparks to her hands. Sorcha stood near her, occasionally glancing at the knife with hunger in her eyes. He himself was also standing, detesting the moment and wishing he were thousands of miles away.

When the Sisu men and women entered the room, some of them curious, others frightened, Moira's eyes flashed.

"Kneel."

The Sisu looked at each other.

"Did you not hear what your queen said?" Sorcha said, her voice echoing around the room of ice. "As subjects of the queen, you will pay your respects. Kneel!"

A man who looked to be in his forties or fifties sank to the ground and touched his forehead on the icy floor.

"My queen," he murmured. "Finally, you have returned to us. I have been waiting every day for your return."

"How touching," Moira said, a slight smile playing on her lips. "You had served me well, Holger. I do not forget."

"The rest of you," Sorcha said sharply. "Why are you not following his example?"

A boy of around ten rolled his eyes. Apparently, he was too young to realize that the witches had power. "Why should we kneel to this old hag?"

Alrik acted without thinking. He grabbed Moira's arm, just as silver sparks began to gleam on her fingers.

"No!"

Time seemed frozen for a second. Moira simply stared at his hand on her arm, as if she couldn't believe he had the nerve to detain her. Then she shook off his hand with a snarl.

"How dare you," she hissed.

"He's only a child; he doesn't know what he's talking about," Alrik quickly said. "And it won't bode well to have blood shed in the beginning of your reign...my queen," he added, hating how he had to abase himself.

The fury in her expression dimmed slightly.

"Child or not, he should be taught a lesson," she said coldly. "But since my dear consort has intervened, I will let it go for once." Raising her hand, sparks flew out to a chair and instantly the chair burst into flames.

"This is an example of what will happen if anyone defies me." Moira's voice, icy and haughty, echoed across the room.

The Sisu stared at the burning chair. Then, one by one, they fell on their knees. Alrik averted his gaze, not wanting to see the fear and despair in their eyes. At the same time he wondered: did the Arksans kneel to his father? Seeing their humiliation, he vowed that when he became king, no one should kneel before him—if he survived to become king.

A triumphant grin played across the witches' faces. Moira folded her arms and raised her chin.

"I am pleased to see that you are not that daft," she said. "Remember that great things can only be achieved by those in power, and to stand in the way of the powerful would be unwise. Twenty years I have spent in exile, thanks to the ruthless treatment I suffered from the hands of other mages. But now, it is time that I am restored to former glory. The first step is to have this castle re-built." She made a gesture at Sorcha, who rose and descended the platform.

Sorcha approached Holger. "Rise."

The man did, but his head remained bowed. "Your command, my lady?"

"The queen assigns you the honor of the chief builder. You are in charge of restoring the castle to what it was like twenty years ago. You are free to use any method to achieve this goal, but make sure it is achieved within a week."

An indignant cry came from somewhere among the kneeling crowd, but was immediately smothered.

"A...a week, my lady?" Holger said. Even a sycophant had to be practical when faced with such a request.

"But of course," Moira said, as if he was the unreasonable one. "I need the castle restored in time for the wedding." She patted Alrik's hand; her touch felt like a spider. He gritted his teeth and tried to look like she had bestowed an honor, not a death sentence. "A queen cannot rule without a handsome consort by her side. Which means, also, that wedding preparations must be done."

At the moment, permanent slumber sounded more preferable.

As if reading his thoughts, something cold and hard wrapped around his ankles. Alarmed, he looked down. Silver chains had appeared, leaving enough space for him to walk, but once he moved his foot, there was a disturbing jingling sound.

Moira did not look his way, but the corners of her lips quirked up.

Escape, which was already difficult, now seemed downright impossible.

CHAPTER 27

"We drink tea with reindeer milk," Piera said, handing Gabi a small pitcher. "But I don't know how long we can afford it, now that she's back."

"We'll bring her down, so you needn't worry," Gabi promised. "So tea is expensive in Sisu?"

"Of course; do you see us growing tea plantations on layers of snow?"

They were staying with Dal's family, which consisted of Dal, his grandmother (Piera), and his father (Ruben). Upon learning Moira was indeed in Sisu, Gabi offered several of Freja's most useful household spells in exchange for food and accommodation. Piera accepted readily. She was nearly sixty, and household chores were becoming more difficult for her. Dal's mother had died giving birth to him, and while Ruben would have liked to re-marry, there weren't many Sisu young women around.

Just when Gabi was pouring milk into the tea, the flap of the tent was lifted.

"He's in the castle," Ruben said.

Moira had ordered every Sisu family to send a representative to the castle. Since Dal was too young and Piera too old, Ruben made the three-hour journey.

When Ruben said those words, it felt as if the sun had broken through the dreary gray sky and shone upon them. Gabi wanted to jump and scream, but since jumping wasn't an option, she screamed.

"Alrik's alive!"

That brought Ulfred and the other two mages running to the tent. Lorenza looked relieved.

"Thankfully he's alive," she said. "Does he look healthy? No signs of torture?"

"He looks all right to me," Ruben said, taking off his fur coat and removing his crimson cap. "I didn't notice if he got any bruises, but it was plain he was unhappy. A boy insulted Moira, and the prince tried to stop her from killing him."

"Nice to see she hasn't changed," Piera said with a twisted smile. "You've missed lunch, but I set a portion aside for you. Sit down. I can hardly wait to hear about the unreasonable orders she has in store for us."

Lorenza went out to call Julong and Ulfred. The four of them shared a tent from Piera's friend, in exchange for a pretty glass bead necklace from Lorenza. The Sisu tent should've been difficult to set up, as Piera said, but for three mages and a retired palace guard, it didn't take much time. In the beginning Gabi was skeptical how a tent could withstand the brutal weather, but the Sisu had lived here for many generations and they'd developed methods that allowed them to survive.

The tent had a wide base and was quite sturdy. They could even set up a small fire inside, as long as there was a small opening in the entrance flap to let the air circulate. Still, this was the coldest spring she had experienced. Arksar had a relatively cool climate, and their winter could be as long as five months. But Sisu basically only had two seasons: a very long winter and a very short summer.

Ruben settled on a cushion. "Where's Dal?"

"He's out playing with the other children," Piera said, passing out mugs of hot tea. "He'll be back when the wind chill's too much."

Gabi wrapped her hands around the mug of hot tea. It had a peculiar taste, flavored with reindeer milk and a dash of salt.

Lorenza took a sip, and did her best not to grimace. In Masaro, where desserts were as common as water, no wonder she wasn't used to the salty taste of the Sisu tea. Julong was impassive. Gabi wondered if they had something similar in Lulan, as it was a huge exporter of tea, or if Julong was simply less emotional. Ulfred finished his tea with one gulp. He was the kind who didn't care about the taste of food, only the amount.

"So what did she want?" Piera said. "A ten-foot ice sculpture of herself, wearing a crown?"

"Worse," Ruben said, grimacing. "She wants us to rebuild her castle in a week. And when the castle is finished—" he glanced at Gabi "—she's going to get married."

"She's marrying Alrik?" Gabi said. It seemed incredible, but now that Ruben mentioned marriage, it made sense. If Moira captured Alrik and didn't kill him, then it was likely she'd take him as her consort. Fitting retribution—marrying the son of the king who once rejected her.

"Obviously she's not marrying one of us," Piera said. "Isla— the first and last man she had her eye on—killed himself before the ceremony."

"I don't get it," Ulfred said, scratching his chin. "No one wants to marry that witch, but surely it has to be better than death."

"You don't understand." Piera set down her cup. "Becoming her husband would mean turning your back against your own people. Those who became her servants could at least get together and comfort each other when she gave tyrannical orders. But if you're her consort, it means your friends and family would be kneeling to you, obeying your commands. Isla's conscience wouldn't tolerate that."

"Not all have a conscience, though," Ruben said grimly. "Holger was the first to kneel. He had no problem calling her his queen."

"That scummy toerag," Piera said contemptuously. "When he was a child, I caught him stealing a reindeer and trying to place the blame on his own brother."

Lorenza set down her cup. Gabi didn't have to peek into it to know that it was half-full.

"Pardon me if this sounds rude, but I can't help wondering, *why* would Moira want to make herself queen of your region? Everything is so different to Arksar. Your dwellings, your clothes, your food...I don't understand."

"Urdu told us the reason earlier," Julong reminded her. "It was easier for her to lord over a smaller place and also elevate her status."

"Yes, but why here? Why not choose a smaller state in Savony or even Masaro? There are parts of Masaro that the king doesn't even know that exist."

"She tried to change us," Piera said simply. "With the power she had, she tried to make us subservient. We were under her reign for ten years, but it felt like a hundred. She detested fish, so no one could serve it to her, and those who lived close by had to either move or survive on reindeer meat only. We weren't allowed to play our flutes, only Arksan music with violins. She burned our flutes. And she destroyed our sacred sites. There was a stone gathering where Ruben used to play, but it's completely gone now. We used to make offerings to our gods there, but she tore the place down."

"Why'd she do that?"

"'Cause she didn't want us to worship anyone than her,"

Piera answered. "She also seized our sheep, reindeer, and even made pets out of wolves. Anyone who dared to defy her ended up with a missing limb, or was thrown to the wolves that were starving. Trust me, if it were a choice between the wolves and obeying her...I'd take my own life."

Silence fell upon them. Nothing could be heard except the wind blowing against the tent. It was warm inside the tent, but somehow Gabi shivered. When they came to rescue Alrik, she hadn't expected that they'd have to deal with Moira's other nefarious deeds.

"Well," she said, since no one else looked like they wanted to speak. "It's obvious. She has to be stopped."

"Obviously," Ulfred said, chewing on his lip. He patted Julong's wrist. "What do you say, Master Julong? Ready to launch an attack with us?"

"You do not attack Moira," the Lulan mage said calmly. "You must take her by surprise. If she is well prepared, there is less chance of success."

Gabi weighed their chances. One week until the wedding. Should they sneak into the castle when Moira was to wed Alrik?

"We'll need to be familiar with the castle's layout," Gabi said. "The surroundings, as well. That way, we can plan the best route to infiltrate the castle and rescue Alrik. Ruben, have you been recruited to rebuild the castle?"

The man nodded. "But they probably will assign me to only one section of the castle. Even if I can explore the entire castle, I don't know if I can remember everything."

"I can do that," Gabi said. "I'll go first and memorize the castle's layout. Then I'll return and we can make plans. We'll rescue Alrik and make Moira pay so that she can never terrorize Sisu again."

Hope shone in Piera's eyes. "Glad that this time we have help from mages," she said. "I don't ever want to see that witch in our region again."

Gabi grasped her hand. "We'll drive her out," she promised, hoping that Piera didn't detect the lack of confidence in her tone. Moira had the Peerless Knife, an extremely formidable weapon that had broken an ancient curse.

But no matter what, she had to try.

CHAPTER 28

*T*ime ticked by in agonizing seconds as Sybil searched through the crowd, asking them if they had seen "a woman in her forties with curly blond hair, about a head shorter than me, and wearing a brown dress." A few women matched her description of Margot, but all of them turned out to be townsfolk.

She didn't want to believe that Margot was trapped inside. And yet, if her cook was inside, they were wasting valuable time asking around. The troll might have found her, might be cornering her and attacking her at this very moment…

A hand caught her elbow.

"I'm going in," Laurent said, his face pale. "She's not anywhere around—she's got to be trapped inside. All I need is something sharp."

"Are you crazy?" a man said. "I saw that creature—it's seven feet tall! We'll be killed if it comes out!"

"Let's burn the house down," another said. "The monster'll be burned too, so it won't be able to harm us."

There was a murmur of approval in the crowd.

"You will not do anything of the kind," Sybil shouted.

"There's a woman trapped inside with the troll. Our priority is to rescue her."

"If she is trapped inside with the monster, she's dead by now," the man who suggested burning the house said. He straightened up, staring at Sybil with hostility. "No one can stand a chance against it."

The townsfolk started hollering.

"Fetch some wood!"

"Gather a fire!"

Sybil ran in front of the house and spread out her arms. "No one is going to burn this house down! I am a magic user. I know a spell that can allow us to kill that troll."

The townsfolk looked at each other. Sybil stood firm, though her heart was pounding. If they tried to pull her away, she was no match for their strength.

"But if we don't burn the house…" a man started.

"Even if the troll is burned, it could still escape the house," Sybil said sharply. "The skin of a troll is incredibly thick. You might think that fire could penetrate its skin and burn it to death, but it's also highly possible that once the walls around the troll start to fall down, it would be able to escape."

Silence. There was a sound inside the house, of something being knocked over. Sybil flinched. At least it wasn't Margot screaming. She prayed that her cook was safe, that she had maybe hid herself in a closet or basement.

"Does anyone have ice? I need some for the spell."

Esteve stepped forward, his face determined. "We don't have any ice, but there's a well near our house and the water is always ice-cold."

"I have some cooling spells," came another voice. Pauline approached, her eyes still red from crying, but she was walking steadily. "I usually serve the guests iced tea during summer. The cooling spells can turn water into ice."

"Excellent," Sybil said. "I'll make the spell right away. Don't anyone of you burn down the house. If the troll escapes before the fire reaches it, we'll all be dead."

Back in Pauline's house, Sybil rolled up her sleeves. Under her instructions, Laurent lit a fire in the hearth, while Esteve brought a large cauldron. Sybil tied a kerchief around her head and started to assemble the ingredients. She had a scrap of paper on which she had carefully copied the makings of the spell, but she had memorized all the details already.

"I need stones as well as ice."

Sybil swirled water in a cauldron, poured ice and stone into the liquid, and muttered a few well-chosen words. Gradually, the mixture in the pot turned into a mist. Sybil sealed the mist into the jar. The glass exterior felt cold against her fingers.

"Will this really work?" Flavien said, looking skeptical.

"It has to," Sybil said grimly. "Let's go."

At the store, the crowd had grown larger. Sybil guessed that the entire town had turned out to watch. However, they were at least a dozen yards away, and all were talking and pointing at the house when they arrived.

"What do you plan to do?" Laurent said. He sounded calm, but his fingers twitched at his side.

"This is the freezing spell that the Otani villagers discovered," Sybil explained. "When the door is opened I'll throw water over the troll. The spell will form an instant layer of ice, and the troll won't be able to move for a few seconds. We must use the opportunity to kill it."

"As long as there is something sharp enough, I'll be happy to perform the honors," Flavien said. Sybil stared at him for a second. He was braver than she expected. Concern for his mother had overcome fear.

Someone found an axe and gave it to Laurent. Flavien was wielding a large kitchen knife. Proper weapons would be ideal, but one couldn't expect proper weapons in a village like this. Sybil uncorked the jar and emptied the contents into the bucket.

The waters flashed for a second, but soon returned to its normal state.

"We're ready."

"Give me the key," Sybil said to the storekeeper. He didn't dare to look at her as he handed over the key.

"Careful, lady!" Pauline called.

With a pounding heart, Sybil unlocked the door. Then she sprang away and reached for the bucket.

Almost as soon as the door creaked open, the troll burst out. It was just as Esteve described—well over six feet, skin mottled green, and bloodshot eyes that were hungry as it gazed upon them.

Sybil flung the bucket of water over the troll. It let out a screech so terrible that it seemed the roof of the store shook.

The screech halted when ice formed over the troll's body, covering its mouth. It tried to lift its foot, but the ice spread so fast that its foot was frozen in mid-air.

"Now!" Sybil shouted.

Laurent and Flavien charged. The axe cut through the ice, hitting the troll over the head. Flavien tried to bury his knife into the troll's chest, but the ice around the troll's body prevented the knife from going in deep.

"It's not dead yet," Esteve said, trembling. "We can't kill the troll through the ice."

Laurent realized this as well. He drew back his hand, prepared to deliver a second blow. But just at that moment the troll roared. One hand broke through the ice and raked at his arm, leaving a deep, bloody gash.

Her footman winced. The troll dashed at him—Laurent ducked behind a barrel—the troll snatched up a dog that streaked past and bit the dog's head off.

Everyone gasped.

"Stand back!" Sybil shouted. "It's going to break through!"

"Stand back," a deep voice said. "Let me handle this."

She knew that voice. She would know that voice anywhere. Sybil couldn't believe her ears. How could he have found them?

But she wasn't dreaming. Prince Gerald had arrived. At that moment, she thought he was the most beautiful creature she had ever seen. He came up to her, carrying a sword.

And he looked mad.

"What are you doing here?"

CHAPTER 29

"Over here, you!" someone barked. "Stop loitering and come here this instant!"

A middle-aged Sisu man was rounding up a group of Sisu men outside the wall. From the missing part of the wall, Alrik perceived that the man was Holger. He suspected that Holger was one of Moira's consorts, back when she was ruler of Sisu.

"Her Majesty wants the wall and castle restored in a week!" Holger shouted, brandishing a whip that was normally reserved for animals pulling a sled. "Get to work, all of you, or you won't be going home tonight."

He turned, muttering how sluggish the men were, and caught sight of Alrik. He bowed, but Alrik detected a spark of hostility in the man's eyes.

I'll be too happy to trade places with you, Alrik thought. *If we were women and Moira a man, you could wear a wedding veil and trick Moira into marrying you.*

The image of Holger wearing a veil and arrayed in an embroidered gown was so hilarious that Alrik clapped a hand over his mouth and turned away. But the lighthearted moment didn't last long. Walking along the glittering ice corridor, he saw Moira coming in his direction. No matter how he wanted to turn his back and run, he had to fake his attitude. She held his life in her hands.

"My queen," he said, managing a smile. Too bad that she was tall and fair—nothing like Gabi, or he could've had an easier job pretending she was the woman he loved. "How are you this morning?"

She wrinkled her nose. "Despite my clearly instructed orders, the kitchens cannot rid the stink of fish."

Alrik wasn't particularly partial to fish, but he'd happily consume an entire salmon in front of her, just to give her displeasure.

"I ruled over them for years," Moira said, grinding her teeth. "Such a long time, and my good intentions had been for naught. Now I return after twenty years, and they have regressed."

"Those barbarians," Alrik said. "They don't know any better." He hoped that no Sisu was nearby. Apart from the castle builders, Moira had also recruited women to serve her and Sorcha. Some of them were to make her wedding dress. There was a mother of four who didn't want to come, but was told that her children would be harmed if she didn't participate. Alrik felt sorry for the mother, and tried to plead with Moira, but it came to nothing. She was adamant that the castle and wedding must be ready.

"The Sisu are a bunch of ingrates," she spat. "I did everything for them. I introduced proper construction—" she gestured at the walls made from blocks of ice "—I made them learn to make fashionable apparel. I corrected their hideous accents. I taught them better ways, and all I get are miserable faces."

Alrik had only been in her presence for days and he felt like jumping out of the window. Imagine being subjected to years of her tyranny.

"But enough of unpleasant talk." Moira threaded her arm through his. He tried not to flinch. "Our wedding apparel is almost done. Let us try on the dresses and see if there are any adjustments needed."

The silver chains around his ankles jingled and clanged as he walked by her side, making his face burn with humiliation. Moira, however, was smiling serenely as if his pain brought her pleasure.

The fitting room, as Moira called it, was a large but crowded chamber located on the first floor, near the throne room. About two dozen Sisu women were employed to sew and embroider the wedding apparel, including the bride, bridegroom, and the bridesmaids. When he and Moira entered, only a young woman wearing a crimson scarf looked over at them. The rest were quietly sewing away, as if uttering a word would bring execution.

Moira swept up to a wooden mannequin in the middle of the room. A white dress was draped over the mannequin. Diamonds of various sizes gleamed over the front. The reason that the diamonds were in different shapes was because they came from different families. Moira had made those families hand over their jewels so she would have enough gems on her dress.

"Well?" Moira tapped her heel on the ice floor. "I need to try on this dress. And so does my new husband."

A few women rose to help her. Alrik turned and faced the doorway; he had no desire to see Moira trying on her wedding dress. He heard her tinkling laugh, filled with amusement, and felt like retching.

The laugh turned into a shriek that sounded like nails on glass. Startled, Alrik whirled around. Moira was wearing a filmy white veil over her head; the next second she ripped off the veil and tossed it on the floor, revealing several ugly red welts running across her face.

"Who did this?" she screeched. "Own up, or I'll have all of your heads!"

The young woman wearing the crimson scarf raised her hand. Alrik was surprised to see that the girl didn't seem frightened.

"I'm sorry," she said, though anyone could see that she wasn't in the least bit apologetic. "I misplaced the veil and got sap from nettles smeared over the fabric."

Moira's reaction was instant.

Smack! A red imprint of a hand appeared on the young woman's face. She flinched, but did not back down.

"What's your name?" Moira said. Her voice was soft, but Alrik was reminded of a viper hissing. Somehow, her calm, controlled fury seemed more frightening than volcanic rage.

"Valta."

"Valta," Moira repeated in that silky soft tone. "Where are your parents? They should have taught you better manners."

"They're dead." Valta straightened her shoulders. "Thanks to you, I grew up an orphan. I don't even know what my parents look like."

That explained her motivation for smearing Moira's veil with poison, and also her lack of fear. Without parents, she had no loved ones who could be used against her.

Nevertheless, Alrik was worried about her. The witch was unlikely to let Valta have a merciful, painless death. She'd torture the girl and break her, physically and mentally.

"Apologize to the queen," he said sharply.

She lifted her chin and kept her lips pressed together.

Alrik hated himself at the moment, but he knew her defiance would only make things worse for her. With a snarl, he aimed a well-placed kick on her ankles. She winced, but did not kneel. "On your knees, you insolent girl."

"That will not be necessary," Moira said, a smirk playing in the corner of her lips. Sparks flew from her hands; Valta was levitated in the air.

To Alrik's alarm, the girl didn't even try to struggle. She

simply glared at Moira with hatred, as if she knew that any resistance was futile.

"Kill me," she said.

"With pleasure," Moira said, circling Valta's floating body. "The question is when and how?" She rubbed her hands together. "Perhaps I should stop feeding my wolves for a day, and then throw you into the same cage with them. Or there's a river with ice floating in it, just behind the castle. I daresay it'd be quite a spectacle to strip your clothes off and toss you into the river."

Valta flinched.

"Kill me," she repeated.

"Oh no, I don't think so." Moira smirked. "You shall be the first to set an example for anyone who dares to defy me."

She flicked her fingers, and Valta was carried outside, still suspended in midair.

The other Sisu women stared in horror, then fell to their knees.

"Please have mercy, Your Majesty."

"She's an orphan, please take pity on her."

"You can banish her from the land—she'll never bother you again."

But no matter how the women pleaded, Moira remained impassive. They turned their attention to Alrik, begging him to save Valta, but he couldn't speak. He knew quite well that no matter what he said, Moira wouldn't budge. He had to keep quiet and figure out a way to rescue her later.

CHAPTER 30

*S*ybil touched her face. She hadn't removed the spell that diminished her beauty. "You recognize me?"

"I'd know you anywhere." Gerald grasped her elbow. If they were in any other place, she would have thrown herself into his arms. But the troll was still there, chewing the remains of the poor dog, making crunching sounds that made her want to throw up.

"We have been tracking the whereabouts of this creature," Gerald said. "Last week several trolls broke out from underground, and we took down every one of them except for this one. It could run and leap like a frog. We were preoccupied with the other trolls, unfortunately allowing it escape into the city. I created a tracking spell from a tree branch it perched on, but it had been traveling so fast that we didn't catch up with it until now."

"Did this breakout cause any deaths?"

"Several soldiers were killed, and everyone was injured, though no one is in critical condition." His left hand still gripping her elbow, Gerald dragged her behind him. "Don't worry, dearest. I have years of experience fighting these monsters."

Rebellious words rose to her throat. She didn't want to stand back and watch him fight, but common sense took over. He was right. What she could do was watch and observe, and provide help when she could. If she got in the way, she'd only distract him while fighting the troll.

Reluctantly, Sybil backed away, but not before giving him a swift kiss on the cheek. "Don't you dare let yourself be killed."

He smiled—a beautiful, brilliant smile that made her catch her breath. His beauty was so radiant that it seemed he glowed under the sun. So *that* was how men felt when they saw her smile. She didn't understand why some men were reduced to gibberish. Now she knew.

As she fell back and took shelter near a house, she saw Laurent and Flavien dart into the store. Her heart contracted with fear and worry. The devastating state of Claude's corpse was fresh on her mind. How could Margot have survived when she was shut in with that monster for so long?

The troll threw down the last bone and raised its head. A drop of blood slid down its chin and fell on the ground with a splat. Its lips stretched into a manic grin as it stared at Gerald.

Everything was quiet now. All the townsfolk had disappeared. They had retreated into their houses, quaking and cowering. Only Gerald and the soldiers he brought remained, though several of the soldiers were white and shaken, looking like they would take off running if the troll attacked.

The sun shone brightly on them all. It ought to be a pleasant day, but somehow the brightness of the daylight made the scene more horrifying.

Gerald bent his knees. He picked a fist-sized stone off the ground and threw it at the troll. The stone struck the troll on its tomato-shaped head, and its wide grin disappeared. Letting out a snarl of rage, the troll chased after Gerald. The prince sprinted away with inhuman speed—he was so fast that Sybil was certain that he had a speed-enhancing spell on his boots.

Her feet moved despite her fear. Following the dusty foot-prints on the ground, she found that the troll had chased Gerald down a narrow alley. Was this what Gerald had in mind? Trapping the troll so it wouldn't be able to leap around and snatch up random people or animals?

It was a clever plan, if it were to minimize the lives at risk, but a stupid one if it were about his own safety.

Sybil bit her lower lip. Wasn't there anything she could do? She was an experienced hunter, but even if there was a bow and arrow available, she couldn't shoot when Gerald was blocking the troll. She racked her brains, thinking about the books she pored over on trolls. But this one was different. Trolls were supposed to be slow, like elephants, but this one was surprisingly agile, an exception to the rule.

If only there was a way to slow it down...

Sybil raced back to the store and found the bucket containing the freezing spell. Some water remained—probably only enough to fill two glasses. Definitely not enough to toss over the troll's hulking figure.

But even a full bucket wouldn't be much use. When she threw the water over the troll when it emerged from the store, the thick layer of ice prevented them from running a knife through its chest.

Nevertheless, Sybil gripped the bucket with both hands and returned to the alley.

Gerald was still facing the troll, his cloak billowing behind him. His sword glinted under the sun. She guessed he was waiting for the troll to make the first move—if the enemy got impatient, it would be easier to discover a chink in its armor.

The troll dashed at Gerald with an earsplitting cry. Instead of backing away, Gerald ran toward the troll, his sword out. He tried to pierce the troll's heart, but the latter was so fast that the sword only met its arm, drawing blood, but hardly causing any significant damage.

At the same time, the troll had taken a swipe at Gerald. The prince averted his face in time—otherwise the troll could've plucked out his eyes—but didn't escape unscathed either. Blood trickled down the side of his face. The troll had snatched away a chunk of Gerald's hair with a bit of skin.

After the clash between the two, their positions were reversed. Gerald was the one trapped against the wall in the dead-end alley. The troll could charge at him and finish him off, or it could escape. Either way, the prince was the disadvantaged.

Gerald saw her. His eyes widened in fear.

On sudden inspiration, Sybil flung the remaining water at the troll's feet. Splash. Immediately, ice formed around the troll's thick, green-skinned ankles, pinning him to the ground.

"Now!" she shouted.

Gerald sprinted forward with his speed-enhanced boots and drove his sword through the troll's chest. It let out a shriek and looked down, seeing the bloodied tip protruding from its chest. It swayed, but did not fall. It swiped at Gerald, its hairy fingers reaching for the prince's neck. The wound was not enough to drain life from its body.

"No you don't!" A soldier rushed up and buried his sword in the troll's stomach. The other soldiers followed, each of them hacking at the troll's body.

Sybil turned away, not wanting to witness the bloody scene. A human could be dead from one fatal injury, but a troll would need several.

As she made way back to the store, a more welcoming sight greeted her. Laurent and Flavien emerged from the store, carrying Margot with them. Amazingly, she looked unharmed. She was disheveled and dirty, but other than a noticeable limp, there was no sign of blood.

"Margot!" Sybil rushed toward them. "How did you manage to escape?"

"Long story," Margot croaked. "I thought I wasn' goin' to make it out alive."

She sank to the ground with Laurent's arm around her shoulders.

"It's all this stupid ankle. I found a box of Masaro chocolates on the top shelf. I was thinkin', we could use some chocolate after that terrible death, but the box was too high. I got a stool, but when I was reachin' for it, someone screamed. I toppled off and twisted my ankle. Everyone was rushing outside, I tried to follow them, but then that monster came in."

Margot shuddered and leaned against Laurent.

"It was standing in the doorway, its hands gripping the frame. I couldn't get out. But there was an empty barrel nearby so I climbed into the barrel. It used to hold sugar." Margot flicked her hair—a few grains fell off. "I closed the lid on top, prayin' that it wouldn't find me. There was a hole in the barrel so I could breathe. When there was no sound, I lifted the lid, but I heard shouting outside. I learned the storekeeper had locked the door, so I prayed with all my might that the troll wouldn't discover me. It was leaping through the room, snarling, and I was thinkin' I was goin' to die of fright, if not as its food. Then the troll found me—don' know how; maybe it smelled me. It tried to pry the lid off, so I rolled across the floor. It was bangin' on the lid, when it suddenly stopped."

"It must be when we opened the door," Sybil said. On a sudden impulse, she reached out and hugged her cook. "Oh, Margot, I'm so glad that you're safe."

Margot returned the embrace warmly. When pulled away, she tilted her head in Gerald's direction. "How did he arrive?"

"He came looking for the troll with a tracking spell, and he killed it."

Margot struggled to her feet with Laurent's support and turned toward Gerald.

"Your Highness." She grasped Gerald's hand in both of hers. "Thank you for saving us from that terrible monster. We can never thank you enough."

"I did what I had to do," Gerald said gently. "Besides, your mistress deserves more credit. Had she not used a spell to halt the troll's movement, I might have ended up with injuries more serious than this." He indicated the wound where the troll ripped off his hair.

"Sybil, is this the spell the Arksan villagers used, way back when the trolls invaded?"

Sybil nodded and told him how she used the spell recorded by the Arksans. "That's why I came to find you. Since the spell was simple yet effective, I thought you could mass produce the spell and use it against the trolls."

"An excellent idea," he agreed. "Write me the list of ingredients and the spell-making process. I must return to the castle immediately."

"I'm coming with you."

He shook his head. "We already talked about this. You must stay safe."

"That was before I saw you battle the troll." Sybil laid her hands on his chest, feeling his steady heartbeat beneath her palms. "When I realized I might never see you again, that you could have *died* fighting that monster, I decided I'm staying by your side. I want to spend as much time with you as possible."

He hesitated.

"If you don't let me come with you, I won't give you the freezing spell."

"Sybil," he growled. "Don't bargain with me at a time like this."

"Then don't argue with me at a time like this. Gerald, this might be the last time we see each other. But if I go with you, we could have at least a few more days."

Gerald stared into her eyes for a long moment. Finally, he nodded.

She slipped her hand through his arm and smiled.

CHAPTER 31

"They'll recognize you."

"You mean they won't be able to recognize me, since they've never seen me before."

"Yes, and they'll know you're an outsider. They'll raise an alarm."

Gabi held up a cracked, handheld mirror to her face. She was dressed in a dark brown cloak, patched in places, and her hair was securely fastened and concealed in a crimson cap. Around her neck was a crimson scarf—if she pulled it high enough, only half her face showed.

"Everyone will be too busy to notice me," she said. "If Moira wants this wedding performed in five days, they'll have their hands full. And the witches never saw me, so they won't notice."

For the past two days, Ruben had tried to gain knowledge about the snow castle's layout. But he was confined to building one of the towers, carrying ice bricks and layering them, and so busy that he barely had time to venture out and explore. He never saw Alrik, though he heard from rumors that the new consort was never seen without Moira or Sorcha by his side—

which meant that if they wanted to rescue Alrik, they couldn't avoid confronting Moira.

In the end, Gabi decided to scout the snow castle. Ruben was becoming tense and apprehensive, and she didn't want to demand too much from him. Lorenza offered to go, but Gabi refused. Lorenza didn't have her picture-perfect memory. Naturally, Julong was out of the question, as he looked nothing like a Sisu.

"Be careful," Ulfred said. "If you sense any trouble, run."

"I can't run," Gabi reminded him. "But I can hide. And I have a few tricks up my sleeves that can cause a diversion. Freja left me some useful spells."

Speaking of Freja, Gabi wondered how she was doing in Savony. Had she used all the collars? Were the trolls bound and sent back to their own lands? Or was there an epic battle, leaving numerous dead and injured?

A chilly wind happened to blow through the flap in the tent. Gabi shivered, then steeled herself. No use worrying about Freja, when she had her own insurmountable odds to conquer.

"Here." Piera handed her a covered basket. "Take care, child. May luck shine on you."

"Thank you." Gabi was supposed to pose as a distant cousin and bring Ruben lunch. "We'll get rid of Moira and make sure she'll never come back."

Piera smiled, but she didn't say anything. Having suffered under Moira's reign, she probably couldn't be optimistic that things would go well.

Gabi emerged from the tent. Lorenza and Julong were practicing combat near a clump of trees.

Although she was on an urgent mission, Gabi couldn't help pausing for a moment. Julong's flying darts whistled through the air, glittering under daylight, and met Lorenza's magical shield in a shower of pinging sounds. Both mages were capable of extraordinary fighting skills, but would it be enough when faced with Moira armed with the Peerless Knife?

By the time Gabi left the dwellings behind, facing a never-ending stretch of snow-covered tundra, she remembered that she had yet to see Dal today. Usually he would be playing by the river with his dog. Perhaps he was off with the other Sisu children. The massive lands offered plenty of space for children to roam and have games.

It was a long walk from Piera's dwelling to the snow castle. Her foot protested, but she used a little magic to make the wooden apparatus travel more smoothly.

She didn't know how long it took, but she rested twice before the snow castle came into sight. Piera had drawn a simple map on the ground, marking out the castle's location, and her photographic memory aided her goal. She had no problem finding the castle.

Considering that most of the Sisu dwellings were tents, the glittering white towers against the gray sky appeared long before she set foot on the castle grounds.

"Queen of Sisu, eh?" Gabi muttered under her breath. "I'll stop you before you make Alrik your Royal Consort."

The thought of Alrik made her insides clench. Without magic or weapons, he was no different from being a pet. Gabi could only hope that his easygoing, carefree character would be useful defense against Moira's tyranny. The kiss they shared before he was abducted still had a phantom presence on her lips. She wanted to kiss him again. And again. Until the time came for him to choose a queen...

Gabi shook her head, quashing thoughts of the future. She didn't even know if she could succeed in getting Alrik out of Moira's clutches.

Trying to walk as naturally as possible, Gabi approached the castle. A snowflake fluttered down and brushed her cheek. Her foot ached. If Moira or Sorcha discovered her and knew she had come to rescue Alrik, she wouldn't get out alive.

A wall around five feet high surrounded the castle. Gabi walked around the wall, keeping away from a couple of Sisu who were fixing a crumbling block in the wall, and came to a larger opening that happened to be abandoned at the moment. She guessed there weren't enough men to be working on every area at all times.

She entered through the opening. One quick scan revealed there were five towers in total—one in the middle, and four others built on the four corners. Two towers were decrepit, two were in relatively good shape, while the central one looked intact. Most of the Sisu were working on the two decrepit towers, while a couple were clearing away the snow on the paths.

Gabi wondered where Alrik was and if he was truly accompanying Moira at all times. There had to be a way to reach him without Moira's knowledge. Despite knowing that Moira planned to marry the prince, it was possible she'd still harm him.

"Who're you and what're you doing here?" someone snapped.

It was a Sisu. From the whip he held, Gabi guessed he was Holger—one of the few men who cheerfully groveled at Moira's feet.

"I brought my cousin lunch." She held up the basket and gestured at Ruben. "He needs more strength. With more strength, he'll be able to do a better job with building."

Holger narrowed his eyes. "Ruben's cousin? Never saw you before."

"That's because I've been living in the western part of the region and don't come often to visit," Gabi said, making her lips stretch into a (hopefully) charming smile. "But I got note that the queen has returned to Sisu, so I wanted to have a chance to come. Is she around? May I pay my respects to her?"

His suspicious expression didn't change. "You don't look much like Ruben."

"My father married a Masaro woman," Gabi said. "She was born of an unusual constitution that doesn't tolerate hot weather. She lived in Linberg for a while but found it too expensive, and eventually came here."

It was a flimsy lie, but it was the best explanation she could come up with. Gabi summoned magical energy to her hands, holding her breath. If there was any sign Holger was to report her to Moira, she'd cast a spell that would confuse his thoughts. Needless to say, this kind of magic that tampered with the mind was forbidden in the kingdoms, but at this moment she couldn't care.

Holger stared at her for a long moment. Gabi took a deep breath, prepared to stun him with mind-numbing magic, when he spoke.

"You know how to sew?"

"What?"

"Sewing," he growled, mimicking the motion of using a needle and thread. "Did your Masaro mother ever teach you?"

"The basics." When Alrik was around, she couldn't mend a torn sleeve by shooting sparks out of her fingers, so she had to learn to sew without magic.

"Fine. After you give Ruben his ruddy lunch, go to the first floor of that tower." Holger indicated the one in the north that was in relatively stable condition. "A girl left yesterday, so they could use another pair of hands with sewing all the wedding finery."

Gabi's heart soared. She had a valid excuse to stay in the castle for a while. Surely, amidst the sewing, she could nip outside for a while and look for Alrik. But she couldn't appear delighted at the prospect of more work.

"Uh…" Gabi tried to look worried. "But I should be going back to help Ruben's mother…"

"Who's more important, the queen or an old hag?" Holger cracked his whip, and she retreated a step, wobbling a little.

"I'm so sorry," Gabi said, putting a hand on her chest. "Of course, it's an honor to serve our queen."

He grunted. "Looks like your head isn't too thick. Now go."

Gabi headed to Ruben. He looked a bit frightened and startled when she reached him, as if he didn't believe she actually had the courage to step into the castle grounds.

"Hello," she said brightly. "Are you doing all right? Aunt Piera sent this; she said it'll fill you up in no time."

"Thanks," he mumbled, glancing at the basket instead of her face. She noticed that the other Sisu men looked either wary (the younger ones) or weary (the older ones). She wished she could pat their shoulders and tell them she was here to help them, but she had to stay silent.

"I'm going over there to help with some sewing. Apparently they need a hand with the wedding apparel."

Ruben nodded, still not looking at her. "Got to get back to work."

Gabi turned and went to the northern tower. It wasn't hard to find the fitting room—the door was left wide open, making it easy to see the white wedding dress, groom uniform, and bridesmaid dresses inside.

Cautiously, she entered. There were two dozen women stitching and hemming with bone needles. Gems sparkled on the wedding gown.

"Hello," she said, giving a friendly wave. "Holger told me you could use an extra hand."

The women stared blankly, as if she talked in Lulanese. Did they understand? They should—the Sisu had their own language, but she knew it was very similar to the common tongue. Or maybe it was her appearance. From a distance she might pass for a Sisu, but in the same room, they could see that her face was "exotic." Her curly brown hair was obscured by the crimson scarf, but her olive skin was distinctly different from the pale, sometimes freckled, skin of Sisu and Arksans.

"Over here," a woman said. She asked a few questions; Gabi told her she was Ruben's distant cousin who came to visit, and she could sew but was no good at embroidery. Soon she was stitching two pieces of fabric together—the part of the brides-maid's dress. She guessed they didn't trust her to work on Moira's gown.

Several minutes passed. Gabi looked out of the window. There was no sign of Alrik, nor any of the Sisu. She could continue sew in silence, but it seemed a pity to waste the time.

"So," she ventured. Her voice sounded loud in the silence. "I heard that a girl left yesterday. Was she ill, or overworked? Or was she ill because she was overworked?"

The women looked at each other. Fear was reflected in their eyes. Gabi had the feeling that the girl who left must have done something to offend Moira.

"Nothing much," a woman murmured.

"Keep focused on your work," another woman said sternly. "Being inquisitive will do you no good."

Gabi bent her head. "Sorry."

So a girl was forcefully removed. Was she dead? It wasn't even the wedding, yet Moira already was punishing the Sisu. She remembered the haunted look in Piera's face when she talked about Moira's reign.

Gabi bit her lip. She had come to Sisu to rescue Alrik, but seeing how Moira treated the locals, she couldn't stand aside and do nothing either. But how could she save everyone from the witches? Getting Alrik to safety was already impossible.

Footsteps came from outside. Startled, Gabi stabbed her

finger. Sucking on the wound, she saw Marianne enter the room.

"Mari..." Gabi hastily clamped her jaws shut. How could she be here? She was dressed in a long, flowing robe that was nothing like an ordinary shopkeeper's daughter.

Then she realized that Moira had performed the forbidden spell on Marianne. The girl from Kardi was no longer living—she was only a hollow shell, hosting Moira's soul.

Shock, disbelief, and anger coursed through her mind. Poor Marianne—she was just getting married and lost her life. Her soul, cruelly ripped away from her body, never to return. And poor Ronnie. How proud and gratified he was when he introduced Marianne as his fiancée. Gabi wondered how long it would take for him to recover—if ever he could recover.

Marianne—actually, Moira—swept across the room. She stopped right in front of Gabi.

Gabi curtsied deeply, hoping that the witch didn't notice her crooked posture. But with her crippled foot, it was impossible that she could perform a perfect curtsy without magic. And at the moment, she couldn't afford to display any magic.

"Raise your head," Moira commanded.

Gabi tried not to flinch. The witch had Marianne's face, but nothing in her expression resembled the young woman. There was a cold arrogance that was more like a ruthless empress.

"What's your name?"

"Piera, my queen," Gabi said. "Holger ordered me to lend a hand with the sewing."

"Ah." Her gaze remained on Gabi's face, hard and piercing. If Moira's gaze were a knife, Gabi would have been cut into two. "So Ruben was telling the truth. A mage has come."

Ruben? How did the witch know...

The truth struck her like a block of ice. Ruben sold her out. That was why he didn't dare to meet her eyes when she brought him lunch. Whether it was under duress or not, he had alerted Moira that she was here.

In a quick, fluid motion, Moira tore Gabi's scarf away. Her dark hair tumbled over her shoulders, eliciting a gasp from the other women.

"The mage from Masaro." Moira sounded calm, as if she had anticipated Gabi's arrival all along. "You should have stayed away, foolish girl."

Gabi summoned all the magical energy she had—it made her hair billow out—but Moira was faster.

Crack! Forces of magic collided. Sparks flew around the room—the women screamed and ducked. One larger spark burned a hole in the wall. Moira's magic was so strong that Gabi was blasted off her feet and flew backward, hitting the wall and sliding to the floor.

"You'll only tire yourself," Moira said, stalking forward. Her hand was stroking something dark on her hips—the hilt of a weapon.

The Peerless Knife. With the knife, Moira could draw an infinite amount of power—power that Gabi, a twenty-year-old mage, could have no chance against.

"Pathetic," Moira said, wrinkling her nose. "But since you're here, we might as well make good use of it. Sorcha!"

In a moment, another young woman entered the room. She was pretty, but when she opened her mouth, large front teeth were shown.

Icy dread trickled down Gabi's spine. Sorcha, Moira's sister.

"Here." Moira jerked a finger in Gabi's direction. "Take her—she's yours. Do with her whatever you want."

A horrifying idea struck her. Would Sorcha take her body, like Moira did to Marianne?

Gabi struggled to her feet. She had a tracking spell on her wrist—Lorenza and Julong would come to her aid. But before she could press her finger on the bracelet, strong cords were fastened over her body. No matter how she struggled, she couldn't free herself.

Where's Alrik? It was the last thought that came to her mind before Sorcha acted. She lifted Gabi's chin and force-fed a potion down her throat. Dizziness engulfed her, and she slumped forward, unconscious.

CHAPTER 32

*G*abi woke up in a spacious bedroom with ice-block walls. She was chained to a wall, her hands and feet bound, and a strange black bowl attached to her chest. She was wearing a loose gown, and a black tube from the bowl ran to a jar filled with a silver liquid.

But she was terribly drowsy. She tried to summon a spark of magical energy, but nothing gleamed on her fingers. Dread filled her mind as she gradually came to realize what had happened. The witches were draining her magic—just like they had done with their own father.

Without magic, she was useless. How was she going to save Alrik?

The door creaked open. Sorcha entered the room. She looked like a seventeen-year-old, too young to be a witch who was several decades old, which meant she also occupied a human body. Gabi clenched her teeth. How many girls did the witches kill and possess?

The witch approached the table and lifted the jar containing silver liquid—her magic. Rage lit a fire and Gabi struggled. Pain shot through her wrists and a rattling noise caused Sorcha to focus on her.

"The more you move, the faster your magic will drain out of your body," she said, indicating the black bowl on Gabi's chest. "Though it would hardly make any difference. I have gathered two full jars of your magic already; what you have left is barely enough to make a feather dance in the air."

Gabi said nothing. Sorcha was right—she couldn't even make sparks glow on her fingers. Inside she was screaming in despair, but she wasn't going to let the witch see her distress.

The tracking spell on her wrist had disappeared as well. If Lorenza and Julong wanted to rescue her, they wouldn't know where she was. They knew she was at the snow castle, but since there were five towers, they'd spend a long time searching.

"Thinking your little friends will come and rescue you?" Sorcha seemed to have read her mind. "My sister stripped off that tracking bracelet and performed a reverse charm. She knows where your little friends are hiding. She'll bring them back at any moment. Are they also mages like you? All the better." She laughed, a cold, cruel, ruthless laugh. While her appearance differed greatly from Marianne's, Gabi could see how they were sisters. Something in Sorcha's expression reminded her of Moira.

Fear ran through her mind. If Moira found Lorenza and Julong—their magic would be drained as well. They'd be permanent prisoners, kept alive to be suppliers of magic. Ulfred, without any practical value, would be killed, his body left to be devoured by wolves or vultures. Piera and the other Sisu probably would be killed for helping them. And Alrik...she didn't even want to think about him.

Sorcha leaned down and took hold of Gabi's chin. "Not bad-looking. I could take *your* body. I'm tired of gazing at these squirrel teeth every day."

Gabi glared, though her insides went cold. Losing her magic

might not be the worst thing. She'd rather die than let Sorcha assume her appearance.

"Better not," Gabi said curtly. "Alrik loves me. If you dare use my body, he might prefer you, and that would invoke your sister's wrath."

Sorcha wrinkled her brow. Moira's wrath was apparently not something she'd want to invoke.

"Why does every man we seize already have a girl?"

* * *

After Sorcha left, Gabi gnashed her teeth, trying to stay calm, but her mind wouldn't settle. The bowl on her chest contracted; she could feel more magic trickling out like the last drops in a glass of water. Soon she would be just like any human—in fact, with her crippled foot, she'd be even weaker than an average human. Dizziness came; she felt nauseous, as if she just performed a dozen pirouettes.

She couldn't stay upright, much less save Alrik. Tears pricked her eyes, and this time she let herself weep. Not only was she stupid enough to get caught, but Lorenza and Julong were also in danger. Could the two of them escape Moira?

When she ceased sniffling, the door creaked open. A young woman entered, carrying a tray of food.

It was one of the Sisu women she worked with on Moira's wedding dress. The woman carefully avoided her eyes, but she looked uncomfortable. The tear stains on her cheeks hadn't dried yet.

Wordlessly, she set the tray near Gabi's feet and left. The chains were long enough that she could reach the bowl of stew on the tray. The bout of nausea had passed; now she felt ravenous. The contents of the stew were better than she expected—almost every spoonful contained meat. She knew it wasn't generosity. The better health she was in, the better quality her magic would be.

Getting food in her stomach did her a world of good. Sisu fish didn't agree with her stomach; besides, the portions Piera prepared were small, since there were four additional mouths to feed. The reindeer stew, however, was filling. She was able to collect herself and ponder on the next step.

From the window, she could see the Sisu working away, Holger brandishing his whip and yelling that they were lazy oafs. The man disgusted her, acting as Moira's lackey and turning on his own people.

But still no sign of Alrik. Gabi wondered where he might be. If she were in Sorcha's bedroom, he shouldn't be far away. Right? But they must know she was here to rescue him. They couldn't have him staying nearby.

Gabi rattled the chains on her wrists. There was no pressure or numbness on her skin, which meant Sorcha wasn't using magic to keep the chains in place. Sorcha probably didn't think it necessary to waste magic on restraining Gabi, as the latter, drained of magic, was no different from any human.

Which meant that she had to rely on something else to free herself.

Gabi thought hard. During the six years she stayed in Brek, she had to pretend she was ordinary. She immersed herself in everything a normal human had to do without magic, and succeeded in most things except cooking.

Apart from magic, her memory was her best advantage. Gabi closed her eyes and focused. An event appeared in her mind.

Two years and seventy-nine days ago, there was a thief in Kardi. He broke into houses and stole valuables. She happened to be in town with Ulfred and Alrik. Using a slight amount of magic (but making it appear that Ulfred did the work), they caught the thief and made him reveal his methods.

The thief had used a simple pin to pick locks. In Linberg, he couldn't break into wealthy family homes, as their locks were more expensive and complicated, but in a distant town like Kardi? It took less than five minutes for him to open a locked door.

At that time, Gabi didn't even know locks could be picked. She watched the thief demonstrate how he inserted the pin into the lock, find the levers, and make them click.

Gabi opened her mouth and yelled as loudly as she could. The same woman who brought her stew came running to the door.

"Yes?" she asked, looking worried.

"Get me a pin," Gabi said bluntly. Having worked with the seamstresses, she knew they had dozens of pins, which were necessary when sewing the wedding apparel. "Right now."

"But why do you need…"

"Just give me one," Gabi said. "I…um…something got caught in my teeth and I need to get it out."

The woman still looked puzzled, but she nodded and ran off. It confirmed Gabi's theory that Sorcha wanted to keep her in good condition. As long as she wasn't demanding the key to the chains, the women had to meet what she requested.

In five minutes, a silver pin was dropped onto her palm.

"Thanks," Gabi said. Trying to imitate what that thief did, she slid the pin into the lock and poked around. It took several tries, but there was an audible click, and the chain fell off her wrist.

Excellent.

The woman, who was lingering in the corner, gasped.

"Not a word," Gabi said, giving her the most lethal glare she could summon. "You know that I'm on your side. Once I get out, I'm going to rescue Alrik and make the witches pay. You don't have to be subjected to their tyranny. Do you know where Alrik is staying?"

The woman looked blank, so Gabi described Alrik's appearance.

"I'm not sure," the woman confessed. "Only time I saw him was when the queen came and told us to take his measurements. I don't know where he is."

Gabi continued to work with the pin and the rest of the chains clattered on the floor. "All right. Do you know where Moira stays at?"

Again, the woman shook her head.

She was on her own, lame and magic-less. Her companions might be in Moira's clutches at the moment. But at least she was free.

Just when she was debating where to go, there was a huge boom and the floors shook. Gabi stumbled and fell on the ground.

What just happened?

CHAPTER 33

"*I* have decided the girl shall be thrown to the wolves," Moira announced. "When was the last time they were fed, Sorcha?"

"This afternoon."

"So soon? Then make it tomorrow afternoon," Moira said, her lip curling. "Another day's time will ensure they are starving to the point they would devour tree bark, not to mention tender human flesh."

Alrik tried his best to look passive. Valta was locked away in an underground cell—one of the places that required little rebuilding, since it was underground, while Moira and Sorcha returned to the throne room. He wasn't required to tag along, but he wanted to hear what would befall the young woman.

"Dear, dear," Moira laughed, seeing his stricken face. "My poor young consort is horrified. You have much to learn, my prince." She leaned forward and stroked his cheek. "To be a ruler, one must be ruthless. A soft heart would only make your enemies bold and give them the power to rebel. Your father, for instance—" she narrowed her eyes, as if recalling Tyrell disgusted her "—behaved abominably toward me. Had he been a kind man, he would not have ordered the mages to come after me."

"Do you still hate him?" He couldn't help asking.

Moira looked as if he threw a bucket of snow on her. "Once I loved and trusted him," she finally said. "And what did he do? He lied to me, pretended that he was going to bring me to meet his parents. Instead, several mages were waiting to ambush me. Were it not for Sorcha's timely arrival, I would have been dead."

Too bad they didn't succeed, he wanted to say. And yet, he couldn't help thinking his father was partly responsible for Moira's deranged behavior. If he hadn't betrayed her trust in the beginning, perhaps she wouldn't have become so embittered, so cruel.

Moira crossed her arms. "It's settled, then. Tomorrow afternoon the girl will be thrown to the wolves. I will not tolerate any rebellious sentiment toward my reign. These primitives must be taught a lesson."

Alrik remembered Valta's face. How young she looked, how vulnerable and helpless. She didn't deserve to die.

At that moment, a servant came in. "A message, Your Majesty. The man said it's important."

"Who is it?"

"Ruben. He asked for a private audience. He said he can't tell you the message until you release his child."

Moira raised her eyebrows. "That will depend on what he has to say."

"Shall I bring him in?"

"Do it."

Alrik stood up. After Moira's announcement of Valta's fate, he had been racking his brains what to do.

"I'm tired," he said. "Excuse me for a while."

Sorcha sent him a searching look. "Planning to escape? Or planning to help that Sisu woman escape?"

Was his expression that plain?

Moira set a lily-white hand on the arm of her chair. She raised her other hand—sparks flew toward his head—he felt something like a wind cut across the air above him.

Startled, he stepped back and a fluff of his own hair fell on the ground, right in front of him.

"I could have aimed lower," Moira said in a lazy voice, as if she was announcing she was going to take a nap. "If I did— which part of your body would have fallen on the floor?"

"Blood would be spilled, at the very least," Sorcha said.

"Let this be a warning, if it hasn't got through your head already." Moira gave him a twisted smile. "If you try to rescue that girl, I will not hesitate to kill you. You have escaped death when you were a babe; it is your choice whether you wish to stay alive."

Alrik bowed, his heart pounding. Once outside, he took a deep breath. He had planned to save Valta—he couldn't walk away from a young woman about to meet her death. But the threat from Moira had shaken him. The witches were ruthless; they might treat him better than the Sisu, but if he put one toe out of line, he'd end up with the same fate.

He wasn't normally prone to emotional outbursts. But at that moment he felt that he wanted to yell out of the window, hurl tables and chairs on the wall, and stamp on the floor. Could he ignore Moira's threat and go ahead with his plan?

Don't be daft, one side of his brain argued. It would be too easy for the witches to find out what he was up to. He'd be dead before Gabi found him.

On the other hand, could he stand by and do nothing? Could he close his eyes, stuff his ears, while Valta was sent to death, torn into pieces by starving wolves?

Alrik drove a fist against the wall. The dull pain made him wince; the ice bricks were solid—more solid than the timber of the houses constructed in Brek. Redness appeared on his skin. If there was something sharp, like an ice shard, he might have bled.

Blood. He cradled his fist—old habits die hard. While he knew he didn't have hemophilia, it became a habit to flinch whenever he was in danger of bleeding.

And it struck him that his twenty-first birthday was tomorrow.

In that moment, Alrik made his decision.

* * *

THE NEXT DAY WAS COLD, yet bright. Alrik had hoped for blurry windy weather, but the daylight streaming in through the window made his spirits sink. He couldn't depend on tumultuous weather to aid his plan.

Throwing off the blankets sewn from reindeer fur, Alrik leaped off the bed. There was much to accomplish today. Moira had left the bedroom long ago—an evil queen needed ample time to perform her nefarious deeds.

As he faced the mirror, the image of Gabi rose in his mind. Never a day passed without thinking of her. Did she miss him as much as he missed her? He wondered where she was. Without a tracking spell to aid her, could she find him? How could she guess that he was trapped in a snow castle, far up north?

The future seemed bleak. Alrik clenched his fists. If Gabi never found him—if she was too late—there wasn't anything he could do about it. But what he could do, at least, was save an innocent girl's life.

Alrik touched the pearl-like explosion spell attached to his tooth. Sorcha had searched him, but she never discovered the spell in his mouth. Today, he would put it into use.

He marched out of the room. A Sisu woman rushed past; it was one of the women who worked on their wedding apparel. She had taken his measurements. When she dropped into a quick curtsy, apologizing for nearly running into him, he held up a hand.

"Do you know where the queen is?"

"She went out this morning."

"Do you know where she went? When she will return?" She shook her head at his questions, looking like she wanted to escape.

"How about Valta?" he said. "Will she be thrown to the wolves, or will the execution wait until the queen comes back?"

"It will take place," she whispered. "The queen's sister is in charge." The woman's shoulders trembled. "I...I should go."

"Wait." Alrik set a hand on her arm. "Do you know of anyone who could help? Someone who doesn't want to see Valta dead?"

She looked up at him, her eyes wide. "What do you want?"

Alrik swallowed. Moira wasn't in the castle—it was better luck than he expected. It was now or never.

"I'm on your side. I want to set Valta free, but I can't do it alone. Tell me if you know anyone who's close to her."

The woman hesitated, her expression filled with anxiety. He guessed what was going on in her head.

"Trust me. I never wanted to marry Moira, never wanted to rule your people at her side. I'm only doing it because otherwise she'll kill me."

"If you try to rescue Valta, she'll definitely kill you."

"Which is why I need help. If more people join in the rescue, she won't be able to discover who did it." Alrik put on a confident face. His charm used to work with girls, and the Sisu seamstress was no exception.

"I know her best friend," she said in a low voice. "Valta's parents are dead, but she has friends."

"Good. Now take me to them before Moira returns."

In a small room on the first floor, Alrik found himself facing several men and women. They regarded him warily, as if expecting he was sent by Moira to test their loyalty.

He made them a low bow, so low that he was slightly dizzy when he straightened.

"I'm sorry," he said. "I'm sorry I'm unable to stop Moira from treating you like slaves, but in truth, I'm not in a much better position. She regards me as a toy, a plaything. If I don't do what she commands, she might kill me too. But now I've had enough. I can't stand by and let an innocent girl meet her death."

Still they stared at him in stony silence. Frustrated, Alrik spread out his hands.

"If I didn't want to save Valta, I could've stayed in my room. I could be outside, brandishing that whip, making you all work harder. Why would I risk my life sneaking down here and asking for your help?"

The Sisu looked at each other. One man shrugged, as if to convey, *Might as well hear what he has to say.*

A woman cleared her throat. "How can we save her?"

"I'll create a diversion. I have a spell that can cause an explosion."

"Explosion?" one man repeated, his face blank.

"It creates a huge noise," Alrik said, trying to explain. "The ice will fly in all directions, so be prepared to duck. Then grab Valta and run." Hopefully. He only knew about explosions through Gabi's description.

A horn blared. Valta's execution was sooner than he expected.

"Remember what I said!" he shouted. "If you don't act, she's going to die."

Alrik raced upstairs. From the window, he could see Valta being led to the wolves' cage. Holger was heading the procession, his expression smug. The cage was in the rear of the snow castle, against one of the walls. Dozens of Sisu were gathered outside the wall, most of them looking frightened and anxious.

Valta was pale. Her fingers grasped the folds of her plain, muddy dress. No matter how indifferent she was to her execution, she couldn't remain emotionless, especially when her fate was to be devoured by starving wolves. If there were poison available, she might have preferred to take her own life.

His gaze traveled to the workers, who were hiding behind the wall. The seamstresses and tailors looked up. Alrik made a gesture—it was time to act.

Alrik yanked the white, pearl-like thing off his tooth. Could this really cause an explosion? There was only one way to find out. Taking a deep breath, Alrik threw the spell at the gates.

Thankfully Ulfred had trained him—the spell flew through the air and hit the gates with a sound much louder than expected, given its minuscule size.

BOOM!

The ground shook; the gates were ripped apart, and bits of the wall went flying everywhere. Agonized cries came from the crowd—he muttered an apology, hoping that no one was seriously hurt. Luckily, the wolves' cage was situated a good distance from the castle walls.

A huge plume of smoke went up in the air. Just what he needed.

Putting his hands around his mouth, Alrik yelled.

"GO!"

The Sisu sprang into action. A tailor hurtled toward Valta as if he were chased by wolves himself, grabbed her, and ran towards an opening in the wall. Valta was still bound, her wrists in chains, but her feet were free. The rest of the workers followed, and soon they disappeared in the crowd. Luckily Sorcha had forced the Sisu to turn up to watch the execution, so they'd know not to defy Moira next time. The crowd made it difficult for Sorcha to discover where Valta disappeared.

Sorcha was looking absolutely furious. She had been waiting by the cage, and when the explosion went off, she had shrieked and hurried to the damaged gates.

"Where is she?"

Alrik took a deep breath. Sorcha grabbed the collar of the nearest man and shook him. Magic blasted from her fingers; the man sank to the ground. Blood pooled on the snow.

"Stop!" Alrik dashed out of the tower. He couldn't bear to see more innocent lives sacrificed. "It was me!"

Sorcha, who was holding up two men by magic, turned around. The men fell to the floor, coughing.

"I set off the spell that ripped apart the gates," Alrik said loudly. All he could think of was to make Sorcha focus on him. The more time that he could keep talking, the more chance that Valta could get away.

Sorcha looked like she wanted to kill him.

"How?" she demanded.

Alrik shrugged. He even smiled. "Guess."

"You ingrate. You were given a chance to become the royal consort, but you chose to side with the barbarians," Sorcha spat. "My sister will have your head."

"Oh, I don't doubt that," Alrik said, feeling like a maniac as he smiled wider. "She never saw me as a partner, only a pet."

Another shout rose—this time from the direction of the castle. Holger hurried toward them and skidded to a halt, panting for breath.

"The queen...has...returned," he said.

Sorcha pushed his back; Alrik stumbled toward Holger.

"Take him to the queen," she ordered. "Tell her he helped the prisoner escape. Let her decide what to do with him." Sorcha's eyes gleamed. "Have fun, little prince. My sister has quite an imagination when it comes to torturing people who betray her."

Everything had gone wrong. Valta might be caught and fed to the wolves. Alrik was going to be tortured; he had no idea how, but it could be worse than being alive. And Gabi still hadn't arrived.

Alrik bent his knees and picked up an ice shard lying on the ground. The explosion had blasted blocks of ice built in the wall; there were thousands of shards scattered around.

Gabi had told him he was cursed to fall into a deep sleep if he were to prick himself before his twenty-first birthday. For years, he had tried to stay away from sharp objects. Now he was choosing to shed blood by his own hand.

"I'd rather die than subject myself to that witch's punishment," he said, loud and clear. Then he plunged the shard into his throat. He took care not to drive the shard in deep; just a prick on the skin, but it was enough. He raised his hand; a single drop of blood had stained the tip of the ice shard.

Amid Sorcha's exclamation of surprise and other gasps from Sisu who were close enough to see him, a heavy drowsiness surrounded him. Strength flowed from his body; he could no longer stand.

Alrik collapsed.

CHAPTER 34

The smell of herbs was so strong that Alix coughed when she entered the queen's chamber. Half the castle had already left, so Alix offered to take the breakfast tray to the queen. As she trudged through the corridor, she noticed bits of dirt strewn on the stone floor, which meant that the servant who used to sweep the floors had left. Just a month ago, she couldn't walk through the corridor without bumping into a laundry maid or page boy.

It was saddening, but she couldn't blame the servants who fled. If it wasn't for her affection for Theo, she would have escaped as well. After the last breakout, everyone had witnessed how horrifying the trolls could be.

Queen Marguerite lay on her bed, a hand over her eyes. Her skin was so pale that Alix was alarmed.

"Are you feeling unwell, Your Majesty? I can get a healer for you."

"No need." Marguerite removed her hand. "I'm not sick. I'm just sad. And how many times have I told you that you should call me Mother?"

Despite the fact that Theo was strongly attached to her, Alix couldn't bring herself to address the queen as "Mother" yet.

She perched on the queen's bedspread, which was a shocking pink embroidered with yellow daisies. "I've brought you breakfast. Do you feel like eating anything?"

Slowly, the queen sat up. Deep bags of purple appeared below her eyes. She seemed to have aged ten years.

"Such a burden I bear," she said with a sigh. "To be able to see the future."

"Have you seen anything?"

No answer. The queen simply stared off into the distance, as if absorbed by the handiwork of the curtains around her bed.

Alix tried another question. "Do you think Gerald will find the troll that escaped into the city?"

Gerald had volunteered to leave with a search team. Theo agreed reluctantly. They couldn't afford to send any mages, but Gerald was a competent magic user and excellent fighter. Of the twelve princes, he was the most capable one of taking down a troll.

"He will survive after taking down that troll. However, something else terrible will happen." The queen shuddered, her shoulders trembling. "To get through this ordeal, more lives will be lost…"

Tears started to stream down her cheeks. Alix looked for a handkerchief, and when she finally found a clean one on the dresser, the door opened. Duchess Claudia appeared. She was the only person in the castle who dared to enter the queen's chamber without knocking. She took one look at the queen's distraught face and waved at Alix.

"I'll handle this."

Alix curtsied and left the queen's chamber. As she went upstairs to her room, wondering if she should go to the healers' ward, she ran into Theo. As usual, he looked deprived of sleep. But there was a softness in his eyes when his gaze fell on her.

She ran up to him and threw her arms around his waist. He returned her embrace, but soon pulled away.

"Did you just come back from my mother's?"

"She didn't look too well," Alix confessed. "However, Duchess Claudia returned and she's keeping the queen company."

"Did my mother make any predictions?"

Alix paused. She wasn't sure if she should tell Theo about what Marguerite said, but he guessed it from her expression.

"Someone is going to die," he said. "Not that it's any surprise, Alix. We only killed eight trolls, and one is on the run. It's impossible that we could get through this battle without any blood shed. I just want to know—did she give any names?"

She shook her head. At that moment, Julian came up the stairs, a light in his eyes.

"Gerald is back. He brought his fiancée with him."

* * *

ALIX HAD HEARD of Sybil's extraordinary beauty, but when she came face to face with the real person, she was still temporarily stripped of speech. Sybil, who stood next to the second eldest prince, radiated a brilliance like glittering jewels. Even Theo paused for a second when he entered the room—something rare for a man who normally shunned women except Alix.

"Theo." Gerald hugged his brother and smiled at Alix. "This is Sybil, my fiancée."

Sybil gave a dazzling smile and extended her hand. "It's a pleasure to meet you."

Her voice was like sweet wine, her accent refined and cultured. Alix could not imagine a more attractive partner for Gerald.

She shook Sybil's hand, trying not to gawk. She remembered that when she first came to the castle to work in the Imperial

Wardrobe, the twins had showed her Sybil's portrait in the gallery. She looked exactly like her portrait, but the lines and colors only captured the details. In flesh and soul, the lady was simply captivating.

"Since you're back," Theo said, "I guess this means you have taken care of that leaping troll."

"We did."

"We?"

Gerald placed a hand on Sybil's back. "Did I tell you that Sybil is also a magic user and great lover of books? She found an ancient spell that could create a layer of ice around the troll's body. The leaping troll was fast, but because its movements were hampered by ice, we were able to kill it."

Excitement spread over Theo's face. "Is the spell complicated?"

"Not at all," Sybil said. "The spell was used by people in a small Arksan village. There are only two ingredients needed— ice and stones. The spell can be prepared early and stored in a jar. Before using it, dissolve the spell in water and toss it onto the enemy."

"Excellent. Tell me how to create the spell and we'll start making as many as possible."

"I can demonstrate how to make the spell. Just bring me the ingredients."

"You should be resting after the journey," Gerald said gently. "Let me do it."

"You were the one holding the reins when we rode on horse-back," Sybil said, with an admonishing look that resembled Theo when he argued with his brothers. "You should be the one to rest."

Gerald opened his mouth, but before he could reply, a huge explosive sound tore through the air.

BOOM.

The earth seemed to shake beneath them. Theo caught Alix's arm, steadying her.

"What was that?" Gerald and Sybil said at the same time.

They rushed toward the window. Alix gasped in horror. Just a few yards from the healers' ward was a giant hole. Green-skinned trolls were crawling through like ants, bypassing the wall that Theo had painstakingly built around North Tower.

An eight-foot troll reached for a soldier and ripped his leg off—the soldier screamed. The rest, horrified by the sight, were backing away.

"We've got to retreat!" Duchess Claudia shouted. She appeared behind them, looking agitated. "We have no chance against the trolls at this moment. We must abandon the castle."

"We can't do that!" Theo exclaimed. "If we don't stop the trolls, they'll enter the city and…"

"Are you that dense? Leaving the trolls in the castle is the only way to prevent them from entering the city," Claudia snapped. "Quick, come on. The mages will cover us. We talked about it last night when you were patrolling."

Down below, the mages had arrived. All three were armed with metal-studded collars, but it was obvious their power wasn't enough. When Freja tossed a collar over a troll and uttered the spell that revealed its true name, the troll would rip the collar away before she could go on to banish it from the kingdom. There were so many trolls that Tamarka and Morkel didn't have time to use the collars; they had to resort to magic, throwing out bolts of power that sizzled and flashed, but the trolls had skins thicker than armor and strength rivaling ten horses. Several trolls were able to get past the three mages—if they got out of the castle and entered the city, just as the leaping troll did—Alix didn't even want to think about the conse-quences.

"Go with Claudia," Gerald said to Sybil. "Theo and I will assist the mages."

"What are you waiting for?" Theo glared at Alix. "You heard my aunt! Off to the drawbridge!"

"I'm not leaving without you."

Theo didn't bother to argue. He gave her a push that sent her stumbling in the direction of Sybil and Claudia, then hurried to his room to retrieve his weapons and defensive spells, Gerald following closely behind.

"Come along," Sybil beckoned her. "I know—I'm worried too, but we can't fight. If either of us are in danger, it'll be the worse for those who are fighting the trolls."

"Well said," Claudia said. "You've a head as well as a pretty face. Gerald has chosen well."

Alix barely heard them, however. When they reached the first floor, she whipped out her invisibility cloak (she had been carrying it in a bag slung over her shoulder) and flung it over her body.

"Go ahead!" she shouted. "I'll be right behind."

Sybil gasped; Alix hadn't donned the hood yet, which meant that her body was invisible but her head was not. Alix grinned, winked at her, and pulled the hood over her head.

She raced off, knowing that no matter how exasperated Claudia was, the queen's sister couldn't follow her.

Trolls were spilling over the grounds. Shrieks and screams filled the air as the remaining servants fled the castle. Familiar with the castle layout, Alix went through every tower, shouting that everyone must make it to the drawbridge. Several servants were huddled in the wine cellar, refusing to come out.

"Are you all insane?" Alix yelled. "The trolls can batter down the door and you'll all end up in their stomachs! Come out— we're going into the city!"

It was then that the servants opened the door. They blinked, wondering where Alix was, but hearing the trolls outside, they broke into a run and raced toward the drawbridge.

Fortunately, there weren't any trolls that could move as fast as the leaping one. They plodded and trudged, making the earth shake, which also warned the castle staff well ahead. As far as Alix could tell, the only ones remaining on the grounds were the mages and the princes, along with a handful of soldiers who were brave enough to face the trolls.

"We've got to leave!" Freja shouted. "Any time longer, and someone might die."

She had a point. Blood was running down Tamarka's left arm; Morkel was favoring his right leg. The princes' tunics had rips and tears, blood dripping down their arms and legs. Freja didn't seem injured, but she was breathing heavily, as if the effort of casting magic was taking a toll on her body.

A troll lay on the ground, apparently dead. But just after Freja shouted, the troll raised an arm, reaching to grab Theo's leg.

Alix gasped. "Theo! Watch out!"

The crown prince swung his sword and chopped off the troll's arm. "Let's go."

Gerald didn't answer. He was still fighting a hulking troll that wielded two clubs at the same time.

Bang! Power burst from Freja's palms and formed a shimmering shield. The trolls that were still crawling out from the hole ran headfirst into the shield and howled with pain, clutching their heads.

But at the same time, Freja swayed and sank to the ground. The force of the shield spell had drained all magic from her body. Tamarka and Morkel caught her arms and hauled her to her feet.

"Quick, let's go!" Tamarka shouted. "Before the shield crumbles."

The mages, princes, and soldiers ran toward the drawbridge. While Freja's shield had blocked most trolls within a ten-yard range of the healer's ward, about a dozen trolls were still lurking on the grounds. They lumbered after the humans with snarls and shrieks, their huge feet making deep prints on the ground.

Alix's heart beat fast, adrenaline coursing through her veins. She was ahead of them all, but she was unwilling to be the first to cross the drawbridge. Theo was in the rear with the mages, his sword glistening with troll blood.

"Come on!" Claudia shouted from the other side of the bridge. Sybil stood next to her, tense and anxious, her gaze focused on Gerald, who had sustained multiple injuries from his battle.

Freja, who was still weak from casting the shield spell, was among the first to cross, supported by the soldiers. Drained of magic, she couldn't protest. Theo and Gerald followed, though they kept looking back. Morkel and Tamarka came last, as they could project magical attacks from a decent range. Morkel was limping, but he stayed near Tamarka, firing jets of magic at the trolls who were trying to follow them.

Crack. A troll landed a heavy, claw-like foot on the draw-bridge. Morkel and Tamarka were only halfway through.

"HURRY!"

Theo darted forward. Grabbing Morkel's arm, he dragged the mage across the bridge. Tamarka managed to throw out a ball of fiery magic that caught the troll in the stomach. It roared and fell down, but its ape-like arm shot out and caught her ankle.

Tamarka screamed. Alix felt in her pockets—there was a second poisoned knife from Beatrice, after she used the first one to rescue Theo. She hurried over and plunged the knife into the troll's arm. In her haste, her hood fell off, revealing her head.

The poison worked instantly. The troll snarled, but its arm became numb—its fingers loosened on Tamarka's ankle. Alix grabbed the mage's arm and they rushed over the bridge to safety.

Once they reached the other end, Alix collapsed. A second later, Theo seized her, his expression livid.

"Don't you ever risk your life again!" He glared, his hand tightening around her waist. Then he raised his head and shouted, "Destroy the bridge!"

Two soldiers with axes came forward.

"Here!" Freja was still on the ground, but she held out a pearl-white ball the size of a goose egg. "It's an exploding spell."

Theo threw the spell.

It struck the poisoned troll on the head and a loud boom sounded. Body parts of the troll, along with wooden planks, fell into the moat below. On the other side, the trolls shrieked in disbelief and despair, but they could not cross the moat, just as they were unable to make past the lake lined with silver trees. While the trolls weren't afraid of water, they couldn't swim. One slid down to the moat and tried to wade across, but fortunately the waters were deep enough. It drowned, arms flailing, and eventually disappeared, leaving a trail of bubbles on the surface.

Queen Marguerite was sobbing quietly. Claudia put an arm around her and glanced at Theo. "The moat will hold them off, but it won't be long before they build a bridge. We must be prepared when they pour into the city."

"Where're we only going?" Alix asked.

"Le Gris' house."

CHAPTER 35

G abi sat on the floor, her heart pounding. An explosion —was it Alrik? Did he use the spell she gave him?

Gasps came from outside. She grabbed the table edge and hauled herself to her feet. Crossing to the other side of the room, she peered out of the window.

Smoke was coming from the gates in the wall. Sorcha was striding toward a Sisu man. Sparks flew; the man was blasted to a tree, hit his head, and sank to the ground.

Seeing how Sorcha used her magic, Gabi was furious. No wonder the Sisu dreaded the witches' reign. They treated the Sisu like cattle to be slaughtered.

"STOP!" someone shouted.

A tall young man dashed to the Sisu's side. He turned and faced Sorcha, and Gabi's heart felt like leaping out of her chest.

Alrik.

Gabi put a hand to her mouth; seeing him alive and well made her want to cry. But her immense relief was soon replaced by intense fear. He confronted Sorcha when the witch was in a foul mood—one wrong word and he could be injured. And she barely had any magic left; she was powerless to protect him.

Footsteps came on the stairs outside. Flinging the door open, Gabi slipped out as fast as her crippled foot would let her. She darted in the opposite direction of the stairs and flattened herself against a wall.

"Get moving," a cold, ruthless voice said.

Moira had returned.

"He can't see," a female voice said.

Gabi put a hand to her mouth. Lorenza was speaking. Her heart sank to the soles of her shoes.

Despite the risk, Gabi tried to peek from behind the wall. Moira, her hair slightly in disarray and her robes splattered with mud, was heading toward the room where Sorcha had locked her up. Lorenza and Julong, both of their hands bound, were stumbling in front of her. Lorenza had a gash on her sleeve, revealing a nasty wound that dribbled blood, while Julong was limping on his right foot.

It had to be the Peerless Knife. Gabi refused to believe that Moira was so powerful that she could disable two mages on her own.

The door was thrown open—in her victorious mood, Moira hadn't noticed the door was unlocked.

"Inside," she barked. "You'd make good company for that Masaro girl…" Her voice died away, as if she were suddenly hit by a silencing charm. Despite the precarious situation, Gabi couldn't resist a grin. It was satisfying that Moira was rendered temporarily speechless.

The next moment, the witch stormed out of the room. "Sorcha!"

Gabi shrank back against the wall. The younger witch rushed up the stairs, her face pale.

"She's gone," Moira said, pointing at the room Gabi was locked in. "You fool—how could you let her get away?"

Sorcha blanched. "I…I don't know. But sister, there's something you have to know. Tyrell's son…he's dead."

Gabi stifled a scream. Alrik was still alive a moment ago! Did Sorcha kill him?

"DEAD?" Moira's hair seemed to crackle as her voice echoed through the walls. "How did it happen?"

"He killed himself," Sorcha said, her voice shaky. "He set off an explosion—he had a bomb spell hidden somewhere, and when I caught him, he used one of the ice shards from the explosion to kill himself."

Darkness clotted her vision for a moment. Gabi blinked; the room gradually returned to focus. Leaning against the wall, she breathed in deeply.

He can't be dead, she told herself. She didn't come all the way to Sisu, only to find that he committed suicide. It was ridiculous. Alrik wouldn't do that. If he were dead, it had to be Moira's doings. He wouldn't hurt himself; they had taught him that even a small scratch could be deadly.

"Bring me the body," Moira was saying. "I must see that he's truly dead."

There was a shuffling noise; Gabi spied four Sisu carrying Alrik's body.

A moment passed. Moira bent over Alrik's body, her hands glowing with magic. Gabi felt her palms grow moist.

"He isn't dead," Moira pronounced, straightening. "But he's unconscious, and I can't prod him awake."

"Probably it's a poison he swallowed," Sorcha said. "I say that we might as well kill him and dispose of his body. I always suspected he was pretending to go along with the wedding. Better get rid of him than having a thorn by your side."

"Not so fast. He's the Arksan prince; he can still be useful. If he is revived, I can use him to make Tyrell bend. He'll do anything to save his precious son."

"I still think it's unwise," Sorcha said. "Have you forgotten what happened when we allowed the Savon prince to live?"

"We allowed him to live because we needed him to lift Sybil's curse at that time," Moira said curtly. "Do not worry, sis. Wait three days; if the prince does not regain consciousness, then you may do whatever you like. Toss him into the river or let the wolves have him."

"What about the wedding?"

"Let the slaves think the prince is currently unwell. Shut him in the spare room. And find the Masaro girl."

"How did she escape?" Sorcha made a noise of disbelief. "She doesn't have any magic left! Wait till I get my hands on her—she can't have gone far!"

"We'll find her," Moira said. "But first you need to secure those two others before they attempt to escape as well. Once you drain them of their magic, the girl won't be a problem."

Gabi flattened herself against the wall. She had to get out of here. Luckily Sorcha and Moira had more important things to deal with. When the noises died down, she ventured into the corridor. Moira had disappeared, though there were sounds coming from the prison chamber where she broke out using the pin. Sorcha must be setting up the equipment to suck out Lorenza's and Julong's magic.

Slowly, Gabi made the painful journey to the stairs. Her heart hammered fast when she passed the door where Sorcha was—there was no other route to the stairs. Time seemed to stretch for hours.

When her feet touched the landing on the first floor, Gabi breathed a sigh of relief. She was exhausted—mentally and physically. But she couldn't afford to relax. Moira and Sorcha were upstairs, and could be coming down at any minute.

There was a smaller tower in the corner of the grounds. Gabi hauled herself to the tower—it was probably used as some kind of storage.

She was correct: it was filled with logs—necessary for the nearly permanent winter here.

Gabi shut the door and hid herself behind the tallest pile,

panting. Her throat was dry and she longed for a drink. But she had a moment to rest and think. The time spent since she freed herself was excruciating.

Alrik was unconscious. She could only think of one explanation: he was "sleeping." Today was his twenty-first birthday—somehow, whether deliberately or not, he had bled and fell into the cursed sleep. If she could reach him, she'd be able to save him with her kiss.

The idea was enticing, but Gabi forced herself to think beyond what might happen next. Even if she saved Alrik, it was impossible to escape Moira and Sorcha. Even if she had magic, she was no match for the power of two witches, not to mention the Peerless Knife.

Without magic, there was no way she could save the prince. The only solution: she had to free Lorenza and Julong before their magic was sucked dry. She needed their help.

Gabi felt in her pocket for the reassuring hardness of the pin. Right now, this tiny pin was more precious than a cellar filled with gold.

Clasping her hands together, Gabi prayed for strength. Alrik's face filled her mind, his smile bright, flirtatious, inviting. She imagined his arms around her body, his voice filled with joy when he outlined his hope for their future together.

You can do this, Gabi.

Gabi rose to her feet. She couldn't walk fast, but she barely noticed. She walked as if having a crippled foot was the most normal thing in the world. Her entire brain was focused on getting to Lorenza and Julong without being caught.

Outside the tower, Gabi gathered a handful of snow and stuffed it into her mouth. The iciness of the snow cleared her head and the moisture soothed her parched throat. It wasn't as ideal as a glass of water or a mug of hot tea, but it was better than nothing.

Gabi made her way back to the main tower. While passing

the room where the seamstresses were working on the wedding apparel, she heard Moira and Sorcha's voices. She halted and ducked behind an ice sculpture shaped into a wolf.

"You already have the knife," Sorcha was saying. "You should let me have those two mages' magic."

"You were stupid enough to let the girl get away when she didn't have any magic left," Moira sneered.

"I'll find her!" Sorcha seethed. "She's got to be hiding somewhere."

"Then bring her head back. Standing here isn't going to achieve anything. Capture her, and I might consider letting you have those two mages' magic."

Footsteps faded away. Gabi crept out of her hiding place, just in time to see the ends of Sorcha's robe disappear around the corner.

A bead of sweat trickled down her spine. Making sure that no one was nearby, Gabi made her way upstairs, ignoring her sweaty hands.

Never had she wished that she could move as easily as a normal person. The journey seemed to take forever, and once she reached the second floor, she felt like collapsing, not from exhaustion but stress. So much was at stake.

Gabi wondered where Alrik was kept in. But the more time it took to set Lorenza and Julong free, the more their magic would be drained.

The door was locked. Gabi used her pin and within seconds the lock sprang open. Luckily, here in Sisu, their locks weren't too complicated. Her elementary lock-picking skills were enough.

Gabi raised her hand to push the door open. But somehow, she couldn't move her hand. Something thick and heavy wrapped around her arm and wrist—ropes had appeared and bound her tight.

"So that was how you got out of those chains." Sorcha's voice, triumphant and mocking, floated in the air.

Gabi froze.

"Did you take me for a fool?" Sorcha said. She snapped her fingers, and more ropes sprang out, binding Gabi's entire body. "I saw you emerge from the tower, and I knew you'd try to save your friends."

Gabi tried to summon magic, no matter how little she had left, but the ropes merely loosened a fraction. Sorcha noticed this and snapped her fingers again. Gabi almost cried out when the ropes tightened around her body, to the point that she almost couldn't breathe.

"Better shut you up in another room," Sorcha said. "I can't have you opening the locks again." She plucked the pin from the door's lock and slipped it into her pocket.

Gabi was doomed.

At that moment, the door was blasted open. Lorenza and Julong stood in the doorway, both of them with sparks shimmering on their hands.

"How did you..." The words were barely out of Sorcha's throat before Julong raised his hands and a bunch of darts flew through the air, pelting toward her with alarming speed. Sorcha ducked—it was too late for her to conjure a magic shield—but one dart caught her squarely on her forearm, drawing blood.

"You forgot we were also in Finsoor," Lorenza said. Both she and Julong looked normal; no chains in sight. "I foresaw that this might happen to us—that if we were taken captive you'd suck magic from us, just like you did to your father. So while we were in Linberg, we put our heads together, and with a little help from your father, we were able to arm ourselves with a counter-charm that repelled the magic-draining spell."

"Why didn't you let me know?" Gabi felt hurt, also rather miffed, that they hadn't bothered to tell her about the counter-charm.

"Sorry," Lorenza said. "It was a highly risky spell, and we had no idea if it would work. We never intended to use it unless absolutely necessary. If it failed, both Julong and I would be seriously injured."

"Let's find the prince," Julong said

Lorenza held a hand over Sorcha's heart. Ice-blue sparks shimmered from her fingers. "Where's Prince Alrik?"

As a mage, Gabi knew that the sparks were just as bad, if not worse, as holding a weapon over Sorcha's heart. Once Lorenza released her magic, the sparks would pierce Sorcha's body like several daggers.

The witch flinched. "It's no use. He's unconscious and nothing we do can make him wake up."

"No matter," Gabi said. "We can't let you have his body. Where is he?"

Sorcha's gaze flickered to Lorenza's hand for a second. "Second door to the right."

"If we find out you're lying, we'll drain your magic as well." Lorenza uttered a few words, and the ropes around Gabi's body flew to Sorcha, binding her instead.

"And what exactly do we have here?" a voice said softly.

Gabi's blood turned cold. Moira stood behind them, her robes flapping in the wind. Head tilted and brow furrowed, she looked more curious than enraged.

"How did you escape? Sorcha is incompetent, but even I cannot believe she'd fail to lock up you two," she said to Lorenza and Julong, then finished with a gesture to Gabi, "after letting *you* escape."

"We have been careless when you captured us," Lorenza said. Her arms were pressed to her sides, but sparks shimmered, as she readied herself to attack. "But this time we will not let you off easily."

"Twenty years," Julong added. "Twenty years I have been longing for revenge, and I will not let the chance slip away."

"Fools," Moira cackled. "Do you think you'd stand a chance against me?"

No. But Gabi wasn't going to give the witch the satisfaction by speaking out loud. Instead, she glanced around, taking in the surroundings and hoping for some way she could slip around Moira and reach Alrik.

"Gabriella," Lorenza said in a low voice. "Julong and I will hold her off. You need to get the prince and get out of here."

"No one is going to leave this place alive," Moira said, raising her hands. The sparks on her hands formed into a huge ball the size of a watermelon. Gabi put a hand to her mouth. The larger the ball, the more powerful the magic it contained. She had never seen any mage, not even the evil mage who killed her parents, cast a ball of magic of this size.

Most mages could only make flame-like magic shimmer on their fingers, but Moira was able to achieve this because she drew power from the Peerless Knife.

The witch attacked. The ball of magic came hurtling through the air—Gabi smelled something like smoke, as if the ball was made of fire. They ducked; both Lorenza and Gabi threw out an arm to Julong, though his hearing was astute enough that he was on the floor before they reached him.

BOOM! A large hole appeared in the wall where the ball of magic struck. Down in the courtyard, there were yelps of pain.

"How long do you think you can keep hiding?" Moira hissed. Magic channeled through the knife concealed in her pocket; the sparks in her hands gradually became a new, bigger ball.

"Can't you summon the knife?" Gabi gasped. As long as Moira controlled the knife and the unlimited magic it contained, they had no chance.

Lorenza shook her head. "We tried that when she hunted us down. Moira has placed a strong adhesive spell around the knife; it won't budge an inch. Watch out!"

During the few seconds of their conversation, Moira had

finished setting up her new attack. The ball of magic was aimed at them crouching on the floor; Gabi rolled to the right while Lorenza grabbed Julong and rolled to the left.

BAM! The ball struck the table they were hiding under; wooden pieces flew everywhere. Lorenza and Julong created a shimmering shield that kept them safe, but Gabi didn't have any magic. Several pieces of wood hit her; one was particularly sharp and embedded squarely in her shoulder. Blood dripped down her arm.

"Gabriella!" Lorenza cried, alarmed.

But she barely felt any pain. The black bowls and tubes that were used on Lorenza and Julong crashed to the floor. They were made of a peculiar hard substance and did not even crack.

On sudden inspiration, Gabi grabbed the black bowl and tube. "Lorenza!"

The other mage understood immediately. Gabi tossed the bowl and tube to her; Lorenza threw the items at Moira. Magic guided the bowl and tube to the knife hilt. Gabi snatched one of the jars in the corner and jammed the tube into the jar.

"Now!"

Lorenza grasped the tube, her hands glowing. She uttered a few words. Magic, silvery and liquid, flowed into the jar.

Thunderstruck, Moira made to pry the bowl off the Peerless Knife.

"Help me!" Lorenza nudged Julong, and he placed his hand over hers. His magic fueled hers, and the bowl remained stuck firmly on the knife. Unable to channel power from the knife, Moira could not defeat two mages at the same time.

This was Gabi's chance.

She struggled to her feet and launched herself at Moira. Moira threw up a bolt of magic—she was still a witch even if she could not use the Peerless Knife's power—but Gabi was prepared for it and ducked in time.

Julong made his move. His right hand was still aiding

Lorenza, but his left hand was free. Plunging his free hand into his robes, he extracted three gleaming daggers. He flung them through the air—one at Moira's neck, one at her chest, the last one at her abdomen.

Moira raised her hands and cast a shimmering shield. The first two daggers struck the shield and bounced off, clinking on the ground. However, the third dagger was wedged in the shield, which glimmered and vanished.

With a cry, Gabi grabbed the two daggers that fell on the ground. With both hands, she drove the daggers into Moira's chest.

The witch gasped; her knees buckled.

"Stand back, Gabriella," Julong said quietly. "Let me be the one to finish this."

She remembered his story, about how his blindness was a consequence of a battle with Moira. She remembered in his culture, revenge was of paramount importance. There was a saying that it wasn't too late to take ten years to seek revenge.

So she stepped aside. Julong headed to Moira.

He spoke something softly—Gabi didn't hear what he was saying, but a moment later, Moira dropped to the ground in a heap. The witch looked deathly pale, eyes tightly closed.

"Is she dead?"

"No," Julong said. "But I stripped her of any ability to wield magic."

"Urdu had sealed Moira's magic, but she regained it," Gabi said.

"This is a special enchantment from Lulan," Julong said with a ruthless smirk. "What I did to her was different from what Urdu tried. If Moira tries to use magic, she'd have trouble breathing. Magic is no different from a gag to her now."

"Make sure to do the same thing to her sister," Lorenza said. "Where're you going?"

"I need to find Alrik."

Gabi's feet felt like lead, blood was still running down her arm, and she was exhausted after the battle, but she couldn't rest. Not when Alrik was still in his cursed sleep.

She hurried to the room as fast as her crippled foot would allow her. She was so eager to see Alrik that she almost tripped. Two Sisu were guarding the entrance, but they parted once she told them that Moira and Sorcha were no longer able to cast magic.

Alrik was lying on a bed covered with silk and velvet. Gabi had no idea how the Sisu procured these materials when all they had were reindeer skins, but perhaps there had been some trade between the Sisu and Arksan travelers. His hands were crossed on his chest, and he looked so peaceful as he slept.

Her Alrik.

The love she felt for him was so strong that she was tempted to imagine a future of them together. Once he woke up, they could return to Brek and live an ordinary life. He didn't have to go to Linberg.

He's the prince of Arksar, her mind repeated. *He needs to return to his family. Be happy that you enjoyed those years with him.*

Gabi went to the bed and sat on the spread. His hand lay near her thigh and she touched his fingers. They were warm.

Would she be able to wake him up? Theoretically, she should be the one. He had declared he loved her.

Heart pounding, Gabi leaned over him. Praying that Freja's magic would work, she bent her head and kissed him.

Heat blossomed, flowing from her lips to his. The paleness disappeared from Alrik's face, and a rosy glow appeared in his cheeks. His breathing became deeper, and as she pulled back, she saw his eyelashes flutter. The next second, his eyes were wide and open, staring at her with utter surprise.

"Gabi?" He blinked. "Why...how did you get here?"

She threw her arms around him and buried her face into his neck, laughing and crying. "It worked! It worked! You're alive!"

His arms closed around her body, as if it were the most natural reaction in the world. Then he drew back, looking alarmed.

"You've been hurt," he said, staring at the red stain on her arm. It was a minor injury, but he looked as if she were stabbed through the heart. "Who did this to you? Was it that witch? I swear, once I get my hands on her…"

"Don't worry; Julong has taken care of her." She kissed him again. It still felt surreal, especially with the ice walls around them. "There was a battle, but everything's all right now."

"Tell me everything."

She gave him the details while he bandaged her arm. When she finished, he pulled her close, resting his chin on her shoulder.

Nothing was said between them; they simply savored the precious moment together.

"I see that true love's kiss has worked," Lorenza said, appearing in the doorway with a smile. Next to her, Julong also wore an affable grin. "Congratulations."

"But we can't rest yet. The trolls are still in Savony. We must head south immediately."

CHAPTER 36

$\mathcal{A}$lix rolled up her sleeves and tied a kerchief over her head, copying what Sybil did. For the past few days since they arrived at Le Gris' house, she had been assisting Sybil with producing the freezing spell.

Le Gris' banishment proved to be surprisingly useful. Since the chancellor was found to be traitorous to the crown, his property and assets were seized and became public property. It was a huge structure of stone and marble, enough to house at least a hundred people.

Under Theo's orders, the servants who had families in the city were ordered to return to their families, while the rest crowded inside the chancellor's former residence. The entire first floor was converted into a healer's ward and kitchen, due to the large number of people injured. Beatrice, Odeon, and the other healers took turns tending to the injured, along with assistance from Ferdinand and several volunteers.

"For each spell, I need eight ounces of stone." Sybil pointed to the scales on a nearby table. "Measure ten servings, please, and arrange them in piles."

"How did you become so good at spell making?" Alix asked.

When the twelve princes were under the curse, only Gerald was a decent magic user and was in charge of making defensive spells to help them survive the trolls' attacks.

Sybil stirred the cauldron without looking up. "Plenty of practice. And also the need to create beautifying spells."

"Beautifying spells? For someone like you?"

"When I was cursed, my skin was gray and covered with scales. Men used to look upon me with desire, but after the curse, they'd run away screaming." Sybil dropped a block of ice into the cauldron. "I spent years trying to look human and failing."

"Tell me more."

By the time they finished creating ten freezing spells, Sybil also finished telling Alix the entire story of how Gerald and she ended up together. It was such an intriguing story that twice Alix forgot to hand Sybil ice or stone.

"Done." Sybil stretched and yawned. "My, it's easier to get tired when your body is no longer a beast."

"I'll take these to Theo," Alix offered. She had taken a nap earlier (Theo insisted), and it did a whole world of difference. "Suppose you go upstairs and rest for a while."

Alix packed the jars carefully in a leather satchel and went downstairs. On the first floor, Odeon and two healers were tending to the patients.

"Have you seen Theo?"

"He's in the gardens." Odeon carried a roll of bandages to a table. "With his brothers."

Alix headed outside. A curious sight met her eyes. Ethan and Enzo were plodding across a bed of grass, trampling dandelions and daisies under their feet. Ethan made a grunt that sounded surprisingly troll-like. Julian was carrying a bucket of water. He tossed the water at their feet—the twins let out a simultaneous grunt and stopped moving.

Freja stepped forward and uttered a few words. A word

appeared on Ethan's forehead, spelling out his name. The same happened to Enzo.

Two collars flashed through the air and settled around the twins' necks. Freja muttered a string of words, ending with a brief command, "Levitate!"

The twins were lifted off the ground, their feet dangling in the air.

Freja turned to Theo, who was leaning against the wall of a tool shed. "How many seconds?" she asked.

"Ten."

The mage frowned. "Too long. A troll might be able to rip off the collar in six or seven seconds."

Theo pushed off the wall, looking worried. "Can you speak faster?"

"It won't be easy. Every word must be spoken clearly to make the spell work, so there's a limit to how fast I can talk." Freja pursed her lips. "Or I could try strengthening the collars—have you a spell that can make the leather tougher? Like the defensive spells used on shields."

"I'll ask Gerald," Theo said, walking away.

"Hey!" Enzo yelled. "We're still up here! Put us down!"

"Sorry." Freja clicked her fingers and the twins landed on the ground in a heap.

Although she knew they were simulating a real battle, Alix had to smile. She approached Theo, but before she could tell him about the spells, footsteps sounded.

Odeon appeared. "Has any of you seen Beatrice? She should have come for her shift an hour ago."

"Did she go out?"

"She mentioned that she was going to get more herbs at the apothecary," Odeon said. "Ferdinand went with her—he's not back either?"

"We haven't seen him anywhere."

Odeon paled. "Do you think they might have...might be in danger?"

"I don't think it's likely," Theo said, though his fingers curled into a fist for a second before letting go. "We'll go look for them. Perhaps Beatrice made a detour to see a friend."

"We'll come with you," Enzo said. Ethan nodded. "The more of us, the sooner we'll find them."

"I'll come as well," Alix said. "I have been indoors all day. I could use a walk."

Theo looked surprised but held out his hand. "Very well."

Just at that moment, a figure burst into the gardens.

"Theo!" Ferdinand hurried toward them. Sweat coated his hair; his face was red from running. "Beatrice...she...I..."

Odeon stepped closer, looking anxious. "What happened to Beatrice?"

"She..." Ferdinand's shoulders shook. "Grevik got her."

"Who?"

"A troll. The one who used to be in charge of the duels when we were under the curse."

Alix covered her mouth. The twins looked at each other in mirrored horrified expressions. Odeon swayed; Freja caught his arm.

"What does the troll want?" Freja said. "If it captured Beatrice but did not kill her, it must have a request."

"It wants to talk to you, Theo," Ferdinand said. "It's...it's at the northeast side, near the opera house."

Theo set his jaw. "Then let's not keep it waiting."

* * *

THE OPERA HOUSE was located northeast of the capital, a short distance from the main road that led to the castle. A large fountain stood in the square in front of the opera house. About a dozen yards from the fountain was a statue of King Antoine built upon a large elevated pedestal.

When they arrived, Alix noticed that the statue lay in pieces on the ground. Grevik stood on the stone pedestal. He had one arm around Beatrice's body, while his other hand was wrapped around her slender neck. Behind Grevik was a mountain of trolls gathered on the steps leading up to the opera house.

It had happened sooner than they expected. The trolls had crossed the moat and entered the city.

"Finally," Grevik smirked. Most trolls weren't intelligent enough to learn human speech, but Grevik spoke as fluently as any well-educated Savon. Alix always had a sneaking suspicion that it was Grevik who found out how to mix poison and use it in battle with Theo. "How about we make an agreement?"

Ferdinand looked like he wanted to chop off Grevik's head. Ethan and Enzo held his arms, preventing him from springing forward and doing something rash. One slight pressure from the troll's fingers could squeeze the life out of Beatrice.

"What kind of agreement?" Theo said slowly. Alix sensed that he was trying to remain calm—a tough restraint for his temper.

"Do you know this is the same place where my ancestor made a deal with your ancestor? That time, it was your king who wanted an agreement. Today, I am going to ask for one."

"Name your terms."

Theo was trying to stall for time. Ferdinand inched forward, but one troll let out a growl. Grevik noticed, and his fingers tightened around Beatrice's throat, causing her to cough and splutter.

"Don't any of you come any closer!" he shouted. "If any of you try to save her, she'll be dead in a few seconds."

Ferdinand held up his hands, his face as white as a ghost. "We promise."

For a moment, everything was quiet except for the running water gushing from the fountain.

Water. Alix had ten freezing spells in her bag, spells she just created with Sybil. The bag also contained her invisibility cloak. Since the first breakout of trolls, Alix always carried her cloak on her, except for the time when she lent it to Tamarka.

Alix looked up. Fortunately, she was small enough that the princes and soldiers blocked her from the trolls. Slipping quietly to the rear of their group, she pulled out her invisibility cloak and put it on. Tiptoeing to the fountain, she emptied a jar into it. The spell dissolved in a flash—the waters glittered—but as the sun was shining, the trolls didn't sense anything unusual.

"No," Theo was saying. "This is unreasonable."

"I see it as leniency," Grevik said, with a nasty grin. "I said I was going to let you live. You and your brothers. All I want is for you to surrender your city to us. My people survived on rats and rushes for years—so many years. All we want is to have a nice meal after all the hardships we have suffered."

"My people are not to be subjected to your torture and slaughter."

"Said with righteous fury." Grevik's tone was mocking. "And yet, you slaughter pigs and cattle without compassion. You are no different from us, Prince of Savony. Listen, you and your brothers can walk away with your lives unharmed. You have been fighting to stay alive all these years; we will show you mercy for your efforts. But if you refuse, none of you can leave this city alive. So, what will it be?"

By this time, Alix had emptied all jars into the fountain. Carefully scooping up some water into a jar, Alix flung the spell-infused water at Grevik's arm. Instantly, a layer of ice formed over the troll's skin.

She pulled down her hood and gestured wildly. "Get him!"

The next second, Grevik let out a grunt of pain. His grip on Beatrice loosened; she fell on the pedestal.

There was an arrow stuck in Grevik's eye, and blood was pouring down his fingers. A figure stood on the balcony of a building facing the opera house. It was Sybil, holding a bow and arrow. The young woman had mentioned that when she was a beast, she had hunted in the mountains. It looked like she had retained her archery skills.

Shouts and yells rose in the air. Her heart pounding furiously, Alix ran toward the pedestal, just when Grevik batted the ice away from his arm. She grabbed Beatrice, who had scrambled to the ground, and flung the cloak around them both.

Grevik roared and lunged at them. Although they were invisible, his arm was long enough that his fingers caught the ends of her cloak. A loud ripping—the cloak was snatched away—she and Beatrice were exposed.

Something spun through the air, heading toward Grevik. A leather collar studded with metal. It attached around the troll's neck. Freja stepped forward and shouted, "Show your name!"

A word appeared on the troll's forehead—*Grevetorik*.

Freja placed her hands together as if she were praying, and began to chant. "Powers of sea and sky, banish the creature *Grevetorik* to the remote region where it came from. Begone!"

Grevik let out a yell. It clutched on the collar, but couldn't rip it off. White mist enveloped its body—poof! The troll vanished in thin air; the mist evaporated and disappeared.

Someone whistled—was it Ethan or Enzo? Considering the previous bloody battles they had with the trolls, this method certainly was more effective.

Alix barely had time to retrieve her cloak. She ran back to Theo and told him that she had poured the spells into the fountain. Ferdinand caught Beatrice in a bone-crushing embrace, telling her to run for safety, before unsheathing his sword.

The battle had begun.

Like a mass of black ants, the trolls stood up and charged.

They ran down the stone steps of the opera house, their faces contorted with fury and bloodlust.

"Stand back!" Freja shouted, handing collars to Tamarka and Morkel.

The mages formed a triangle, while the soldiers and princes behind them surrounded the fountain. The latter unhooked their water skins, filling the skins with the magic-infused water, and tossed it onto the trolls. The mages would get the trolls' names, use the collars, and then chant the transportation spell.

But there were too many trolls, and too little time. One by one, the trolls in the front vanished, leaving wisps of white mist, but at least two dozen made it past the mages and escaped into the city.

Screams of anguish. Grunts of pain. Yells of warning. Alix barely could pause or think, as she kept filling her own water skin and trying to freeze as many trolls as possible. Most of the time, the trolls would break free of ice on their body parts, but it was enough to halt their movements and lessen the damage. And with her cloak, she could sneak up unexpected at the trolls. A troll which had grabbed Julian's foot was forced to let go, when her freezing spell formed a thick layer of ice around its wrist.

But wearing the cloak was not without risks.

A troll with an unusually keen sense of smell snatched away her cloak, tearing the material from her body, and she gasped in surprise and horror. It looked upon her, fury in its bulbous yellow eyes.

"You," it spat. "You caused so much trouble for us. We were nearly there. We could have crossed the lake, but you had to cut off the tree. And now, you shall pay."

It raised its hand, claw-like fingernails gleaming in the air. Alix closed her eyes. Theo and the other soldiers were held up by the other trolls. No one was close enough to save her, not even Sybil.

But the killing blow never came.

Alix opened her eyes. The troll stood like stone, several daggers buried in different parts of his body. It twitched, then crashed to the ground.

"Don't touch it," a voice said. "My daggers are fed with poison. It's a surefire way to kill a troll when one wound is usually insufficient."

It was a man with smooth dark hair and fine features. He reached into his robes and more daggers appeared, wedged between his fingers.

"Find a safe place, little one," he said. "We will handle this."

Help had arrived.

Freja had talked about the other mages she invited to fight the trolls. This must be Julong, the mage from Lulan, who could wield several weapons at once.

"Don't use your flying weapons unless necessary," a woman said. She had olive skin and dark eyes—a Masaro. Which meant she must be Lorenza. "There are too many trolls. You'd run out of weapons."

"Stand back, all of you." An old man stepped forward, his arms stretched out, with glowing balls of magic on his palms. Leather collars studded with metal hung from his arms like huge loopy bracelets. Urdu, the one who invented the powerful counter curse.

Urdu let out a cry. Twelve collars flew through the air and found twelve trolls' necks. The trolls' names were revealed. Urdu chanted so fast that no one could hear what he was saying, but it was efficient all the same.

Poof. Poof. More poofs.

Twelve trolls vanished in a puff of smoke. For the first time since she arrived at the opera house, Alix felt relieved. With three powerful mages joining the battle, they'd stand a better chance against the trolls.

* * *

Sʏʙɪʟ ꜱᴛᴏᴏᴅ ᴡᴀᴛᴄʜɪɴɢ from the balcony. In the beginning she was able to kill with her bow and arrow, but as the trolls and humans clashed, she was reluctant to shoot anymore, afraid that her arrow would find one of the soldiers instead.

Now and then she looked for Gerald. Luckily, her fiancé was an experienced fighter, and despite some minor injuries, he seemed to be holding up well. She also saw that Urdu, Lorenza, and Julong had arrived, joining in the battle. Urdu seemed to have recovered from his imprisonment in the Finsoor islands. He was the fastest of them all, firing collars and banishing trolls with amazing speed.

Perhaps she should go downstairs. She had several freezing spells; they could be used on the trolls that escaped into the city.

But just as she put down her bow and arrow, there was a huge, booming sound, followed by terrified screams..

Sybil froze. A gigantic troll came trudging toward the opera house, leaving craters the size of round tables on the ground. It was so tall that it seemed like a tower itself. When it passed her (she was on the top balcony of a five-story building), she was at eye level with its shoulder. Even the other seven-foot trolls seemed like dwarves.

How could they take this troll down?

CHAPTER 37

For a moment, the world around Sybil went dark. The giant troll's shadow blocked out the sun. It raised its foot. A huge, sickening crunch followed, as it trampled three soldiers, rendering them into minced meat.

Boom! The troll punched a building near the opera house. Pillars shook. Walls crumbled. Screams came from the building. The troll bent and fished out a man, who screamed and struggled. It bit the man's head off, blood and bones flying everywhere.

Sybil screamed, catching the troll's attention. It turned and faced her, its jaws pulled wide into a manic grin, the unfortunate man's blood smeared over its lips.

She had to run. But she couldn't move—the shock and fright had paralyzed her legs. The troll reached out toward her, its fingers as thick as the branches of a tree, reaching to wrap around her body.

Arrows flew fast and thick, but they all bounced off the giant troll's body, which seemed similar to a coat of armor. Jets of magic hit the troll's body—it grunted in pain, but its hand didn't stop. It knocked away the balustrade—pieces of stone fell away

—Sybil was going to be crushed under its strength at any moment…

A horse galloped to the giant troll. A mage with brown hair and olive skin raised her arm, a black dagger gleaming in her hand. Power burst from the blade and hit the troll's wrist. It yelped and clutched its wrist, which was red and covered with blisters.

Sybil had never seen this mage, but she recognized the Peerless Knife. Moira was the last person who had the knife. Which meant that this young woman must be Gabriella, Freja's niece, who was supposed to save the Arksan prince from Moira.

"Over here!" Urdu shouted. "We need to band together to vanquish this troll!"

Gabi spurred the horse forward and reached the other mages in a matter of seconds. The seven mages formed a semicircle and held up their arms. Magic in several colors and shades burst from their palms—in Gabi's case, she also provided magic from the Peerless Knife—and seven collars were merged together, producing an enormous collar.

The collar flew toward the giant troll and wound around its neck. The troll roared and tried to tear off the collar, but Gabi, wielding the knife, fired huge balls of magic that burned the troll's hands, leaving them blackened and charred.

Urdu chanted. A word formed on the troll's forehead: *Joringa*.

"Powers of sea and sky, banish the creature Joringa to the remote region where it came from. Begone!"

With an earsplitting roar, the gigantic troll disappeared. The mist left behind was so large that no one was able to see or do anything until it dissipated.

Sybil sank to the floor, feeling like she had aged ten years. A piece of stone that remained from the balustrade cracked and dropped to the ground five stories below. Realizing the balcony was unstable, she scrambled back inside.

Halfway down the stairs, she met Gerald. His face was pale, his clothes covered with dirt and blood. But when he smiled—a smile radiant with relief and happiness—she had never seen him so beautiful. The next second, she found herself in his arms, his cheek damp against hers.

"You're alive," he whispered, his voice hoarse.

"So are you."

* * *

GABI LOWERED THE PEERLESS KNIFE. A troll lay nearby, head severed, blood spilling over the ground. Hopefully, this was the last one. She sheathed the knife and tucked it into her belt. Good thing that she retrieved it from Moira. The infinite power from the ancient weapon was mind-blowing. And it was only because she had the knife that she was able to convince Alrik to stay in Arksar. He had been determined to accompany her to Savony, but after nearly losing him to the witches, she was adamant that he stay in Linberg. He argued like a housewife trying to drive a bargain in the market. Only when she destroyed one of Moira's ice towers, using the power of the knife, had Alrik finally agreed to let her go.

Brushing a strand of sweat-soaked hair from her face, she looked around. Bodies—battered, bruised, and broken—scattered around the ground. Cracked blocks of wood and stone lay separated from houses. Somewhere a lone child wailed like a wounded kitten, until a neighbor came and comforted her.

A magnificent horse galloped into the wrecked marketplace she was in. Freja appeared. As she normally looked like a middle-aged working woman, her position on the horse looked rather incongruous.

"I didn't know you could ride," Gabi said.

Freja rode to her side. "I couldn't very well make Alrik suspicious. A village woman might be able to know how to mix spells, but it would be unusual if she could ride a horse."

"You can't fool him anymore, now that he knows the truth. Did you happen to banish a troll close by?"

"No, I came to look for you. I believe we have banished every troll in the capital, though a few could have escaped into the countryside." Freja jerked a finger in the direction of the opera house. "Suppose we head back to the princes?"

Gabi was glad to comply. She longed to dismount after riding all the way from Arksar.

"So how did you defeat Moira?" Freja said, glancing at the Peerless Knife strapped on Gabi's belt. "Was Alrik harmed?"

Gabi related how they pursued Moira in Sisu, and how she worked with Lorenza and Julong to take down the witches. By the time she finished, they had arrived back at the opera house.

It was a disheartening scene. The mages, all except Lorenza, were gathered in a circle, healing each other with magic. Beatrice and Odeon were hurrying around with the other healers, applying salve to the wounded, and bandaging broken arms and legs.

Freja led her over to the mages. Julong smiled in their direction, having heard them approach. Urdu raised a hand. Two other mages, she didn't recognize, but Freja soon performed introductions: the woman with brightly painted nails was Tamarka, and the lanky young man wearing glasses was her brother, Morkel.

"Gabi. How wonderful it is to finally meet you," Morkel said, grasping her hand. He had a nice smile, she conceded, but he wasn't Alrik.

"You're so pretty," Tamarka said. "And powerful as well. We couldn't have banished that gigantic troll without your help."

Gabi blushed. "I didn't do much, it's all thanks to the Peerless Knife."

"Nevertheless, your timely arrival allowed us to get rid of that troll," Morkel said admiringly.

Gabi didn't mind his appreciation, though by instinct, she felt she could become good friends but not lovers with him. He was just as nice as his letters, but Alrik kept invading her mind.

Just then, the sound of hooves reached the square. Lorenza came galloping up to them. Her dark hair whipped in the wind like a banner; her blue-gray eyes were bright and sparkling.

Morkel instantly rushed to her side and offered his hand. "May I help you down?"

He hadn't offered to help Gabi dismount. Plus, the eagerness in his face was more than proof that he was interested in Lorenza.

Gabi laughed softly to herself. And to think that Freja wanted to introduce him to her. It didn't matter, anyway. If Morkel did end up with Lorenza, they could still produce mages with undiminished magic.

Lorenza accepted Morkel's hand, but the first thing she did was go to Theo.

"I've been to the entrance gates of the capital," she reported. "I haven't seen or heard any trolls around."

"Excellent. We'll send out messengers to the entire kingdom, and dispatch a squad if any trolls are sighted." Theo drew a hand over his forehead and exhaled deeply. Making a low bow to the mages, he said in a hoarse voice, "I cannot thank you enough for helping us get rid of the trolls."

The mages returned the bow, Gabi holding on to Freja.

"It is our mission to help when it is needed," Urdu said. "We could not let the kingdom be destroyed under a troll invasion."

A messenger came racing up to them. "Your Highness—outside the walls, there are troops from Arksar."

To Gabi's surprise, Ulfred appeared. He winked at her and made Theo a bow. "Greetings, Your Highness. I am Ulfred, retired captain of King Tyrell's guards. He sent me with Prince Arksar to offer assistance."

"Thank you, Ulfred." Theo said, after receiving a nod of approval from Freja. To the messenger he said, "Let them in."

Within minutes came the sound of horse hooves stamping and bells jingling. Heading the troops was Alrik, dressed in full warrior gear. Gabi almost couldn't recognize him, being used to him in his farmer's clothes.

When Alrik dismounted, Gabi hurried toward him as fast as her foot would allow.

"Why are you here?" she demanded. "How did your father let you come?" She had met King Tyrell before she started on her journey to Savony. After being reunited with his son after twenty years, it was unlikely that Tyrell would let him out of the palace.

Alrik grinned. "I told him that I couldn't live without you."

Gabi rolled her eyes.

"Well, he finally said yes when I said I'd bring an army, and that I'd stay behind if there were any trolls." Alrik's cheeky expression disappeared. "It looks like those trolls have wreaked enormous damage on the city."

Theo approached them. Alrik held out his hand.

"Hi there." Gabi elbowed him and whispered that he was talking to the crown prince. Alrik grinned sheepishly and scratched his head. "Haven't quite got used to my new role yet." Raising his voice, he said, "Well met, Prince Theo. I am Prince Alrik of Arksar. My father sent me to help Savony recover and rebuild."

Theo grasped Alrik's hand and gave it a hearty handshake. "We are greatly obliged to your help."

Alrik shook his head. "If you didn't defeat the trolls, they would have made way to Arksar, so we are the ones who should be thankful."

Looking around at the carnage, Gabi closed her eyes for a

second. They had prevailed eventually—the witches were defeated and the trolls gone, but what a bloody price they paid.

Alrik touched her arm. She let herself go and leaned against him, wishing nothing but to climb into bed and fall asleep.

* * *

SEVERAL DAYS PASSED. Gabi was kept busy as she helped to restore the castle and the city. The Peerless Knife was useful in battle, but it wasn't the answer to everything. It could attack with amazing power, but it couldn't heal. It couldn't mend a broken leg or fix twisted joints. Nor did it stop Alrik from popping up whenever he could, offering his arm and insisting that she should take it easy on her foot.

About a week later, a letter came from King Tyrell. Alrik had brought breakfast to Gabi's room when the letter was delivered. He read the contents, and his face fell.

"What is it?" Gabi asked, though she had a good idea what the letter was about.

"He wants me to return," Alrik said, with a shrug of his shoulders. "He said that I could leave Ulfred in charge and return to the palace. "

"It has been twenty years since he saw you. Naturally, he'd be eager for your return."

"Naturally," Alrik agreed. He stashed it into his pocket. "Well, I suppose it's about time. I'll tell Ulfred to ready the horses. Have you much to pack?"

"I'm not coming."

Alrik stared at her as if she were crazy. "What do you mean? We have to thank you for everything you've done, and we must have an engagement ceremony, and…"

"Listen to me," Gabi said. It pained her, especially when he was looking at her with wounded puppy eyes, but she hardened her resolve. She had begun preparing this speech long ago, when he confessed his feelings to her. "You have spent all your life in the village. You didn't know any girls— well, there were some girls, but I'm the only one you truly knew well. You never had the chance to meet noble ladies—you'll inevitably meet many of them when you becoming king. You might fall in love with someone else, some noble lady who would be a better candidate for queen."

He winced and pressed his lips together. "What can I do to convince you that I only want you?"

Gabi swallowed. She knew he had a stubborn streak, but she wasn't prepared for a question like this. Pacing the room, she finally turned and held up three fingers.

"Three years. Use this time to meet as many people as you can, and if three years later you still want me, then come and find me. I'll be waiting."

Alrik looked like he wanted to take her by the shoulders and shake some sense into her brain, but Gabi stared right back. She was a mage. He couldn't force her to stay.

"Can't you make it three months? Three years is an eternity."

"If you want to argue with me, I'll make it five."

Alrik let out a long sigh. "Fine, fine, three years if you must. I'll do what you want. But you have to promise me also to stay away from that fellow."

"Who are you talking about?"

"That Morkel fellow you've been corresponding with. And that Julong—he looks like he's going to stay for a while. Or just any man who wants to court you."

Gabi laughed. "I promise."

She took a step forward, sagging a little, but Alrik had antici-pated what she was going to do. His arms came around her, strong and comforting, and when he pulled back, it was not to let her go but to tilt her chin and capture her lips.

She didn't want the moment to end. His lips were soft and warm, kissing her with a passion that made her want to melt in his arms. When she finally broke away, Gabi had to steel herself before gently extracting herself from his embrace.

"Gabi, darling," he said. "I love you."

"I love you too," she whispered. "But I must go. Goodbye, Alrik."

Alrik let his hands fall to his side, his disappointment evident. "Three years, don't forget. I'll be coming for you."

CHAPTER 38

*I*t was a typical day in Panola, Masaro. The air was dry and hot, the sun baked the bricks yellow and the paint was peeling from walls. Panola was the westernmost town of Masaro, and during summer the town was sweltering and uncomfortable. Yet visually it was an appealing place, with baskets of flowers hanging over street lamps, and the houses painted in bright colors of pink and yellow and green.

Gabi wiped sweat from her brow as she limped into the town square. Her employer had sent her to buy cinnamon and cardamom. He didn't trust her with baking, but Gabi proved that she was valuable when it came to figures. When selling bread in the store, she never had to use pen and paper—she added up the amounts in her head and was never wrong. She might not be fast when buying food stuffs, but she never forgot what to buy and never made mistakes. For Masaro people, who generally were laid back and lacked the precise mind of Arksans, Gabi's assistance was much appreciated.

When she entered the store selling baking supplies, the owner was busy handling a few middle-aged customers haggling the price of fine white sugar, so Gabi went ahead. She had visited the store many times; she knew where the goods were kept.

To her surprise, the aisle containing spice jars was blocked. About a dozen fat sacks labeled "Best Quality Flour" were piled in the aisle like a small mountain. The end of the aisle was a wall, meaning that the only way to get to the spices was to remove the sacks.

It was tempting, so tempting, if she could use a little magic. But a voice burst that bubble.

"Hello, Gabriella." Turning around, she met the gaze of a startlingly handsome young man. "Did you miss me so much that you came to visit this store in hopes of running into me?"

It was Cristian, who owned a bakery with his mother and sister. Like Gabi, he sold bread instead of doing the baking, but he relied on his amazing good looks to attract customers. Most of the customers in Cristian's bakery were female, and he was nicknamed "Cristian the Heartless" because of the many girls who wanted him but failed to be the sole recipient of his affections.

Sometimes she couldn't help comparing Cristian with Alrik. Both of them were flirtatious, but in her opinion, Cristian was more arrogant, more self-centered. She sometimes caught him preening in the mirror, smoothing his hair and straightening his collar. Too foppish for her taste. There was still pain when she thought about Alrik. Three years, and she still missed him. Luckily, in Panola, news about the long-lost Arksan prince wasn't frequent. An ocean separated Masaro from Arksar, and Panola was far from the coast.

Forcing herself to forget about her childhood friend and lover, Gabi returned her attention to Cristian. "How did you know I've been patrolling the store every day, just so I can see you?"

The sarcasm was palpable in her tone, but he merely

grinned. "Let me help you, sweetheart. What're you looking for?"

Reluctantly, she pointed at the last shelf. Usually she appreciated when people tried to help her, seeing that she was lame, but in Cristian's case, she'd rather not accept his assistance and listen to him sing praises of himself.

"What are you doing over there? You're supposed to be shelling walnuts for Mama."

A petite young woman stood behind them: Chiara, Cristian's twin sister, though she wasn't half as stunning. Barely reaching five feet, and with her pink cheeks and round eyes, Chiara made people think she was cute, rather than beautiful.

"Chiara!" Cristian looked as if his shirt was on fire, and Chiara suddenly appeared with a bucket of water. He beckoned to her and said in a whisper, "Can you lend a hand? Gabriella needs help reaching the shelves in the end. I'll keep watch."

Chiara rolled her eyes. "Don't you want to impress her with your bulging muscles?"

"I would, but since Gabriella already knows about your *ability—*" he shrugged "—I don't fancy wasting my strength unless necessary. I need to be full of energy to charm those ladies at the storefront."

Grumbling that he was useless except for his face, Chiara issued a simple command to her brother: "Move."

The petite young girl picked up a sack of flour as easily as if it were filled with cotton, and dropped it to the side. She picked up another sack, and another, and in no time the aisle was cleared.

"Thank you," Gabi said, smiling at the other woman. Unbeknownst to most people, Chiara possessed the gift of super strength. Gabi had sensed the girl had a strange aura—an aura that only another mage could detect. On one occasion she confronted the girl, displayed a bit of magic, and soon wormed out the truth. Chiara's father had done a good turn to a mage, and when the mage approached dying age, she granted the twins a wish.

Originally, the mage was supposed to grant Chiara the gift of astounding beauty, and Cristian super strength, but as babies they looked so alike that she got them wrong. Worried that men would find her strength unattractive, Chiara kept her power a secret. However, it didn't prevent Cristian from taking advantage—whenever it was laborious tasks like moving furniture or carrying weights, he'd ask Chiara to do it, while giving all credit to himself. Naturally, Chiara resented the treatment, but she couldn't do anything about it.

"What's this about?" The owner of the store came over. "Why's the flour dumped in here?"

"No idea," Cristian said, shrugging.

"They were lumped in the middle of the aisle, but Cristian came along and moved them to make way for me," Gabi said.

The confusion in the owner's face cleared. "Must be that scoundrel we hired last week—he was supposed to put the flour in the storage room! Didn't even wait till I was done. Must have a word with him...anyway, glad you're here, lad." He thumped Cristian on the back. "Always there when a pretty damsel needs help, eh?"

"Always." Cristian grinned. Chiara rolled her eyes.

"Thank you for coming to my rescue," Gabi said sweetly, but as she turned to pay for her purchases, she threw Chiara a wink.

Both girls knew what it was like, forced to conceal magic in order to avoid unnecessary trouble.

* * *

LIFE IN PANOLA was similar to her "previous" life in Brek, yet different in many ways. Here she could stay anonymous and keep a low profile as a mage. As long as she didn't complain about the low pay and long work hours, she could live peacefully in this Masaro town.

Though, in the beginning, there were difficulties. Her Arksan accent, for one thing, made some people suspicious. Her skin and features were Masaro, but her style of dress and manners all evoked of Arksar. It took her nearly a year before she was able to open her mouth without someone raising an eyebrow and asking where she was from.

"Gabriella!" the baker hollered. "Get your rump here this very instant!"

Gabi rolled her eyes. The baker was bad-tempered and ill-mannered, but he was actually decent compared to the other men she worked for. Her first employer was a creep, the second one with appalling hygiene. Domenico might have the patience of a flea, but he was honest and treated her like a normal person, not a vulnerable young woman who could be taken advantage of.

Limping to the front, she stopped at the counter, where Domenico was glaring.

"You've a customer." He jerked his finger at a young man, who was perusing a basket of brioche. A few young girls hovered in a corner, jostling and giggling.

Her heart caught in her throat.

"Al—Alrik?"

He turned around, and his smile was brighter than the scorching sun that baked the dried tomatoes outside.

"Hello, Gabi."

She was instantly conscious of her sweat-soaked hair, her flour-dusted apron. He was immaculately dressed and was miraculously fresh in the hot Masaro summer. Knowing him, he must have put in the effort to dress up to impress and attract her. He was staring at her as if she were the most delicious item in the store, making her cheeks flame.

"Who's this?" Domenico asked, regarding Alrik with a wary eye.

"An old friend," Gabi quickly said. If the girls knew that Alrik was the prince of Arksar, they'd descend upon him like hawks discovering prey. "We haven't seen each other for three years."

"Which is far too long," Alrik said, smiling, but his tone carried a reproachful note.

She felt like taking the end of her apron and wiping her face, but resisted the urge.

"Can we talk?" Alrik said. "In private."

Domenico frowned. "I'm not sure if that's all right with Gabriella."

"There's a public park nearby," Alrik said. "We won't be too far."

"But she's on duty."

"How much are you paying her?"

"Three ducats a day."

"Fine." There was a clink of coins. Alrik set a handful of ducats on the counter. "Here're ten ducats. I'll buy the rest of her day. Will you let her come with me now?"

Domenico raised an eyebrow, but didn't pocket the money eagerly, as most other sellers were likely to do. "Gabriella? You sure you want to step out with him?"

She nodded.

"Fine." Her employer folded his arms. "Mind you get back in time for dinner."

Gabi removed her kerchief and dusted her hands.

Once they were in the park, Alrik turned and faced her.

"Three ducats a day?"

She raised an eyebrow. "I'm an assistant baker in a town that has dozens of bakeries. That's fairly common."

He shook his head. "I know we're no longer on the farm, but three ducats! The buttons on my cuff cost more than your daily salary."

"It's enough to live on." She put her hands on her hips. "How did you find me?"

He grinned. "Freja told me. I wouldn't give her peace of mind till she agreed."

"But how did the palace let you come? I didn't think they'd be willing...after you nearly lost your life..."

"Well..." He gave a sheepish grin. "Notice anything strange around?"

Gabi looked. There was a man fanning himself under a tree. Another was reading a paper in the park bench. A few others loitered nearby, chatting casually, but she detected the hilt of a sword poking from their trousers.

"Are they all your bodyguards?" she whispered.

"They're not doing a good job of keeping a low profile, eh?"

"Only elderly men retired from their jobs have the leisure to idle about in working hours."

Alrik grinned. He stepped closer and gazed at her intently.

"Three years ago, you told me that I needed a choice. That I needed to be around more women, that my affection for you was borne only because you were the only girl I knew well. I was mad at you in the beginning, but since I realized I couldn't make you stay, I had to accept it." He took a deep breath. "Three years have passed. And I still want you."

Gabi opened her mouth, but no words came out.

"The truth be told, I was more worried that you mightn't wait for me, though since I set foot in this kingdom, I haven't seen any man as charming as I."

Gabi rolled her eyes. This was the Alrik she knew. "What about your parents? Do they know that you don't plan on marrying a woman from a noble family?"

He shrugged. "Father says that as long as you're willing and I'm certain, he'd have no objections. Mother's happy with whoever I pick, even if I chose a scullery maid. In a way, we have Moira to thank. Because she threatened my life, my parents don't care about who I marry, as long as I'm alive and well. Besides, they wouldn't mind having a mage in the family. Magic can be awfully handy in a time of crisis. If you didn't wake me, I'd be trapped in that horrible snow castle for ages." He shuddered in a comical manner that made her smile.

"So," Alrik coughed, apparently from the effort of speaking so much in the hot, dry climate. "After all that I've said, have I convinced you? Come back to Arksar with me, darling. I know, it's not going to be easy, but I promise that I'll protect you with my life—as you did with mine."

"Fool," Gabi muttered, but she couldn't keep the smirk off her face. "I protected you because I promised Freja I would. Because I owed her my life."

"Liar." Alrik wagged a finger at her. "You'd have protected me whether Freja made you do it or not. Because you love me."

Gabi went red. She limped toward him, tripped on a rock— he strode forward and encircled her in his arms.

"It's stifling," she informed him, her voice muffled against his chest. "I'm going to suffocate from heat."

"Sorry." Alrik loosened his grip, but his hands rested firmly on her waist. "See what happens if I'm not around you? Who's going to catch you every time you fall? Seriously, Gabi. Make me the happiest man alive. If you don't say yes..." There was a desperation in his tone. "I won't marry. There will be no heir. Then the entire kingdom of Arksar will be on you, and you won't be able to have a day's peace."

"They won't. They'll just parade hundreds of women in front of you, and you still won't get a day's peace."

He sighed. "I was only joking, you know. If you really don't want to marry me..."

"I never said I didn't want to."

"...you can still move back and we can find...what?" Alrik leaned back, staring at her face. "Did you just say that you'll marry me?"

Gabi laughed. Placing her hands on his shoulders, she popped up on her good foot and kissed him.

For that moment, time stood still. Beads of sweat trickled down her neck, but she barely noticed. He was passionate and demanding, burning hotter than the ruthless Masaro sun.

When she pulled away, he made a noise of protest. "No, not that fast! I've been waiting for three years."

Gabi laughed—he was so adorable when he looked at her like that. Ignoring the hoots and catcalls around the park, she wrapped her arms around his neck and kissed him again.

When both were finally satisfied, she rested her forehead on his collarbone.

"I won't be able to dance at balls," she said.

"That's a relief. You don't know how many toes I trod on when they taught me those Arksan dances."

"And I can't help everything with my magic."

"How about setting up a trade? For the requests you don't want, we'll charge them with exorbitant amounts of money. The palace treasurer will be eternally grateful."

"And if I can't give you an heir…"

"I've got a few cousins. The oldest one has two sons already. They can have the throne."

"Well then, what are you waiting for? Take me back to Arksar this very instant."

The joy that shone in his eyes was the last straw. A tear leaked from her eye and she didn't bother to wipe it away. After all these years spent in emotional turmoil, she was finally going to be with the man she loved.

Alrik swung her up in his arms, into the air, and the happiness reflected in his eyes was infectious.

"Let's go home."

THE END

AFTERWORD

Dear readers,

Hope you've enjoyed *The Cursed Prince*! The Reversed Retellings had been difficult to write (well, most of the time writing is tough for me), but I hope you had fun with the gender-bend take on fairy tales! My next book is going to be pure fantasy, though it'll be set in the same world. You've met the heroine already--remember in the last chapter there's a young woman called Chiara, who's gifted with super strength? The next book, *Power Born*, will be Chiara's story.

To learn when it'll be out, sign up here: http://www.ayaling.com/newsletter.html

What you'll get for joining the club:

1. Receive exclusive short stories written to accompany my novels.

2. Be the first to know when I have a new release.

3. Be the first to know when I give away free stuff, run a poll, or other fun activities.

See you next book!

~Aya~

BOOKS BY AYA

REVERSED RETELLINGS
Till Midnight (Book 1)
The Beast and the Beauty (Book 2)
The Cursed Prince (Book 3)

UNFINISHED FAIRY TALES

The Ugly Stepsister (Book 1)
Princess of Athelia (Book 1.5)
Twice Upon a Time (Book 2)
Ever After (Book 3)
Queen of Athelia (Book 4)

THE PRINCESS SERIES
Princesses Don't Get Fat
Princesses Don't Fight in Skirts
Princesses Don't Become Engineers

GIRL WITH FLYING WEAPONS

Girl with Flying Weapons

ABOUT THE AUTHOR

Aya is from Taiwan, where she struggles daily to contain her obsession with mouthwatering and unhealthy foods. Often she will devour a good book instead. Her favourite books include martial arts romances, fairy tale retellings, high fantasy, cozy mysteries, and manga.

www.ayaling.com

facebook.com/ayalingwriter

twitter.com/ayalingling

Printed in Great Britain
by Amazon